D1560342

SHADOWS OF A SOUND

SHADOWS OF A SOUND

STORIES BY
HWANG
SUN-WŎN

EDITED BY
J. MARTIN
HOLMAN

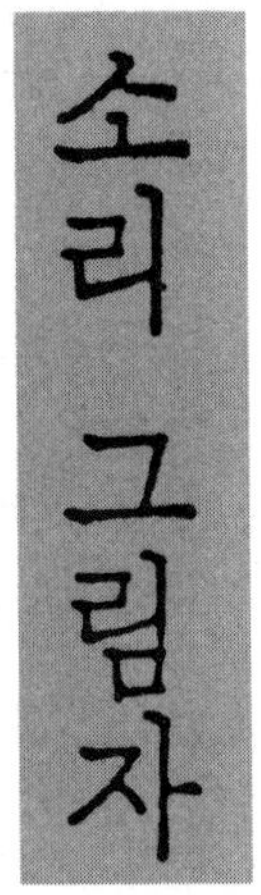

Mercury House, Incorporated
San Francisco

This is a work of fiction. Names, characters, places, and incidents either are the product of the author's imagination or are used fictitiously. Any resemblance to actual events, locales, or persons, living or dead, is entirely coincidental.

Stories translated by David Brunette, Douglas A. Clark, Stephen J. Epstein, Heinz J. Fenkl, Bruce and Ju-chan Fulton, Neil Hoyt, Kim Chong-un, Edward W. Poitras, and Suh Ji-moon are used by permission of the translators. "Widows" previously appeared in the fall-winter 1988–1989 issue of *Fiction Network.* "In a Small Island Village," "Blood," "Masks," and "Shadows of a Sound" previously appeared in *The Book of Masks,* published by Readers International.

Published in the United States by
Mercury House
San Francisco, California

Distributed to the trade by
Consortium Book Sales & Distribution, Inc.
St. Paul, Minnesota

Manufactured in the United States of America

Library of Congress Cataloging-in-Publication Data

Hwang, Sun-wŏn, 1915–
[Short stories. English. Selections]
Shadows of a sound : short stories / by Hwang Sun-wŏn;edited by J. Martin Holman.
p. cm.
ISBN 0–916515–65–6 : $17.95
1. Hwang, Sun-wŏn, 1915– —Translations, English. I. Holman, J. Martin. II. Title
PL991.29.S9A24 1990
895.7'33—dc20 89–32146
CIP

CONTENTS

INTRODUCTION

Hwang Sun-wŏn, roundly praised as the master of the Korean short story, has been an influential figure in Korean literature for most of its modern history. His first published work appeared in newspapers in P'yŏngyang (the capital of what is now North Korea) in the early 1930s, not long after the emergence of modern Korean literature. Today, at the age of 74, he continues to write, as well as to teach at Kyung Hee University, where he has been a professor of Korean literature since 1957.

Hwang's output includes two volumes of poetry, eight collections of short stories, and seven novels spanning the storms that Korea has suffered in the twentieth century. By the time Hwang was born, in 1915, Korea had been firmly under Japanese rule for five years. For many centuries before, Korea had been governed by native kings, but in a tributary relationship with China. The last of these dynasties, the Yi Dynasty, had been weakened by internal factionalism, largely precipitated by the encroachment of Western powers and Japan at the end of the nineteenth century. In 1910, Japan was finally able to exert colonial control over Korea.

The Japanese rule was harsh; Hwang's father was jailed for eighteen months for his participation in the March First Korean Independence Movement of 1919. The movement failed to dislodge the Japanese, but it provided a rallying point for Korean nationalism that is still recalled today. During the thirty-five years of Japanese control, efforts were made to "assimilate" Koreans into the expanding Japanese empire: The Japanese language was used in schools, Korean activities that seemed nationalistic were curtailed or completely oppressed, Koreans were required to take Japanese names, and men were conscripted into labor corps and the Japanese army. Korea's economy was transformed to make it a supplier of agricultural products and raw materials to feed the Japanese people and the war effort.

Hwang was educated in Japanese-language schools in Korea. He went on to take a degree in English literature at Waseda University in Tokyo. Soon after returning to his homeland, he published his first collection of short stories, *The Marsh,* in 1940. Hwang continued to write, even during the war years, when all writing was prohibited by the Japanese authorities. He hid his manuscripts against the uncertain hope that his work would someday see the light of day. "Snow," dated December 1944, captures the mood of attenuated despair near the end of the Pacific War.

With the surrender of Japan, the liberation of Korea from colonial rule was replaced by an ideological division between the Soviet-controlled North and the American-controlled South. Hwang had remained in the North, but soon fled to the South with his family as conditions grew hopelessly worse. *The Dog of Moknŏmi Village,* which appeared in 1946, less than a year after the end of World War II, was actually his third in order of composition. His stories from the war years, under the title *Wild Geese,* ironically or appropriately, had to wait until 1951, during the height of the Korean War, to see print.

In June 1950, North Korean forces invaded the South, occupying Seoul and sending masses of Koreans fleeing for refuge in the southernmost part of the peninsula. Hwang lived as a refugee with his family while the Korean War raged across the land.

"Clowns," the title story of his fourth collection, published in 1952, reflects the conditions the refugee population faced, while stories such as "Drizzle" and "Time for You and Me Alone" depict the war from the soldiers' viewpoint. Before the outbreak of the war, Hwang also began to turn his energies toward the novel. His first, *She Lives with the Stars,* was published in 1950, and his second, *Descendants of Cain,* a semiautobiographical account, in 1954.

The end of open hostilities in Korea brought only an uneasy peace. No armistice had been signed, and the Korean people seemed more hopelessly divided than ever; the Demilitarized Zone that divides the peninsula represents a spiritual rent that is yet unhealed. The tumultuous postwar years saw the publication of Hwang's fifth collection, *Cranes* (1956), the title story of which captures the poignancy of a nation divided, and his sixth collection, *The Lost Ones* (1958), as well as the novels *Human Grafting* (1957) and *Trees on the Cliffs* (1960).

After the war, President Syngman Rhee's increasingly dictatorial regime led to the 1960 Student Revolution. The democracy that followed, however, was short-lived. A military coup established another dictator, Park Chung-hee, who remained in power until his assassination in 1979. Since then Korea has experienced another military coup, the first elections to bring a peaceful transition of power, and world attention for its economic achievements.

During these years of political turmoil, Hwang has continued to write but has largely ignored the current political situation. His 1964 novel, *The Sun and the Moon,* takes up the question of human loneliness exemplified by the traditional outcast class of Korean society. His 1964 collection, *Time for You and Me Alone,* is most notable for stories of wartime Korea, while his last collection, *Masks* (1976), is perhaps his most unique, often experimental but at the same time firmly grounded in the same context as his earliest work. His last novels, *The Moving Castle* (1973) and *Dice of the Gods* (1982), are also experimental works. Though Hwang may touch on contemporary political or social problems, as he does on the Student Revolution of 1960 in his story "For

Dear Life" (in *The Book of Masks,* published by Readers International), political events in the postwar period serve only to guide his characters toward introspection of a more universal nature. In one of his last stories, "A Shadow Solution," written in 1983, he alludes to the campus strife of the 1980s, but the story can be read as a statement—a troubling, intriguing, and beautiful one—Hwang's personal faith in literature.

Hwang bases his literature in the deepest, most personal questions of human existence rooted in unmistakably Korean experience. Loneliness is a constant theme. Characters are frequently solitary, isolated either physically or emotionally. In *"Ringwanderung,"* Hwang likens human life to the kind of circular wandering that disoriented hikers experience in the wilderness. Each circle is distinct, and each person travels his or her circle alone. The outer reaches of these orbits may be vast and desolate, but Hwang's emphasis is not on the emptiness. Rather, he values the brief instants when paths cross and produce a moment of illumination. At these times there is warmth and communication, an exquisite juncture.

Such junctures form memories, or they may open windows of memory, and memory has the power to transform the heart. For many of Hwang's characters, childhood and youth hold the most significant recollections of life. Memory provides the base from which to interpret and appreciate life; it fortifies the traveler for the lonely stretches of road.

Hwang Sun-wŏn's work is notable for its fine attention to detail. In a conversation with Hwang Sun-wŏn at his home in 1986, I praised the aesthetic sensibility of a certain Japanese writer, and Hwang responded that he too had been impressed by the sensitivity of this author's work; nevertheless, he had reservations. "A writer should seek beauty," Hwang said. "But that is not his only purpose. A writer must also seek the salvation of man."

This book is the result of the efforts of many people over a number of years. My thanks go to each of the translators, who have labored to bring Hwang Sun-wŏn's short stories to an international audience. I am indebted to the Korean Culture and Arts Foundation in Seoul for providing me with grants on two occasions that allowed me to work on these translations. I am grateful to Virginia Burnham and Richard Markley for typing part of the manuscript. I would also like to thank my wife, Susan James Holman, for the many hours she contributed by reading the translations in manuscript and offering invaluable criticism and suggestions. I am grateful to Thomas Christensen for bringing Hwang's literature to the attention of Mercury House. And I wish to thank Kim Jung-sup for introducing me to Hwang Sunwŏn himself. Those of us who have worked with Professor Hwang have soon found it impossible to separate our admiration for him from our admiration for his literature. He and his wife have been gracious hosts on many occasions during the preparation of these translations of his stories, and he has exhibited the patience of Job in the face of countless questions about his work.

J. MARTIN HOLMAN

A NOTE ON THE TRANSLATION

Korean personal names are given in Korean order: family name (usually one syllable) followed by given name (usually two syllables). The romanization system used is a somewhat modified version of the McCune-Reischauer system.

In Korea, women keep their maiden names after marriage, so the terms "Mrs. Han" and "Mrs. Pak" in "Widows," for example, are somewhat misleading. Han and Pak are the women's maiden names. "Mrs." is used to indicate that they have been married.

CRANES

鶴

The village just north of the thirty-eighth parallel was quiet beneath the clear, lofty autumn sky.

A white gourd lay where it had tumbled, leaning against another on the dirt-floored space between the rooms of an abandoned house.

An old man Sŏng-sam happened to meet put his long tobacco pipe behind his back. The children, as children would, had already fled from the street to keep their distance. Everyone's face was masked with fear.

Overall, the village showed few signs of the conflict that had just ended. Still, it did not seem to Sŏng-sam to be the same village where he had grown up.

He stopped walking at a grove of chestnut trees on the hill behind the village. He climbed one of the trees. In his mind, from far away, he could hear the shouts of the old man with a wen. Are you kids climbing my chestnut tree again?

Had that old man died during Sŏng-sam's absence? He had not seen him among the men he had met so far in the village. Hanging onto the tree, Sŏng-sam looked up at the clear autumn sky. Though he did not shake the branch, some of the remaining chestnut burrs burst open, and the nuts fell to the ground.

When he reached the house that was being used temporarily as the Public Peace Office, he found someone there bound tightly with rope. This was the first young man he had seen in the village. As Sŏng-sam drew closer and examined his face, he was taken aback. It was none other than his boyhood friend Tŏk-jae.

Sŏng-sam asked one of the security guards from his detachment who had accompanied him from Ch'ŏnt'ae what the situation was. The guard answered that the prisoner had been vice-chairman of the Communist Farmers' Alliance and that he had just been captured while hiding in his own house here in the village.

Sŏng-sam squatted by the house and lit a cigarette. Tŏk-jae was to be escorted to Ch'ŏngdan by one of the young security guards.

After a while Sŏng-sam lit a cigarette from the one he had been smoking, then stood up.

"I'll take the guy myself."

Tŏk-jae kept his face turned away; he did not even glance at Sŏng-sam.

They left the village.

Sŏng-sam kept smoking, but he could not taste the tobacco. He just sucked and puffed. He suddenly realized that Tŏk-jae might like a smoke. He recalled when they were boys how they had shared a smoke of dried pumpkin leaves, hiding from the adults in the corner of the wall around the house. But how could he offer a guy like this a cigarette?

Once, when they were boys, he had gone with Tŏk-jae to steal chestnuts from the old man with the wen. Sŏng-sam was taking his turn climbing the tree when suddenly they heard the old man shouting. Sŏng-sam slid down the tree and got chestnut burrs stuck in his rear end. Yet he dashed off without doing anything about them. Once they had run far enough that the old man could not catch them, he turned his backside toward Tŏk-jae. It hurt even more to have the prickly chestnut spines pulled out. Tears ran freely down Sŏng-sam's face. Tŏk-jae held out a fistful of his own chestnuts, then thrust them into Sŏng-sam's pocket.

Sŏng-sam had just lit a cigarette from the last one he had smoked, but he tossed it away. He made up his mind not to smoke anymore while he was escorting this bastard Tŏk-jae.

They reached the mountain ridge road. He had often come to the ridge with Tŏk-jae to cut fodder before Sŏng-sam moved to the area around Ch'ŏnt'ae, south of the thirty-eighth parallel, two years before the Liberation in 1945.

Sŏng-sam felt an inexplicable urge. He burst out shouting. "You bastard, how many people have you killed?"

Tŏk-jae glanced toward Sŏng-sam, then looked away again.

"How many people have you killed?"

Tŏk-jae turned his face toward Sŏng-sam and glared. The light in his eyes grew fierce and his mouth, which was surrounded by a stubble beard, twitched.

"So, is that what you've been doing? Killing people?"

That bastard! Still, Sŏng-sam felt a clearing in the center of his chest, as if something caught there had been released. But then he said, "Why wouldn't someone like the vice-chairman of the Farmers' Alliance try to escape? You must have been hiding out because you had been given some assignment."

Tŏk-jae did not respond.

"Well? Answer me. What kind of mission were you hiding out to do?"

Silent, Tŏk-jae just kept walking. The guy certainly seems cowed. At a time like this, it would be good to get a look at his face. But Tŏk-jae did not turn toward Sŏng-sam again.

Sŏng-sam took hold of the pistol in his belt.

"It's no use trying to explain your way out of it. You'll have to be shot anyway, so go ahead and tell the truth."

Tŏk-jae began to speak. "I'm not trying to get out of anything. First and last, I'm the son of a dirt farmer. I was made vice-chairman of the Farmers' Alliance because they said I was a hard worker. If that's a crime worthy of death, there is nothing I can do. The only skill I've got is tilling the ground." After a moment he continued. "My father is sick in bed at home. It's been six months now."

Tŏk-jae's father was a widower, a poor farmer who had grown old with only his son by his side. Seven years ago his back had already been bent, and his face had dark age spots.

"Are you married?"

"Yes," Tŏk-jae answered after a moment.

"Who to?"

"To Shorty."

Not Shorty! Now that's interesting. Shorty, a fat little girl who knew the breadth of the earth but not the height of the sky. Always such a prig. Sŏng-sam and Tŏk-jae had hated that about her. They were always teasing and laughing at her. So that's who Tŏk-jae had married.

"And how many kids do you have?"

"Our first is due this fall."

Sŏng-sam tried to stifle a smile that rose to his lips in spite of himself. Asking how many children Tŏk-jae had and having him answer that the first was due in autumn was so funny he could not stand it. Shorty – holding up her armload of a belly on that little body. But Sŏng-sam realized that this was not the place to laugh or joke about such things.

"Anyway, don't you think it looks suspicious that you stayed behind and didn't flee?"

"I tried to go. They said if there was an invasion from the south, every last man who was a man would be captured and killed, so all the men between seventeen and forty were forced to head north. I really didn't have any choice. I thought I would carry my father on my back and go. But he wouldn't stand for it. He said if a farmer leaves the fields he has already tilled and planted, where can he go? My father has always depended on me alone. He's grown old farming all these years, and I have to be the one to close his eyes when the end comes. The truth is, people like us who just till the ground wouldn't be any better off even if we *did* flee . . ."

Sŏng-sam himself had fled the past June. One night he secretly spoke to his father about escaping, but his father had said the same thing as Tŏk-jae's. How could a farmer flee and leave his work behind? Sŏng-sam fled alone. As he wandered along the strange roads through strange towns in the south, he never stopped thinking of the farm work he had left to his old parents and his wife and children. Fortunately, then as now, his family was healthy.

They crossed the ridge. Now, somehow, Sŏng-sam was the one who kept his eyes averted. The autumn sun was hot on his forehead. What a perfect day this would be for harvesting, he thought.

After they had gone down the far side of the ridge, Sŏng-sam hesitated.

It looked like a group of people wearing white clothes were stooped over working in the middle of the field. It was actually a flock of cranes, here in the so-called Demilitarized Zone at the thirty-eighth parallel. Even though people were no longer living here, the cranes remained as before.

Once when Sŏng-sam and Tŏk-jae were about twelve years old, they had secretly set a snare and caught a crane. They even bound its wings with a straw rope. The two boys came out to the place they kept the crane almost every day; they would hold the crane around the neck and raise a ruckus trying to ride on its back. Then one day they heard the adults in the village talking in whispers. Some people had come from Seoul to hunt cranes. They had special permission from the Japanese governor-general to collect specimens of some kind. When they heard this, the two boys raced off to the field. They were not worried about being caught by the adults and scolded. Now they had only one thought: their crane must not die. Without stopping to catch their breath, they scrambled through the weeds. They took the snare off the crane's leg and loosened the straw rope from its wings. But the crane could hardly walk, probably because it had been tied up for so long. The boys held the crane up between them and tossed it into the air. They heard a gunshot. The bird flapped its wings two, three, four times, but fell back to the ground. It was hit! But in the next instant, another crane in the grass nearby spread its wings. Their own crane, which had been lying on the ground, stretched out its long neck, gave a cry, and rose into the sky, too. They circled over the boys' heads, then flew off into the distance. The boys could not take their eyes off the spot in the blue sky where the cranes had disappeared.

"Let's go catch a crane," Sŏng-sam said abruptly.

Tŏk-jae was bewildered. He did not know what was going on.

"I'll make a snare out of this, and you drive the cranes this way." Sŏng-sam untied Tŏk-jae's bonds and took the cord. Before Tŏk-jae knew it, Sŏng-sam was crawling through the grass.

At once, Tŏk-jae's face went white. The words "you'll have to be shot" flashed through his mind. At any moment a bullet would come from wherever Sŏng-sam had crawled.

Some distance away, Sŏng-sam rose and turned toward Tŏk-jae. "What do you mean standing there like an idiot! Go drive some cranes this way!"

Only then did Tŏk-jae realize what was happening. He started crawling through the weeds.

Above, two cranes were soaring, their vast wings spread against the high, blue autumn sky.

tr. J. MARTIN HOLMAN

IN A SMALL ISLAND VILLAGE

조그만 섬마을에서

Seven-year-old Ugi had gone down to the shore to set adrift a piece of pine bark shaped like a boat. The waves were rather strong in the west wind, and each time they washed up toward him, Ugi watched the boat to see how it would be dragged under the water. Some time ago, the boat on which Ugi's father was working had been caught in heavy seas and sunk. As in most cases, the body was never found. And now, in his own way, Ugi was trying to play out that moment.

In another spot Chini was squatting before a seaweed doll. She was pounding the surface of the sand with both hands and wailing as if in lamentation. "*Aigo, aigo, aigo,*" she sang out her dirge. Chini's father had gone to sea with Ugi's, also never to return. She was imitating the way her mother had grieved. Chini's darkly tanned chest, left bare by her clothes, was still that of a six-year-old girl, flat like a boy's.

"What a fit you're throwing." Ugi walked up beside the girl.

"Someday, when you die, I'll cry like this for you." Chini looked up at Ugi. Her eyes were unlike those of a child; they were misty like the distant light off the ocean.

"I won't die, but if you want to die, you little shrimp, go ahead."

Ugi trampled on the doll, smashing it. Then he scampered off.

Chini gazed at Ugi's tanned back, which glistened in the sunlight as he ran away. Then she stood up and walked around the edges of a net that had been spread out on the sloping sand to be dried and repaired. It was better than walking on the sand because the net was not as hot. She enjoyed the ticklish sensation on the soles of her feet.

Chini was not aware that Ugi had come back, and now he gave her a sudden shove. She tumbled sideways. Then Ugi nimbly tossed the net over her and scurried off again. Chini squirmed and kicked to free herself from the net, but the more she tried, the more entangled she became.

The summer Ugi turned eleven and Chini ten, Turtle Rock was often a playground for the mischievous boys. It was shaped like a giant turtle crawling up onto the land from the sea.

When the boys jumped off the back of Turtle Rock, Ugi always swam the farthest. They leapt into the water again and again without resting. Then, tired of swimming, the boys would bet on who could stay underwater the longest. The only time Ugi ever lost at any competition was at these diving contests.

One day, however, after several rounds of diving, Ugi did not reappear, although the rest of the boys had all come up. One boy struck the back of Turtle Rock with a stone, shouting down into the water, "Get out, damn you! Right now! That's enough!" But there was no sign from beneath the waves. Suddenly one boy picked up his shorts and began to run toward the village. Then all the other boys turned pale with fear, grabbed their shorts, and ran after him.

A little way off, Chini was gathering clams. Seeing the boys' serious expressions, she called loudly, asking what had happened. But the boys ran on without answering. As soon as she realized that Ugi was not among them, Chini tossed aside her bamboo basket and raced toward Turtle Rock. No sooner did she reach it than she jumped into the sea. Ugi was under the water, just as she had thought. She found him immediately. He was holding fast to a rock beneath the surface, not stirring. Since he would not loosen his arms, which were wrapped around the rock, she was barely able to pull him free. When she dragged him up to the beach there seemed no doubt he was dead.

Suddenly Chini was clutched by fear, but without thinking, she began to suck at Ugi's nose to remove the water. Some time ago a grown-up did this to a drowned boy, and she remembered seeing it. Chini sucked and spit and sucked again. Now it was no longer distasteful or frightening.

Chini was sucking and spitting frantically when a gurgling sound suddenly emerged from Ugi's throat. She sucked at his mouth. His chest moved, and a vapor flowed from between his lips. Again and again he vomited water. Chini turned his head to one side to make it easier for him to spit up. Then she waited for him to open his eyes. She watched his chest rising and falling, and for the first time her eyes moved below his stomach where he had nothing on. His small member stood out, moving by itself. Quickly Chini picked up Ugi's tattered shorts and tossed them over him.

Seeing villagers in the distance swarming toward her, Chini began to run back where she had left her basket.

Just like her mother and all the other village women, Chini had to live with the knowledge that the men had to go to sea when they turned seventeen. Feelings of loss or sorrow were out of the question.

The more Ugi went to sea, the more muscular his build became, and the rougher his face grew from the salt. Only on the nights they slept together, when he was home from the sea, could Chini regard him as her husband. That alone satisfied her.

Ugi had not even been going out to sea for three years before he began to feel dissatisfied with their meager catch. He complained incessantly when he returned from sea, "It's no good using rowboats. We have to get a motorized boat and go far out to sea." These frequent grumblings pierced Chini's breast. Ugi seemed to be a man driven mad by the sea, dreaming only a desperate dream of going far out in the ocean. Chini's feelings changed until she could no longer think of Ugi as her husband even when they slept together.

She wanted somehow to bring Ugi's heart back. If only she could have a baby. If she did, Ugi would forget his vain ideas of going out to the distant sea. Then she could have him look after the child when he was in the village, like other husbands. How wonderful it would be then, to be able to tend to some of the outside work. But it did not turn out the way she wanted it to.

After a while, it sometimes happened that Ugi would not return with the others when he went out to sea. He stayed on other islands, then came back several days late, looking as though he were about to die. After he got home, he would do nothing but mutter about motorboats.

One night Chini heard someone calling from outside. It was Ugi's voice, the voice of her husband, who had been away at sea for several days. She opened the door quickly. No one was there. The late autumn moon, just past full, shone down unobstructed.

Maybe he's beyond the wall, Chini thought. She went out to look but saw not so much as the shadow of a person. Chini stood in the moonlight gazing about for a moment. Then, as she was about to go back inside, she heard Ugi's voice calling again. This time it came from the direction of the nettle tree not far from the house. She ran to see, but she could find no trace of anyone. There was nothing there except the leafless branches of the tree drawing sharp, tangled shadows in the moonlight. Again she tried to go back to the house, but once more Ugi's voice called. This time it came from about ten or twelve yards ahead, though she could not tell exactly where. When she went to where she thought she had heard the voice, however, the sound withdrew about the same distance from her. Chini passed by the grove of camellia trees and walked to the strip of sand, then on to the shore. The light of the moon was full on the ocean, and the myriad ripples in the water glimmered like the scales of a fish. And there, about the same distance out in the sea, Ugi's voice called to Chini.

She got into a nearby boat and set out into the sea, drifting about here and there, following the voice in the bright moonlight. She never once doubted her ears or thought it impossible that Ugi's voice should be heard there.

The next morning a villager discovered Chini collapsed in a boat far from shore. She was six months pregnant at the time.

"It wasn't until later that I found out what had happened. They had been fishing near Komun Island but hadn't caught anything, so they were going to head back. They say only Ugi wanted to go farther out. He was so insistent that the others on the boat could not persuade him otherwise. That night the moon was shining brightly there too, they say, but after he went out in the boat, quite unexpectedly, a storm blew up."

The woman who kept the tavern paused for a moment. "I couldn't even cry. If only he'd been in a motorboat, then even a considerable storm would have been no problem."

I looked at her eyes. They were like the misty light off the ocean, but her gaze was fixed on one spot. I saw no expression of emotion in her eyes that might reflect her words.

Not far away grew a single nettle tree, casting its dense shade, and some distance from there a grove of camellias stood in a black shadow. Beyond that was a strip of sand, and beyond that the water. A rather large fishing boat, which had returned from the sea to avoid the typhoon that had been predicted, was moored at the shore. It was a motorized boat, and most of its white paint had peeled off. Ahead lay a long island shaped like a horse's back, which cut off the way south. The east was occupied by islands of various sizes, so this place was adequate to take refuge from a southern or eastern wind, but it offered no shelter from the west. Despite the typhoon warning, the sapphire waters of the sea, oil floating on its surface, stretched out quietly in the distance as though the storm would never come this far.

Out to the left, at a bend in the wide curving shoreline, stood Turtle Rock. Viewed from here it was nothing more than a crag jutting out to the sea. Now a great number of young Ugis were playing on the rock, taking not a moment's rest. A distance away from them in this direction, many young Chinis were gathering clams.

I lit a cigarette and asked the tavern keeper something I had been hesitating to inquire about. "Are you living alone now?"

I was not asking if she had remarried. When she lost her husband at sea she was six months pregnant. I was wondering about the baby she had been carrying.

"I live with my son."

I felt she had been fortunate.

"He's fifteen now. The years have passed so quickly. It's hard to believe he's that old."

The woman looked out at the sea. Her unwavering gaze was misty and firm.

"That's him over there. He's been swimming like that all morning."

I had not noticed earlier, but someone was swimming near the motorized fishing boat. When I looked out at him, he dove under the water and instantly bobbed up on the opposite side of the boat.

"Something might happen . . . him swimming like that." I frowned, thinking there could be trouble if he were accidentally to be caught under the boat.

"That's right, but whenever that kind of boat comes in, he always dives around it like that."

With my head turned toward the sea, I thought about her son being fifteen.

"Your son can't go out fishing yet, can he?" I asked.

The woman was silent for a moment, "He always pesters me wanting to, but I won't let him."

Now I understood why she had to run this small tavern.

After a moment the woman continued speaking, serenely, as though to herself.

"When he sees a big boat like that, he makes a fuss wishing he could ride in it, but I was hoping to get him away from the water. Still, whatever I do, I can't keep him from it forever. These days I even think that the night his father drew me outside, he was not actually calling me—he was luring the baby inside me to the sea."

I was startled to hear a woman talk as she did on this remote island.

Her son was diving underwater as if he would pass beneath the bottom of the boat again. Even from this distance, I could see the rippling circles in the water following one after another.

tr. J. MARTIN HOLMAN

BLOOD

피

The boy had caught a honeybee. The bee had crawled inside a pumpkin flower, and he caught it by pinching together the ends of the petals. It was a nimble feat for a six-year-old.

The boy picked the pumpkin flower that enclosed the honeybee and put it to his ear. The bee buzzed inside the flower. The child's mouth fell wide open. He grinned and rows of wrinkles appeared on his face, tanned golden by the sun.

The pumpkins had been planted in a small piece of open ground in front of his family's tent. Houses were to be built throughout this area in the future, so trash had been hauled from the city to make a landfill. This made the pumpkins bear well.

Some time ago, the boy had tried quite innocently to catch a bee in his hand, but he sprang back in shock and burst out crying. Where did that little bee get such a dreadful thing? His mother pulled out the stinger from his hand and applied soybean paste, but it had smarted for a long time.

The boy learned from his mother to grasp the ends of the petals instead, but bees seldom came to this tent village. If by chance he happened to see one in a flower, it would fly away before he could catch it. Every time this happened, the boy would gaze off into the endless sky where the bee had disappeared. He had thought a honeybee would never come again, but today, having caught one quite skillfully, he could not help but be overjoyed.

The boy wanted to show it to one of his friends, but the child he always played with next door had been sick in bed for several days. Another friend's family had sold their tent and moved away. The new child who had moved in was a girl. The boy had not yet made friends with her.

As he was putting the buzzing flower bag to his ear, he heard the sound of ground squirrels scampering about in his family's tent. They seemed to have eaten all their food. The boy's mother had gone to the trash heap to gather rags, but he wished she would hurry back with food for the squirrels.

Thinking his father had said this morning that the squirrel buyer would be coming, he walked between the tents and climbed the path up the hill behind them. He was barefoot, and he was only wearing a tattered shirt. His belly bulged out enormously, and his navel protruded even farther through his torn shirt. The boy's family, having lost their home in the flood the previous year, had come to live in this tent village. Here the boy was able to fill his empty stomach by eating all the pumpkin gruel he wanted, so he grew potbellied. When he walked, it looked as if a huge belly were walking by itself. His arms and legs were thin and gaunt in comparison.

At the end of the tent village was a sweet potato patch that one of the refugees was cultivating. Bindweed flowers bloomed on the embankment around it. The boy felt a need to urinate. Why would looking at these trumpet-shaped flowers make him have to urinate? The boy wore no pants, so it was no trouble at all; he simply stood there to relieve himself. The yellow stream struck the flowers.

Just beyond the sweet potato patch, the boy's father was digging up large pieces of rock, preparing to plant autumn vegetables. The boy walked up to his father and made a big show of holding out the pumpkin flower.

"Papa, . . . a bee. I caught a bee."

The boy's father stopped his work and stared at the pumpkin flower. "Oh, that was quite a trick." Then, hobbling on his lame leg, he picked up a large rock to move it. "Hold it carefully while you're playing with it. And don't get stung again."

"I won't. I caught it the way Mama taught me to."

The boy climbed up the hillside path. He was not bored today even though he was alone. Over and over he put the pumpkin-flower bag to his ear. When he could hear no sound, he shook the flower. Then the buzzing started again. No matter how much he thought about it, the boy could not get over his pride at having caught a honeybee.

When he reached a spot where rugged stones stuck out of the ground, the boy started to rub the sole of his foot on a rock. This was his habit when he came to this rocky place. I'm not going to break my leg like my father broke his. He rubbed one foot for a while, then changed to the other.

Trees stood sparsely above this spot. There were almost no pines, but various other trees grew there, mostly brushwood, scrub oak, and overcup oak.

The boy walked up to the trees. The full leaves cast cool, luxuriant shade. The boy felt around in the grass with his foot, looking for acorns. They could hardly be plentiful. If he happened to find one, it was usually rotten. And the occasional sound ones were all black and hard as rocks. When he put one in his mouth, it cracked and a bitter liquid seeped out. Still, it was better than nothing at all. As the boy put the bee to his ear again, he thought how wonderful it would be if the acorn were a piece of candy.

The boy looked for acorns a while. Then something darted out in front of him. It was a squirrel. The boy stiffened and watched. The squirrel climbed nimbly up one of the scrub oak trees. The boy held his breath as he watched the squirrel's movements. It went out on a branch about halfway up the tree, stopped there, then turned toward the boy, its tail curled up over its back.

Great. I should hurry to tell Papa, thought the boy, but before he could turn to go, the squirrel scampered down the tree. The boy stiffened again, observing the squirrel's behavior. The squirrel did not rest at the bottom of the tree but ran off in the opposite direction. The boy found himself chasing after it in spite of himself—the skinny legs and potbelly went tottering off. It was impossible for him to keep up with the squirrel. Still, he pursued it with all his might. The squirrel came in and out of sight among the grass and bushes and finally darted into a hole under a tree stump. The boy stopped and scrutinized the hole, then turned and began to race down the hill. "The squirrel went in a hole! The squirrel went in a hole!"

The boy emerged from the shade of the trees into the blazing sun. He passed the spot where the rugged stones stood embedded in the ground.

His father should have been working in the field, but he could not see him. He ran on. Just as he was about to pass the sweet potato patch, the pumpkin flower he had been holding in his hand suddenly slipped to the ground. "What should I do?" He stopped running. Only the tips of the petals were left in his hand. The bee in the pumpkin flower on the ground was covered with pollen. It buzzed and tried to fly, but could not. Still, the boy could do nothing. The honeybee buzzed again. This time it flew away, drawing circles as it rose up high in the sky. The boy did not even bother to follow the bee with his eyes as it disappeared; instead, he ran down toward his house.

The squirrel buyer had stopped his bicycle in front of the boy's tent and was talking to the boy's father. I'm just in time, the boy thought. "Papa!"

"Stop talking nonsense," the squirrel buyer was saying. "You complain that ten won is too cheap for one squirrel, but to tell the truth, if I pay that I'll only make two won profit. Two won! Do you know how much squirrels go for on Kanghwa Island? I can buy all I want there for a single won each." The squirrel man fanned his face in great gusts with a mountaineer's cap.

"Even so, if you take them to the city you can get at least thirty won apiece."

"How ridiculous! Who on earth told you such a wild story? Why don't you go there yourself and see. You'd probably have a hard time selling a single squirrel, even if you spent the whole day."

The boy's father answered with an unsatisfied look, "When you send them over to Japan, can't you get a dollar apiece in Western money?"

"Well, I don't know how much they bring in Japan, but it would take all kinds of trouble to send these squirrels there. They'd have to give them shots and build lightweight cages to ship them by air. And that's not all. Ten percent or more would die on the way, so if I sent a hundred, ten would be lost and . . ."

The boy's father showed no reaction. He stood staring at one spot.

The boy became impatient. "Papa . . ."

"Besides, they wouldn't just die of disease . . . I mean, some would kill each other. Since the shippers send them by plane, they're afraid of even the slightest extra weight and don't put water in the cages. So when the squirrels get thirsty they kill each other and suck the blood. It's hard to believe. Even microscopic creatures do it. How do they know there's blood inside other bodies . . . and that they can live by sucking it?"

The boy's father stood there silently without changing position. He had lost the welcoming expression he had worn when the squirrel man came. "Do you think that's limited to squirrels? What about us people? Anyway, give me twenty won each for them."

"This is frustrating . . . You mean I should put out my own money to pay you? . . . invest my own money to no end? Well, at that last house over there, they sold them to me with no complaints. Why are you acting like this today?"

The squirrel man seemed to be thinking about something for a moment. "Look, do you think this business of sending squirrels to Japan can continue forever? The Japanese have already started breeding Korean squirrels. And me . . . how much longer will it be before I can no longer make a living at this? Please, don't complain."

The squirrel man put his mountaineer's cap back on as if he had nothing more to say. He lifted the edge of the tent door, then, without asking permission, picked up the family's squirrel cage, which was bound with bush clover, and walked to his bicycle.

"So this time you've got four."

The boy's father said nothing.

The squirrel man pushed aside the grass that covered the top of the wire cage on his bicycle rack. Then he put the boy's family's squirrels inside. The new squirrels and the ones that were already in the cage raised a fuss.

"Papa . . ."

The boy wanted to speak before the squirrel man left, but his father just stood watching the man's actions expressionlessly. Sweat appeared on the boy's father's sleek face and neck. He had an absent look, but there was also something uneasy about it as well. The boy could say nothing more as long as his father looked like this.

After he finished tying up the load, the squirrel man took four ten-won bills from his inner pocket and handed them to the boy's father, who accepted them without a word. Then the squirrel man weighed the boy's father's stare. He picked a green pumpkin from the patch, broke it into several pieces, and put them inside the cage. The boy looked up at his father. How strange he was today! It was a rule that the boy could not pick pumpkins for the squirrels they caught and kept in the house, but his father had said nothing at all when the squirrel man did it. He just stood there not paying any attention.

He was sure his father would want to hear about the squirrel he had seen on the hill. The boy now grabbed his father's arm and shook it. "Papa, there's a squirrel up there."

Before he could respond, the squirrel man asked where.

The boy pointed toward the hill in back of the tents.

"You mean it's caught in a trap?"

"No, I just saw it there."

"Do you think it's still waiting there saying, 'Catch me, catch me'?"

"Well, it went into a hole . . ."

The boy's father, who had seemed indifferent to his son's

words, picked up a long pole that was standing beside the tent. A horsehair noose was attached to the end.

The father gave the boy a glance, as if to say, "Let's go." Half running, the boy led the way. The squirrel man quickly picked up the family's woven basket and followed.

Not a word passed among them as they reached the place where the trees stood on the hill. When they arrived at a spot where they could see the hole beneath the tree stump, the boy gestured and nodded toward it. The father had the boy and the squirrel man stay behind while he approached the hole alone.

The father stopped. He put the end of the pole into the hole and pulled it out two or three times. Then he put the snare at the mouth of the hole and held it motionless.

The squirrel was not quick to appear.

"Are you sure it went in there?" the squirrel man asked impatiently.

The boy nodded.

"I don't think it's still there. It's probably already run off somewhere."

The boy, too, thought that was what had happened, but still the boy's father stood immobile. Then, something popped out of the hole.

"There . . ." The boy started to speak, but the squirrel man covered his mouth with his big hand.

The boy's father carefully moved the snare in front of the squirrel's nose. "Put on the crown. Put on the crown," he muttered, telling the squirrel to get into the noose. As if in response to his words, the squirrel played with the snare with its foreleg. Then, in a bound, the squirrel put its head through.

Determined not to miss this chance, the boy's father raised the pole. The squirrel wiggled in the air.

The squirrel man ran over immediately and put the struggling squirrel in the woven cage. "It's a female with young ones. The teats are full."

The boy, whose mouth had been covered by the squirrel man's hand, had tumbled backward from the force of the man's movement as he dashed over to the squirrel. With his huge belly facing the sky, the boy could not get up right away, so he was unable to see the squirrel man put the snared animal in the cage. The boy lifted himself to his feet with a sullen look.

"We'll have to catch a male, too, since you caught a female," the squirrel man said.

"Would we catch it as easily as this?"

The boy did not understand what was meant by "male" and "female."

They went down to the house without exchanging a word, just like on their way up. The boy thought his father was limping more than usual on his bad leg.

The squirrel skittered about when the man put it in his wire cage. This time it seemed only the new squirrel made a commotion.

The squirrel man gathered his load together again and took two five-won coins from his pocket. He jingled them in the palm of his hand as he offered them to the boy.

"I'll give this to the kid. It's just as if he caught the squirrel himself."

The boy gladly accepted the money. The coins felt cool in his palm. He grasped them tightly. An image of the candies and sweets in the tiny shop farther down the hill flashed through his mind. But his father immediately took the money away.

"Well, shall I give you a ride on my bicycle?" The squirrel man took the boy under the armpits and lifted him onto the saddle.

The boy was a bit frightened.

"Hey, there's nothing to be scared of . . . nothing to be scared of."

The man had the boy hold the handlebars while he pulled the bicycle along. The bicycle rattled. The boy was exhilarated, but he was disappointed that he could not show the other children in the neighborhood. Why were there no children out, today of all days?

After he had pulled the bicycle for a while, the squirrel man said, "Why doesn't a big boy like you cover his little red pepper? Why, you're all belly." The man stretched out his finger and snickered as he poked the boy sharply in the navel. He seemed to be in an extremely good mood.

The boy laughed, too. His whole face wrinkled.

"You watch that hole and see if another squirrel goes in there, okay?"

The boy nodded.

"If you do what I say, I'll give you a ride again next time."

The boy nodded again, and the wrinkles filled his face again. The squirrel man stopped his bicycle at the end of the tents to let the boy off, then got on himself.

The boy stood there, his eyes following the man's bicycle as it wound along the narrow road and around the far side of a trash pile where women sat in clusters under the blazing sun diligently poking through the heap. His mother was probably there, but he could not tell which one she was from this distance. The boy turned his eyes back toward the bicycle and followed it until it disappeared.

The boy thought about going inside the house to eat whatever pumpkin gruel might be left, but instead he started back up the hill. He stopped at the border of the sweet potato patch where the bindweed was blooming and urinated as quickly as he could.

His father was digging out rocks as before.

When he got to the place where the rugged stones stuck out, he rubbed the sole of his foot just a bit, then went on to where the trees stood.

He had no intention of looking for acorns but went directly to a spot where he could see the hole under the stump. He watched it for a long time. His legs hurt, so he sat down. He thought of the joy of riding the bicycle. Next time I'll ask him to take me a little farther, where Mama is.

Though he waited for some time, there was no sign of a squirrel. He looked around, then crept toward the hole and peeped inside. He flinched. Something was wiggling in the pitch black of the hole. He peered closer and saw tiny creatures. They looked like squirrels. The boy put his hand inside and took them out. There were three in all.

The boy cupped them in both hands, held them close to his chest, and started to rush down the hill, but thinking he might drop the squirming baby squirrels if he ran, he slackened his pace.

As soon as he saw his father, he called out in a loud voice, "Papa, look at this!"

His father kept at his work. The boy could not tell if he had heard or not, so he went over to him quickly.

"Look at this, Papa."

Only then did his father turn his head. He seemed surprised.

"Where did they come from?"

"I caught them."

"Where?"

"Right up there where we were before."

"What?" His father shouted. "In that hole?"

The boy was disconcerted. He had thought he would hear praise.

"Please sell them."

"Son, who would buy them?"

"We'll raise them until they're bigger. Then we'll sell them."

"What a blockhead! Stop your babbling. Hurry up and put them back where you found them."

The boy hesitated.

"Right now! Go put them back! What would you feed them? These are newborn babies. Hurry up and take them back up there."

The boy finally seemed to realize the reason for his father's anger. He hurried away.

Oh, that's right. They have to have mother's milk. They'll have to have mother's milk soon. Then we can sell them when they're bigger. Then the squirrel man will take me even farther on his bicycle, he thought.

The boy hugged the baby squirrels to his chest and headed up the path at a fast clip.

"What a silly boy! He thinks he has to catch the male. What's he going to do? . . . use those as bait?"

For a moment, as the boy's father focused his gaze on his son's retreating figure, his eyes were misted with tears.

tr. J. MARTIN HOLMAN

MANTIS

사
마
귀

One by one the baby rabbits had disappeared. That morning the last one seemed to be gone. Hyŏn could hear his landlady scolding the mother rabbit: Maybe a praying mantis would devour its young or its mother, but who had ever heard of a mammal, even a vicious one, gobbling up four of its own babies? The woman asked herself once again why she had ever told Hyŏn to leave the mother rabbit home until the babies were grown. Hyŏn had bought the rabbit to use at the laboratory, and then a few days ago, it had spent an entire night pulling fur from its breast; it had made a nest and given birth in it. Now the landlady was cursing the rabbit. She was probably poking a stick into the rabbit hutch again, jabbing it in the side. Hyŏn then heard the little girl who lived in the house ask the landlady, whom she called "Grandmother," whether eating its babies had made the rabbit's eyes red. "Damn peepers, those damn peepers," she kept saying. It sounded to Hyŏn as if the girl wanted to skewer the rabbit's eyes.

The girl never failed to call the landlady "Grandmother" while the young lady of the house was away; after the young lady returned she changed to "Mother." Whenever Hyŏn asked this little girl her age, she would say "Six" and spread the five fingers of her hand before him.

The only one the girl always called "Mother" was her doll. She never carried the doll piggyback, as other little girls might have done. When playing house, she would make food out of dirt and serve it in broken pieces of porcelain. Bringing the potsherds to the doll's mouth, she would say, "Eat, Mother." This, too, happened only when the young lady was out.

Whenever the young lady returned, an unfamiliar pair of men's shoes would appear on the narrow veranda outside her downstairs room. The shoes changed in color and size each time. When these unfamiliar shoes appeared, the lives of the little girl and the landlady also changed. The little girl's round face became prim, and she would come upstairs, where Hyŏn lived. The landlady's face, with all its tiny wrinkles, would grow tense. And she would leave for the market earlier than usual, a basket hanging from her arm. She would still emerge from the smoky kitchen wiping her eyes with the breast-tie of her Korean jacket, but unlike other times, she could not cry out that her eyes were smarting. She would quietly finish all the dishes, then go straight to Hyŏn's room, creeping up the stairs without making a sound. Only when the young lady's room became still did she tiptoe down the stairs with the girl and go to sleep in the back room next to the kitchen.

When the landlady came upstairs on such occasions, she would sit silently for a while, her back to Hyŏn. Then she would turn to the glass fishbowl in the corner of the room as if seeing it for the first time. The girl would look at the fishbowl and the landlady for a moment, then would start picking at her hangnails. With a look of amazement the landlady would observe how the swimming goldfish became huge or tiny according to its distance from the glass. She would then turn her eyes to the girl as if to draw her attention to the fishbowl. But the girl never looked back toward the bowl, although she would gaze upon it with great joy when the young lady was out.

When the young lady was away and the girl came upstairs to Hyŏn's room, the first thing she would do was go to the fishbowl. The goldfish, which usually was swimming in one place slowly moving its fins, would suddenly become skittish and start swimming back and forth. When it settled down again, the girl would catch a fly and place it on the surface of the water. The first time she did this, Hyŏn told her not to feed the goldfish such filthy things. The goldfish darted to the surface and nibbled at the twitching fly, descended, and returned to nibble again, but it never swallowed it. The less the fly twitched, the less the fish would nibble at it. The nibbling finally stopped when the fly was dead. When the girl caught ants crawling next to the fishbowl and put them in the water, though, the goldfish would dart up and gulp them down. She would also go outside to catch little ants and put them in the bowl, too. The goldfish swallowed only the live, wriggling ants, ignoring the dead ones.

The girl would tire of toying with the flies and ants before the fish would. Then she would entertain herself by dredging scales from the bottom of the fishbowl with a long, pointed stick. She would press one of the scales against the glass and pull it up little by little. But the scale would slip away before it reached the mouth of the bowl. When this happened, the girl would quickly reach into the water and remove the sinking scale. She would glance at Hyŏn, and when he pretended not to see, she would swirl the water with her stick to set the other scales astir. Then she would remove them with her hands. Having recovered all the scales, she would hurry outside to dry them in the sun.

Whenever Hyŏn went out to the well to change the murky water in the fishbowl, the girl would run to him and pick up the goldfish as it flopped in the empty bowl. As the fish struggled in her hand, she looked down with satisfaction at its shiny scales. After filling the bowl, Hyŏn would hold it close to the girl's hand. Only then would she put the fish back in.

Once, though, he had had another goldfish: it had slipped from the girl's hand and fallen into the sewer drain as she was about to put it into the bowl. Just before Hyŏn could grab the fish, it disappeared down the sewer pipe, drawing a line in the muddy water. The girl looked down at the scales remaining in her palm. Hyŏn was afraid she would burst into tears if he stood there any longer, so he hurried upstairs, all the while looking at the remaining goldfish, which was moving its fins and swimming spiritedly in the fresh clean water as if unaware its mate had disappeared.

Once Hyŏn was out of sight upstairs, the girl became cheerful. She added the old scales she had collected to the new ones in her palm and arranged them all on the back of her hand. Next, she turned her hand toward the sun to make the scales sparkle. She repeated this movement again and again. Finally she stuck the scales to her cheeks, forehead, and nose, and pretended to dart and swim like a goldfish, rounding her lips over and over and working her arms like fins. But the girl lost interest in this game too. So she found the cat and began scratching its face with her fingernails.

The young lady had a different way of playing with the cat. After returning from one of her sojourns she would take the cat in her arms, hold one forepaw, and caress her own cheek with it. The paw, claws retracted, would brush gently across her cheek. Closing her eyes, the young lady would stroke more forcefully. Red marks would gradually appear on her face, and a faint smile would rise on her lips, forming a dimple on her left cheek. The round outline of her face looked quite smooth from the front, but her profile was a different story altogether, revealing her sharp nose, mouth, and chin. The slight upward slant of her long eyelashes was charming when seen from the side, but from the front, the first thing Hyŏn noticed in her eyes was the fatigue that had settled there.

One day, after the owner of an unfamiliar pair of shoes had left, Hyŏn, on his way downstairs, made the chilling discovery that the dimple on the young lady's cheek was actually a deep scar. The young lady was standing outside her room, smiling, her arms extended toward the girl. Hyŏn was curious. This was the first time he had seen the young lady open her arms to the girl. Perplexed, the girl stared up at the young lady's face. Then she looked back just in time to see the cat run out from behind her and jump into the young lady's arms. "Oh, my daughter," the young lady might have been murmuring to herself as she held the cat to her breast.

This black cat was the only one allowed to enter the young lady's room when a pair of men's shoes sat outside her door. Inside, the cat would nestle in her arms, crawl around her bosom, climb to her shoulders. And after attaching itself to the young lady, it would often lick the rims of her ears and her rouged cheeks. The young lady would then go into the kitchen, slice several pieces of raw meat, and place them on her palm in front of the cat. The cat would eat them, the blood staining the edges of its mouth like lipstick. Finally, it would stretch, yawn, and withdraw, leaving a couple of slices of meat uneaten. The young lady would then take the cat to the sunny part of the yard and give it a bath. The cat was used to this and merely blinked when its fur was lathered with soap; it was more docile than the girl was when the landlady washed her hair. The cat was carried to the young lady's room, where it played with the flowers.

The flowers were as various as the shoes of the men who visited the young lady. Only when a man left and the young lady went out on one of her visits could the little girl have the flowers of her choice. The girl would plant sprigs of these flowers around the sewer drain. There she left them, not removing a single one, until they withered.

Once Hyŏn gave the girl a vase so she would have a place to put her flowers. For a moment she didn't know what to do with it, but then she set in down and raced downstairs. She came back a little later with the sprigs she had planted near the drain and put them in the vase. Either the flower petals were torn, or they were wilted. The torn petals must have been the work of the cat, as it played with the flowers with its claws and teeth. The girl changed the water in the vase as often as possible. If the cat tried to bat at the flowers, the girl grabbed it and threw it to the floor. But the sturdy cat would land on its feet and stand its ground, as if to prove it was a match for the girl. Then it would stretch and yawn, extending its middle and hunching its back.

As time went by, the young lady's sojourns got longer and longer, and the cat began to grow thin. When the girl threw the cat away from the flowers, it was barely able to land on its feet. Then it would climb onto the windowsill. One day the girl crept up behind the cat and tried to push it out the window to the ground below. But the cat managed to flatten itself against the sill and escape back inside, tipping over the vase. The vase broke at the neck, and the flowers, which were already withered anyway, fell out, their petals scattering. As Hyŏn picked up the petals floating in the water on the floor, the young lady's dimplelike scar kept appearing in his mind. He placed the petals and sprigs in the broken vase, then took it to a vacant lot at the corner of a nearby alley. He threw it onto a pile of dung, dead rats, and broken dishes under a sign on the back wall of a house that said, "Don't Anybody Urinate Here."

As the cat wasted away, it sometimes came home from the vacant lot with a dead rat in its mouth. When that happened, the landlady cursed the cat and chased it with the stick that she used to poke the mother rabbit. But not for its life would the cat part with the rat—it would climb up the outside of the chimney and hide in a corner of the roof. The landlady would rap the chimney with her stick and yell at the cat to get it to let go of the rat and come down. Finally she would throw the stick aside and go into the kitchen. The cat would come down from the roof licking blood from its mouth and begin sunning itself under the veranda.

Once the girl stole up to the cat and poked at its half-closed eyes with a sharp stick, but the cat just batted the stick away. The girl then started clawing the cat's face, but the cat clawed the backs of her hands. The girl clawed more forcefully, then, when the cat was about to run away, she grabbed it around the middle and rolled it on the ground. The cat got covered with dirt. The girl then tied a piece of colored fabric to the cat's tail. The cat chased its tail, trying to catch the fabric in its mouth. The girl went around in circles, too. Soon, after tottering several times, she keeled over. The cat kept going. Exasperated, the girl got up and started turning in circles again, trying to outlast the cat. But then she plopped down again and couldn't bring herself to get up. She was even dizzy lying down. Her upper body swayed round and round. The cat kept turning in circles, trying to catch the colored fabric. The girl was clearly the loser in this circling game. A few minutes later she rose, picked up the landlady's stick, and hit the cat's belly as hard as she could. The cat rolled over with a howl and scurried away.

When the girl had nothing else to do, she could play with the mute boy who lived next door. The landlady called him an opium addict. The boy had come here to live with some distant relatives after his parents died from opium addiction. Though mute, the boy could hear, and he would look down with shame when the landlady declared that the little bastard had turned his parents into addicts and destroyed them; it was rotten luck, but that's what happened when you had a boy whose nose turned up toward the sky. When the boy played with the girl, he undertook all the drudgery—kneading mud into the shape of food when they played house, putting the food in one of the larger, prettier-colored potsherds, and serving it to the girl and her doll. The girl never shared this food. Even so, the boy watched in satisfaction, with no sign of displeasure, as she kept touching the mud to the lips of the doll and saying "Eat, Mother." But this sight had him drooling before he noticed it. When the boy's father had started taking opium, the mother nagged him trying to get him to stop. The hounding ended when the father forced her to become an addict as well. The two then had to compete for opium, and finally the father sold the mother away. But the mother secretly visited the boy and had him steal his father's opium. The boy was caught by his father and beaten again and again. In the end the father ripped out the boy's tongue to prevent him from communicating with his mother. Since then the boy had been unable to talk, and he drooled helplessly without realizing it. Whenever the girl saw him drool, she scowled and jumped up. "Filthy!" The boy understood and sucked in the spittle. But the girl would disappear inside without looking back. At such times the boy also went home, never waiting for the girl to come out.

After one such incident, the boy came to play with the girl, offering her a broken piece of porcelain he had smoothed. She accepted it as if it were her due. The boy then took a shiny blue potsherd from his shabby vest, placed it on a rock, and began smoothing its edges. It was a piece of the vase Hyŏn had thrown away in the empty lot. Whenever the boy struck one of the sharp edges with a stone, bits of porcelain flew up. The girl stood far enough away to avoid them. The boy kept smoothing and didn't seem to mind when the chips flew in his face or down his neck and inside his sleeves. Suddenly he lifted his left hand, the one holding the potsherd. He had struck his thumb by mistake, and immediately blood had begun to well up from the cut. In no time it stained the piece of porcelain. The girl retreated a step and wrinkled her nose at this awful sight. But the boy flicked his hand back and forth once or twice and went back to smoothing the potsherd. The bits of porcelain flew faster than before. Finally he was done. He polished the smoothed potsherd on his threadbare pants and handed it to the girl. The girl received it as if this were only proper and added it to her other potsherds.

Sensing that the girl was about to become bored with the potsherds, the boy took two clamshells from his vest. After fitting the shells together, he began rubbing the hinged side against a crock of soy sauce to make holes to blow through. The rubbing produced a ringing screech. The girl covered her ears, withdrew farther than before, and watched the boy. The landlady came out of the kitchen wiping her hands on her skirt and yelled that the damned addict ought to be grateful he was allowed to play with the girl, but instead he had the nerve to make that terrible racket. But before the landlady could make the boy stop, the girl snapped at her to go away. The boy kept rubbing the shells. The landlady went back to the kitchen mumbling to herself that the handicapped didn't have an ounce of kindness. Finally the boy stopped rubbing, his hands worn out. But he had made holes in the shells. He started to bring the place with the holes to his mouth, but then he noticed that he was drooling again. His face crinkling in alarm, he offered the girl the shells. "Filthy!" The girl spat, then took them. Showing no desire to blow into them, she threw the shells under the soy-crock terrace, breaking them to pieces.

After a few moments, the boy suddenly ran out the gate. The girl picked up some of the prettier and more shapely pieces of shell as if nothing had happened and added them to her pieces of porcelain. She had started playing house with her doll when the boy returned, panting. He took a handful of sawdust from his vest and held it in front of the girl. He had gotten it from the sawyers' workplace at the corner of the empty lot. After removing the rest of the sawdust, which filled both pockets of his vest, he buried one hand in the sawdust and began patting it with the other, firmly and evenly. Then he carefully withdrew his hand from the sawdust. Instead of forming a cave, however, the sawdust crumbled. Again the boy buried his hand in the sawdust and patted it, and again the sawdust crumbled. Impatient, the girl scattered the sawdust with a sweep of her hand. The sawdust flew into the boy's face. A smile of enjoyment rose at the corners of the girl's lips, and she sprinkled the boy's face with a handful of the sawdust. The boy didn't move, merely closed his eyes. The girl sprinkled his face with another handful of sawdust. This time the boy recoiled as if surprised. Her interest heightened, the girl now sprinkled the sawdust with both hands. The boy flinched again. The girl raked the sawdust together again and again with both hands and showered the boy with it; by now she was giggling. The louder she giggled, the more forcefully the boy ducked. Eventually the girl lost interest in this game and her laughter faded. The boy got up with a sudden look of satisfaction and dashed out the gate without glancing at the girl. That was the last time he came to play with her.

On his way home from the laboratory, Hyŏn sometimes saw the boy playing near the two elderly men who sawed logs in the empty lot. A sign saying "If You're Not a Dog, Don't Urinate Here" was now posted beside the sign saying "Don't Anybody Urinate Here." The two men worked their saw lengthwise down a large log that was propped up at one end, dusting the hair of the boy and the lower man. The boy heaped sawdust into a mound. A keen scent of wood rose from the sawdust. The log, the bent back of the elderly man standing on it, and the saw being pulled and pushed — all were in dull silhouette against the glow gathering in the evening sky. The sawdust was like falling snow. Whenever he saw them, Hyŏn thought that real snow whiter than the sawdust would surely begin to fall before the men finished sawing all the dark logs piled in the corner of the lot.

Hyŏn returned from the laboratory exhausted and sprawled on the floor of his room. The late-summer evenings were darkening more and more quickly. Suddenly he could smell the rats he had been handling at the lab. Surely the smell was coming from his hands. Hyŏn raised his head and looked at his hands, but it was already too dark to see them. The walls and ceiling seemed to press in on him. The corners of the walls and ceiling were not square but round. He could not sense which way he was lying. Sometimes he would awaken, his heart quickening, to find he wasn't lying where he thought: the window that should have been above his head was at his feet, things that should have been at his right were at his left. But today he hadn't even fallen asleep before he sprang up in alarm, thinking that the blur of the window was in the wrong place.

"Damned cat! That damned cat!"

The thumping of the landlady's feet on the stairway followed her voice into Hyŏn's room. Hyŏn turned on the light. The stairs he thought to be at his feet were at his head. He opened the door. The cat came in with something in its mouth, the landlady in pursuit with the stick she had used to poke the mother rabbit that morning. It was a dead baby rabbit. The landlady's wrinkled face twitched, and she tried to grab the cat, saying she hadn't realized the damned thing was eating all the little rabbits. The cat easily eluded her.

The girl ran into the room and grabbed the cat by the middle; the animal tried to squirm free. When she yanked at the dead rabbit, the cat arched its back, hissing spitefully through clenched jaws. Hate filled its eyes. Hyŏn now grabbed at the rabbit, and part of it tore free. The girl went down the stairs clutching the cat in her arms. "I'd better kill that damned cat," muttered the landlady. "All it's good for is bringing dead rats into the house and eating up baby rabbits." Hyŏn went down the stairs holding the piece of rabbit. In the darkness outside he could barely see the girl hurl the cat to the ground. The cat howled and disappeared beside the rabbit hutch. Hyŏn went to the hutch and showed the remains of the baby rabbit to the mother. The hutch was quiet, as if the mother rabbit, like the goldfish that had lost its mate, knew nothing. Hyŏn had to kick the hutch to make his point, and only then was he able to startle the rabbit. He decided to take it to the lab the next day.

Hyŏn took the piece of rabbit to the open sewer beside the street leading to the park. The farther his eyes traveled down the ditch, the darker it appeared. The smell was foul and repulsive. Hyŏn dropped the rabbit into the ditch. There was a soft plop and the ditch became still again, filling the air with its stench. The goldfish the girl had dropped down the drain at his boardinghouse would be dead and rotten before coming this far, he told himself. While gazing into the dark sewer, he had a recurring illusion that it was flowing upstream. He walked on toward the park.

At the park Hyŏn went to a broadleaf tree and stretched out his hand. The dewy leaves infused him with their damp coolness. Hyŏn withdrew his hand, but then stretched out both hands and rubbed them with the leaves. He went to a bench and sat. The clouds had not parted for even an instant. With the moon cloaked, the sky was as black as the ditch. The shadows in this part of the park were darker because the few lights along the paths were screened by trees.

Hyŏn left the park and went to a well-lit market. An elderly woman in a stall near the entrance to the market was sitting among some brightly colored toys amusing herself. A toy tank wheeled about, knocking down other toys. The woman sent a self-righting doll rolling down a slide. The tank knocked the doll over at the bottom. The doll rolled away and righted itself again.

Hyŏn returned to the park. A boy and a girl were sitting on the bench he had occupied. They were laughing in a shrill, affected manner. Hyŏn turned away. His hands still felt sticky, as if exuding a bloody smell. He returned to the broadleaf tree. This time he picked some leaves, rubbed them between his palms, and wiped the backs of his hands and each of his fingers with them. Their grassy smell was stronger than the bloody stink. Then he noticed a different smell, not blood or grass—the scent of cheap face powder. He lit a cigarette. No one was there. He was about to reach up to the leaves again when something whitish appeared right in front of him. He stepped back in surprise. A woman next to him laughed nervously and asked for a light. But her outstretched hand snatched the cigarette from his mouth before he could hand it to her. The area around her nose, which looked reddish in the glow from the cigarette, was discolored with a mark that her thick facial powder could not conceal. The tips of the cigarettes fell away from each other, and the woman's face disappered in a cloud of smoke. The woman held Hyŏn's cigarette out to him in the darkness. He reached for it. She brushed his hand aside. Her hand, which held his cigarette, probed for his mouth. Hyŏn stuck out his lips, only to find that the woman was trying to pass him the lighted end of the cigarette. He slapped the cigarette from her hand and strode away. Behind him, the woman giggled.

Hyŏn slipped out of the park. Just before reaching the sewer, he took a shortcut down an alley next to a small shop, and he was home in no time. He went upstairs to his room and found the cat inside, licking the floor—probably some blood had dripped from the baby rabbit. The cat noticed Hyŏn and lifted its vigilant eyes to him, but soon its red tongue was diligently licking the floor again. Hyŏn decided he would give the cat to the woman he had just seen at the park. He approached the cat, petted it briefly, then grabbed it. The cat licked its mouth, unconcerned, twitched its ears this way and that, and started licking the backs of Hyŏn's hands—still that smell. Hyŏn tied a small towel around the cat's eyes. The cat struggled a moment, then licked Hyŏn's hands some more.

Hyŏn held the cat to his chest and stole from the house. This time he took the long way to the park, following the sewer. Moonlight suddenly appeared as he walked along the ditch.

Hyŏn tucked his jacket tightly around the cat. It grew dark again. Hyŏn entered the park and went straight to the foot of the broadleaf tree. The leaves, damper and cooler than before, brushed against his ears, chilling them. Hyŏn placed the cat under his arm and struck a match, but the flame touched a moist leaf and went out. He struck another match, but there was only the blackish gleam of the leaves; no one was there. Hyŏn lit a cigarette and went to the bench where the boy and the girl had been laughing. He sat down. The market had closed, and it was dark there now. Hyŏn spied something shadowy moving back and forth in the gloom in front of him. Wondering if this was an illusion, he looked carefully and discovered two dogs mating. Locked end to end, they were taking turns trying to move forward. The moon reappeared. The thin dog nearer Hyŏn, its eyeballs and long, drooping tongue glistening, pulled the other dog a couple of steps forward. The other immediately pulled the first dog back those few steps. This action was repeated over and over under the moonlight.

Clouds covered the moon again and Hyŏn got up, but there was a weight on his shoulder. It was a drunken woman – whether the same woman, he couldn't tell. Hyŏn tried to move aside, but the woman wrapped her arm roughly about his neck and brought her lips close to him; they reeked of liquor. "Bet you thought no one knew. You're abandoning a baby. Yes, indeed." Instead of explaining, Hyŏn gripped the cat more securely and tried to avoid the woman. But she kept after him, asking whether the baby was a boy or a girl. Hyŏn heaved the woman aside. She staggered and then squatted in a heap. "This is the best time of year to abandon a baby," she said. She herself had given birth to twins, a boy and a girl, and gotten rid of them here. The woman broke out in hollow laughter. Hyŏn escaped before the moon came out again.

He reached the edge of the park, and it occurred to him that giving the cat to the woman with the cigarette might be tantamount to returning it to the young lady in his boardinghouse. The cat would be better off as a stray, he thought. He decided to set it loose in the park. He removed the towel from the cat's eyes and flung the animal into the darkness as hard as he could. Then he ran from the park. When he got to a street that had some lights, he took a good look behind. The cat wasn't following him. Hyŏn took the shortcut home rather than the route next to the sewer. He wondered what would happen when the young lady returned to find the cat gone.

But when he got up to his room, Hyŏn found the cat lapping the water in the fishbowl. He turned off the light. Moonlight filtered through the window. The cat kept on drinking. Hyŏn approached the cat as if to pet it, then grabbed it around the belly. But as he picked it up, the cat's forepaws hooked the fishbowl, and it toppled over. In the moonlight, the goldfish looked like a single huge fish scale flopping in the spilled water. Hyŏn seized the cat by the neck. It had eaten up all the baby rabbits, now it would be the goldfish. The cat licked the hands clutching its neck. Hyŏn gripped harder. Die! The cat clawed at Hyŏn's hands, its eyes burning blue in the moonlight. Hyŏn squeezed the cat's throat harder and harder. Die! Die! He finally let the cat go when he saw sparks in its eyes. The cat fell to the floor, and after clawing at the air, it bolted up and slinked out the door, which had been left open a crack.

The goldfish had stopped moving. Hyŏn returned it to the bit of water remaining in the fishbowl and took the bowl outside to the pump. Its white belly listing to the side, the fish lay motionless in the water, which was too shallow to cover its back. Hyŏn ran fresh water into the bowl and was about to turn around when he spotted something at the dark opening of the drain. Something was moving among the flowers the girl had planted there. Hyŏn gently parted the stems, whose petals had already fallen, and picked up a small fish. Could it have come up from the sewer through this pipe? Did it mean there were fish living in the sewer? And if there were, how could this one have gotten all the way here? He quickly rinsed the fish, placed it in the bowl, and took it upstairs.

Hyŏn turned on the light and examined the fish from the sewer pipe. In the place where its eyes should have been there were faint hollows like festering sores. Blind and dark all over, the small fish wriggled about. Time and again it collided with the goldfish, which had barely been able to right itself and was moving its fins anxiously. The goldfish's reaction was to wiggle briefly. Indifferent to the blind fish, it came to rest, finning vigorously. The blind fish got more jumpy, butting the sides of the bowl and almost leaping out of the water. Suddenly it turned on its side; soon it had stopped finning. The goldfish now began to swim about animatedly, as if completely recovered. The blind fish rocked slightly in the churning water, its tail resting on the surface.

Hyŏn picked up the blind fish. Its belly had already begun to swell. He went to the window and threw the fish out. It continued to shine like a muddy scale as it fell in the moonlight. The cat dashed over from the rabbit hutch, took the fish in its mouth, and ran back under the hutch.

The day Hyŏn took the mother rabbit to the laboratory, he passed the empty lot on his way home and saw the sign reading "If You're Not a Dog, Don't Urinate Here." Next to it, "Dogs' Toilet" had been written on the wall. Decomposed rats, dung, and broken dishes were scattered every which way. He got to the place where the sawyers worked. Today the boy was sitting apart, his back to Hyŏn. Probably making a mound of sawdust, Hyŏn thought. But then, as he passed behind him, he caught a glimpse of what the boy was doing. Hyŏn stopped in surprise. Wasn't that a baby rabbit? The boy was about to serve the rabbit some sawdust in an attractive, smoothed potsherd. But the rabbit didn't budge. It was dead. Had the boy taken the baby rabbits one by one after losing the girl as a playmate? Had he been playing with them like this? Hyŏn was about to leave before the boy noticed him, when the cat suddenly appeared and snatched away the rabbit in its mouth before the boy could lift a hand. With a guttural shout, the boy set off in pursuit. Hyŏn joined the chase, following the boy into the evening shadows.

tr. BRUCE AND JU-CHAN FULTON

REEDS

갈대

Last year's broken reeds trembled above the new grass.

In a vacant lot, little more than black dirt, a swarm of mosquito larvae rose, then sank in a dark puddle; maggots squirmed out of the puddle and then were submerged once more in the thick, black, muddy water.

A mangy dog holding a bone in its mouth skirted the edge of the puddle. Curling up by a large, rotten log, the emaciated dog began to chew on the bone but could not gnaw through it. The dog left the bone and sniffed around before coming back to it again.

While the dog was licking the bone, a young girl hurled a clod of dirt in its direction. She missed, but the dog flinched and yelped.

The girl plopped down on the ground and squeezed a sore on her calf. Sunlight leaked through a gap in the clouds, touching her back. The girl pulled her elbows up toward her armpits as if she were being tickled and broke into a laugh that seemed much older than her years.

The weather was as mild as could be.

The dog approached the dirt-walled hovel where the girl lived at the back of the vacant lot. The girl's grandfather was coming out of the hovel. He called to her across the lot.

"Child, come have a look at your father!"

The girl just sat there, biting back the laughter on her lips.

Now the old man saw the bone the dog had dropped at his feet. He lifted a large rock next to it, placed the bone in the depression, and stamped it down firmly with his foot.

The dog went into the hovel through a flap of canvas that served as a door.

Inside, the girl's father was lying down. He put an opium needle to his gaunt, bruised, jaundiced arm, but he trembled and slipped as he tried to insert it. Yellowish snot dripped from his flaring, black nostrils and pooled on his upper lip. He barely managed to inject himself. He became very quiet with the needle still stuck in his arm.

With its pale tongue, the dog licked the man's face, then went out.

At the edge of the puddle, the dog was licking the bone.

The girl walked past the rotten log, accompanied by a boy bearing a knapsack. "Do you know what that dog's got in its mouth?" she asked.

The boy looked at the dog. Then he turned back to girl and shook his head.

"It's a bone! A human bone!" said the girl. She observed the boy's anxious expression and smiled to herself. "You know, once that dog eats a hundred skulls, it'll turn into a human being. There's plenty of bones here if you just dig a little ways. This place was all graves before. That puddle's a gravesite, too. My grandfather used to be the gravekeeper. He still makes his rounds every night. They say soon this place is going to be packed with big houses. Ghosts will come and wander around then. My mother ran away because she was haunted by a ghost and my father's dying because he's possessed by a ghost."

A weak rain began to crumble down from the sky. The dog tried to shake off the raindrops, but it staggered and collapsed.

After the rain stopped, the dog kept on whimpering all through the black night.

The girl's grandfather sat on the rotten log and looked in the direction of the dog's whimpering.

Suddenly, at his side, there was a cackling sound. A street woman had appeared. She sat at one end of the log. Her white face and hands seemed to be floating in a pool of darkness.

The old man got up and went toward the dirt-walled hovel. The cackling sound behind him stopped abruptly. He turned his head. Something like a hand gestured vaguely from near the log. The old man changed directions and walked toward it.

The vaporous hand and the woman were both gone. The old man had nearly bumped into a pine tree. He stopped short. When he looked, he saw that the tree was still a few paces ahead of him.

The dog whimpered in the dark.

The dog went back into the hovel. With its tongue, now dark and mottled, the dog licked the snot that dripped onto the upper lip of the girl's father, who lay there shivering, not even able to open his eyes.

The dog dropped the bone by the log and staggered around in circles.

The girl walked toward the dog, limping on her sore-covered leg.

Before she reached it, the dog yelped and tucked its tail between its legs.

The shivering dog crouched by the water, chewing the bone, then dropping it again.

Sitting on the log with another boy who also had a knapsack, the girl asked, "Do you know what that dog's eating?"

The boy quickly shook his head.

"It's a human bone. Once it eats a hundred skulls, it'll turn into a human being. This place was all graves before. It's still full of skeletons if you dig a little ways. Want to try?"

The girl looked into the boy's face as he quickly shook his head again. She laughed to herself and said, "My grandfather still makes his rounds here every night, he used to be the gravekeeper, big houses are going to go up here and ghosts will come and wander around. My mother already ran away because she was haunted by a ghost, and my father's dying because he's possessed by a ghost, and when Father dies Grandfather will take him out and bury him, and then the dog will suck on his bones."

On the day the clear weather ended and the cold rain poured down again, the dog fell dead.

A thin, cold rain continued to fall well into the evening.

The girl's grandfather came out with a shovel and walked toward the puddle.

Something black was moving at the place where the dog had fallen dead. There was a cackling sound.

As the old man hurried over, the street woman, her white face turned toward him, ran toward the road and vanished with the dead dog.

In the vacant lot, the grass grew over last year's broken reeds. The gnarled, spreading branches of the pine tree were greener.

The sun's rays stung, and in each crack in the rotten log, poisonous-looking green moss grew once more. Tiny red worms crawled through the moss.

New mosquito larvae swarmed in the puddle. Maggots began to appear in the filthy, stagnant water. Whether or not there were clouds, the sky was never reflected in the puddle.

The bone that the mangy dog had once carried around in its mouth had been carelessly cast aside. When the girl's grandfather saw it, he covered it with dirt and firmly tamped it down.

Shards of celadon ceramic buried in the dirt shone green in the sunlight.

The girl stretched her sore-covered leg out to yet another boy with a knapsack. "Hey," she said, "squeeze this for me. Hard, huh?"

Before the the dazed boy had even touched her, the girl lay back, and not caring that she was on the spot where the dog had died, she laughed and laughed as if she were being tickled.

tr. HEINZ J. FENKL

EVEN WOLVES

이리도

Between my second and third years of middle school, after I got home from school each day, I almost seemed to live at the home of my friend, who had recently moved into the neighborhood. Since he lived nearby, surely the boy Man-su must have come to my home as well, but as far as I can remember now, I only visited him. Why would that have been?

Man-su lived in a small house with his mother. The president of a successful rubber company in P'yŏngyang, his father had set up a separate household for his concubine and seemed to have broken ties with Man-su's mother. The only time I saw Man-su's father was at the funeral for Man-su's mother, just before Man-su moved away from the village, which would have been late spring of our third year of middle school. Even then, no one pointed out Man-su's father to me. On that day—I think it was a Sunday—when I went to the funeral, I was able to pick out Man-su's father from among the few people gathered there. His face, appearing from beneath a hempen mourning hood, looked like Man-su's. With his clear features, this handsome young man wearing a smart-looking coat over his suit did not look old enough to be anything but Man-su's brother.

Compared with her husband, Man-su's mother had looked quite wrinkled and old. There was no way you could think of the two as husband and wife. It seemed, if Man-su was her son, he must have been born late in her life. But Man-su was the couple's first child, born after their rather early marriage. They had no other children.

What's more, Man-su's mother always seemed to be ill. Since she didn't have many mouths to feed and care for, she was always tidy, but the shadow of illness never left her face. Thinking about it now, I wonder if she looked that way because of the grayish cast of her complexion. Perhaps it grew more severe with the failure of her marriage. Her death in her early thirties may have been due to the shock of her husband's leaving her.

What I am going to talk about, however, is not Man-su's family. I want to begin by talking about the house Man-su lived in—more specifically, the room he occupied.

Man-su's room was at the east end of the house. From the time Man-su came to our village until he moved inland with his maternal uncle—just over a year—I grew fond of this room, which I visited every day. Since the room faced east, when I dropped by in the morning on the way to school, the sliding paper door in front would catch the full sun, invigorating us with its brightness. But this room really became ours after dinner.

We studied together. We talked together. Man-su was not a particularly cheerful boy. Still, he was by no means melancholy. This was true in class as well. He was not the kind of boy who would stand up alone and cause a disturbance, but he would laugh and talk with others.

Man-su played the harmonica well. I also enjoyed the harmonica then, so we played together. But we didn't play with the music book sitting in front of us. The two of us played at random, not the way we had learned to play from sheet music. We played songs we had learned at school, popular songs we had heard on the street—every song we knew.

It didn't matter who started the song; the other would follow along. Out of breath and heedless of our aching cheeks, we kept playing. Over and over we played songs we had played just moments before. These two boys at the height of their youth could not deny this season of their lives—we played and played again, exhausting our energy, until it seemed the house would be blown away. I think that probably, if we could have seen it from the outside, the once quiet home would probably have appeared to have taken on some strange animated spirit from the sound of the harmonicas.

Only when we were exhausted did we stop playing. Neither of us decided in advance how long we would play before quitting. When one of us stopped, the other followed suit and put down his harmonica.

Then we would lie on the floor with our hands behind our heads. For a moment neither of us would speak. Compared with the clamor up to that time, the silence was sudden and extreme. Finally, along with the whole house, our room once again seemed to sink down to the bottom of the sea. Sometimes Mansu's mother would come and break the stillness. She brought us watermelon or yellow *ch'amoe* melons, apples, chestnuts, or oranges.

Whenever we had exhausted ourselves playing the harmonica or were tired of studying or talking and lay down with our hands behind our heads, our eyes always rested on a picture of the sea hanging on the wall. It was a rather large color photograph.

At first glance, there seemed to be nothing in the picture but a few waves with large and small whitecaps spread across the boundless sea. Where the water met the sky, several fragments of clouds floated like bits of cotton strewn carelessly across the horizon. Several other spots of white, which seemed to have broken off from these clouds, drifted in the sky. They were sea gulls. There was nothing else.

But actually, that's not quite true. Far off, on the distant horizon, there was a black spot. It looked like a flaw in the photograph, but it was not. If you examined it closely, the spot appeared to be producing wispy smoke. It was a ship. It was hard to tell whether it was sailing off beyond the horizon or moving this way, but it was undoubtedly a boat.

As I think about it now, it was not particularly interesting as photographs go, but it was enough to spur our hearts to dream. Or was it to yearn? Back then, Man-su was sure of the dream he had his heart set on, more than you would expect at his age.

Man-su always said he would become a sailor and travel the whole world. Even then, his eyes held a curious gleam. In those eyes I could read the names of the ports I had heard him speak of. Nearby, there were Shanghai, Hong Kong, Singapore, Colombo, Bombay . . . A little farther, through the Suez Canal, Athens, Naples, Marseilles. . . . And farther distant, London, Hamburg, and Capetown.

Man-su was good at rowing a boat. Once or twice during summer vacation he came to my house wearing white running shorts and lured me down to the Taedong River.

That's right! Even if he didn't come at other times, he *did* come to my house for this reason. But now that I recall that he actually did come to my house at least a couple of times, why do I still feel as though he never came to my house and that I always went to his? I don't know. It must be because I can't think of anything to say about my relationship with Man-su outside that house and that room.

Our room. The time we spent there, though not long, was a part of our lives in the prime of our boyhood. It was a dream like the wisp of smoke that streamed from the ship — that one spot on the boundless horizon in the photograph on the wall. Was it the incomprehensible vitality of boyhood? Or the radiation of continual passion? In our many talks, dreams and vitality and passion all merged together. The memory of all these things appeared and disappeared like foam on the water of the sea in the photograph, like a conversation that was erased from my memory long ago . . .

Even now, however, if I close the door tightly and search thoroughly inside, I can still breathe a bit of something that is left there, but it's not that I grope through that room trying to touch something. Rather, I am trying to communicate with a world that was newer and wider than our small room — a world broader than the ocean on our wall. And it was not the newness or the wideness that we had learned of in geography at school, and yet it was a world apart from our misty dreams of those days. Our temperaments made us feel our one small room was insufficient, and it made us open up a new world as big as could be, one we could not see on the wall.

The person who made us communicate with the wide world from our room was Man-su's uncle. What remains now in my memory is the impression of a man with a dusky complexion, a little on the short side but otherwise average in build. His eyes sometimes flashed strangely, which was his way of making us feel close to him, but they did nothing to help me know his inner feelings. I knew only what Man-su had told me, that his uncle had gone to Manchuria and Hingan Ling long ago and had led a wandering life. I had no way of knowing why this man had lived in such a way. Indeed, I was very young then. But, even if I had been old enough to understand such things and had had the chance to learn about his life, and even if it had remained in my memory until now, I would still not write about him in any detail, because his life has no great bearing on the story of us boys.

The first time I met him was in our room on a cold winter evening. I say "first time," but I only met him twice all together. The second time was when I saw him at Man-su's mother's funeral, standing with his head bowed beside Man-su's father, so that cold night was really the first and last time.

He told us all kinds of stories. Thrilling stories of Manchu horsemen, legends of mysterious Chinese men and birds. One night, in a blizzard in northern Manchuria, he heard a jackal's bark and the sound of horses in a stable shuffling their hooves on the frozen earth and the jingling of bells on the sleigh of a late traveler. He suddenly felt the desolate isolation of the place, and thoughts of home burned in his heart, but he said his memories grew more dear to him after he returned to his Korean homeland. As soon as the funeral for Man-su's mother was over, he took Man-su inland with him. I do not know if Man-su stayed there or became a sailor as he had long wanted to do.

Of all the stories he told us, one allowed us to open the door of our room, revealing a great, fresh view of a new, wider world; it was his story of Hingan Ling.

Hingan Ling is a range of hills covered with white birch trees in Hulun. It opens out onto a vast plain where packs of tens and hundreds of wolves roam.

To protect themselves from attack by wild beasts at night, cows sleep in a circle with their horns facing outward and their calves in the center. Horses, as one would expect, stand around the young ones with their heads inward to sleep.

The Mongolians there led a uniquely simple life, though it is probably quite different these days. In some ways these Mongolians' features resemble those of our people, and their language, too, has some similarities, words like "mother," "father," "baby," and "soybean." I would give you other examples, but I've forgotten them. Once, when Man-su's uncle had traveled somewhere (when he told us the story, he said the name of the place quite clearly, but I've forgotten that too—would it have been Wangyamyo?), he was taking a nap on a summer day. He awoke to the sound of a commotion outside. He heard loud voices arguing in what sounded like the Kyŏngsan dialect of the southern part of Korea. Wondering why some Koreans would be fighting like this in a foreign land, he stuck his head outside and discovered that they were not from Kyŏngsan Province at all, but an old Mongolian couple.

The story Man-su's uncle told us took place in an area where he had recently traveled. There was no inn, so when he finally arrived at a house in the evening, he explained his situation and arranged to stay there for the night.

There was one other guest in the house, a Japanese man about the same age as Man-su's uncle.

The kind and cordial master of the house even treated his guests to wine, a special wine made with sheep milk and served with mutton. The master of the house spoke Chinese, as did the

Japanese man, so the three of them spent the evening talking, not noticing the passing time as the wine cup made its rounds.

By the time the fading light of the beef tallow lamp revealed the lateness of the hour, they had dozed off. Suddenly, the two dogs outside began to bark. Once they started they would not stop, barking as if to announce impending doom. Opening the door, the master shouted, "What is it?" Then he turned back to the two travelers and told them that a wolf pack was about.

Then a smile played about the almost naive face of this man with his characteristic dark red Mongolian beard. He told them that the dogs cowered and barked like that when wolves or other animals were around. He said the dogs would face the same direction and bark if they saw a stranger, but when it was someone they knew, they would bark just once.

The dogs had stopped when the master shouted at them, but now they began to bark and growl more frantically than before. It seemed the wolf pack was close by.

The Japanese man had been sitting facing the master, but he abruptly sprang to his feet. In his hand was a pistol that he must have been hiding somewhere.

The master of the house looked startled. He put out his hand to block the Japanese guest. His face red from drinking, the Japanese man turned toward the master, as if to say, "What do you think you're doing? Just stay here and watch me."

As the master withdrew his hand, he told the Japanese man quietly that if he were to fire, one shot into the air would scare the wolves away. Hearing these words, the Japanese man did not argue, but merely stuck the pistol outside, fired one shot at random, then returned to his seat.

The conversation turned to beasts of the wild. The master ended up doing all the talking while the other two men listened. In these mountains it was considered something of a virtue not to kill any animal indiscriminately, whether it be bird, beast, or even insect. One point that travelers from other lands had to take particular care about was that they should not shoot directly at the wolves if they were to come upon a pack. If the wolves gave them trouble, the best thing to do would be to fire into the air to scare them away with the sound. You might think that firing directly into the wolf pack would be the best method, but it most certainly was not. Of course, it would do no harm to bring down one or two wolves that might be wandering near a house, but if a person out in an uninhabited area shot at a pack of wolves just for the fun of it, he would be injured. Wolves, like all other animals, hate and fear the smell of gunpowder, but you must realize that once they have seen blood – whether the blood of one of their own or the blood of another animal – once they have seen it or smelled it, they don't just come after you – they lunge at you, crazed. Then, saying that there had been an incident like that some five years earlier, the master told this story.

Three soldiers on border patrol got drunk and were taking a walk one night when they met up with a wolf pack. They knew if they just stayed calm and fired a single shot in the air, then found a house nearby, that they would be safe. But they had had a lot of wine. They faced the wolves head on and began to fire. Once it came to this, the end of their bullets meant the end of their lives. The next morning there was nothing left of them but three guns and a few tatters of blood-stained clothing.

When the two men had heard this much of the story, the dogs began to cower and bark again, as if the wolves had appeared once more. Then, almost simultaneously, the master shouted outside and the Japanese traveler got up, pulling out his pistol as he had before. This time the master did not put out his hand to stop him. He seemed to think the Japanese man had gotten up to fire into the air as he had done the first time.

But, even in the dim light of the lamp, the master could see the sudden excited movement of the Japanese traveler and the expression of scorn that had risen in his face. Then the Japanese man spoke. "They were fools. It wasn't just one man – there were three. On top of that, they had guns. And, still they were attacked and eaten. When I was in the army, I was famous for my shooting. I want to show you the ability of a citizen of the great Japanese empire." He told them to watch him closely. An unspeakably bloodthirsty look appeared on the Japanese traveler's face.

Finally, looking alarmed, the master put out his hand to block the Japanese traveler's way. He asked the Japanese man not to do it. He asked him to sit down and have another round of wine. With his other hand the master poured a new cup, but the Japanese traveler said the wine could wait. He told the master that they could have a drink together as a toast after he had driven away the wolf pack. Pushing aside the master's hand, he went outside.

The master seemed confused, he didn't know what to do. But, in a dignified manner, as before, he told Man-su's uncle that they should let him go outside to shoot a wolf since he was near a house, if it would give the man so much satisfaction.

Man-su's uncle listened closely to the echo of a gunshot. He could not hear it very well. Why was that? The master appeared to be listening, too. Finally, from a distance they heard the sound of a gun again, followed by the cry of a beast, like that of a baby.

The master jumped up. "This is terrible. It sounds like he's rather far away. I didn't know he had that in him," he murmured. An anxious look appeared on his face, and he dashed outside.

Man-su's uncle also dashed out. The air outside was suddenly thick—a change that often occurred on the continent. It struck his face and cleared his head after all the wine he had drunk. But, in the darkness, he could distinguish nothing, though the sky was strewn with stars.

The master shouted, "Quick! Come back!" Then he cried out several times. Though Man-su's uncle did not know what the man had said, he guessed that he had shouted to keep the wolves from approaching the Japanese traveler.

Again, a gun sounded. This time the master faced the direction from which the sound had come, calling for the man to come back quickly. Then he repeated the same strange cry over and over and started running in the direction of the sound. Man-su's uncle chased after him.

The gun kept on firing. It suddenly stopped. Then there was a queer scream mixed with the sound of a shot. Man-su's uncle faced in that direction and heard a sound like the driven wind.

The master instantly halted his steps and muttered to himself, "This has all gone wrong." Turning around, he urged Man-su's uncle to go back to the house, saying it was dangerous here, too, if it had gone this far.

As soon as they got inside, the master asked if the Japanese man might have been insane. He had taken pains to warn him. What else could he have done? Why would the Japanese traveler have acted the way he did? Again he looked outside. His face was unsophisticated and good. Tears had appeared in his eyes.

It had all happened so quickly. Man-su's uncle could not believe it was real. Could it be that the man who had been sitting there so confidently until moments ago was no longer of this world? He asked the master if there were any houses in the direction the shots had come from. Perhaps the traveler had fled to some house when he fired his last shot. But the master said there were no houses within ten miles in that direction. Man-su's uncle wondered, if there was no house, then perhaps he had climbed a tree.

There was nothing to do now but wait until daylight. "When it gets light, I'll hurry out to check." Whatever country this traveler was from, and whatever he had come to such a place as this to do, all Man-su's uncle wanted was for the man to be alive, if only for one day, if only for a few hours. It did not matter what sort of proud smile he had worn or whom he had scorned.

That was what Man-su's uncle genuinely desired. And he intended to sit up waiting until dawn. But, he had had several exhausting days and the effects of the wine he had drunk earlier gradually returned. He collapsed into sleep in spite of himself.

By the time Man-su's uncle awoke, it was already completely light. "Oh, it's late!" He stood up. The master was holding something before Man-su's uncle's eyes. It seemed he had been waiting for him to wake up so he could show him something.

It was a gun. Without asking, Man-su's uncle knew it was the gun the traveler had been carrying the night before. The realization that the man had actually died seized the uncle's chest. The master said that he had found the gun by itself. There was not so much as a scrap of cloth or a strand of hair left near it. In that moment Man-su's uncle shuddered; he could not suppress the hatred and rage he felt toward those animals.

Continuing to hold the gun in front of Man-su's uncle's eyes, the master asked him to look closely. Red-black blood was dried on it.

"Do you know what these are here on the gun?" the master asked him.

Man-su's uncle peered at it. Weren't there countless marks on the gun, so that the gun looked as though it had been scratched all over with a file?

The master turned the gun over once. The other side was the same, covered with marks. Man-su's uncle asked what they were. When he lifted his eyes from the gun, the master answered in a pathetic tone that they were the tooth marks of wolves. A shiver went down the uncle's spine.

"Wolves' tooth marks? These are really the tooth marks the wolves left when they attacked the gun?" He did not need to listen to the master's explanation. "So wolves feel that way, too — even wolves."

tr. J. MARTIN HOLMAN

CLOUDBURST

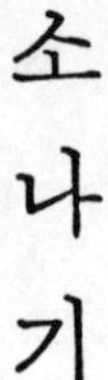

The boy stood by the stream. As soon as he saw the girl, he knew she must be Yun's great-granddaughter. She was playing with her hands in the water, as though she had never seen such a clear stream in Seoul.

For several days now, she had been playing in the water on her way home from school. But until yesterday she had stayed on the bank. Today she was squatting on one of the stepping-stones in the middle.

The boy sat on the bank. He decided to wait for her to move out of the way.

Luckily, someone came, and the girl made room for him to pass.

The next day he came out to the stream a little later.

Today the girl was squatting on one of the stepping-stones, washing her face. The sleeves of her pink sweater were rolled up. Her arms and the nape of her neck were pure white.

When she finished washing her face, she stared into the water. She was probably looking at her reflection. Suddenly she scooped up some water, as though trying to catch a passing minnow.

Whether or not she knew the boy was sitting on the bank of the stream, the girl just kept nimbly scooping up water. But she never caught anything. Even so, she did it over and over. It seemed she would only move if someone came by, as on the day before.

The girl picked up something out of the water. It was a white pebble. Then she jumped up and scampered across the stepping stones.

When she reached the far side, she turned back and faced the boy. "You silly fool."

The pebble flew at him. He leapt to his feet in spite of himself.

The girl ran off, her bobbed hair flapping. She went down the path between the reed fields. All he could see was the reed tops beneath the cool autumn sun.

Maybe she'll come out at the end of the field. It seemed like a long time, but the girl did not appear. He stood on tiptoe. And still, he waited a long time.

Some reed tufts moved at the end of the field. The girl must be carrying an armful. Now she was walking slowly. The unusually bright autumn sun shone on the tufts of the reeds. It looked as though the girl—no, the reeds—were walking along the path through the field.

The boy stood there until he could hardly see the reed tufts. On the ground he happened to see the pebble the girl had thrown. It was dry now. The boy picked it up and put it in his pocket.

The next day, the boy came out to the stream even later than before. He saw no sign of the girl. He felt fortunate. But a strange thing happened. As the days passed, unable to see the girl, he felt an emptiness somewhere in his chest. He got into the habit of fumbling with the pebble in his pocket.

One day the boy squatted on one of the stepping-stones where the girl had played in the water before. He put his hand in the water. He washed his face. He stared into the water. His dark tanned face was reflected in it. He hated it.

The boy scooped up the face in the water with both hands. He scooped again and again. Startled, he jumped up. The girl was crossing the stepping-stones.

She's been hiding, watching me. The boy started running, but he missed one of the stepping-stones, and one foot went in the water. He kept running.

I wish there was a place to hide myself. There was no reed field down that road, just a buckwheat field.

The fragrance of the buckwheat flowers stung his nostrils. He felt giddy. A salty liquid was running onto his lips. His nose was bleeding. He wiped the blood with one hand and kept running. From somewhere a voice followed him. "Silly fool! Silly fool!"

It was Saturday. When he reached the stream, he found the girl, whom he hadn't seen for several days, on the far side playing in the water.

Pretending not to notice her, he started across the stepping-stones. He had made only one misstep the other day in front of the girl, but now he crossed carefully, even though he usually skipped across these stones as confidently as he walked a wide road.

"Hey."

Pretending not to hear, he climbed the bank.

"Hey, what kind of clam is this?"

He turned around in spite of himself. The girl's clear, dark eyes met his. He shifted his gaze to the girl's palm. "It's a silk clam."

"Even the name is pretty."

They came to a fork in the road. From here the girl had to go a mile along the upper road, while the boy went three miles along the other.

The girl stopped walking. "Have you ever been to the far side of the hill?" She pointed beyond the end of the fields.

"No."

"Why don't we go? I've been so bored since we moved here to the country, I can't stand it."

"It might look like it's right over there, but it's really far."

"How far is 'far'? When we lived in Seoul, we used to go for long walks." The girl's eyes seemed to say, "Silly fool. Silly fool."

They turned down a path between the rice paddies. They passed some people who were harvesting the autumn rice.

A scarecrow stood in one of the fields. The boy shook one of the straw ropes supporting it. Several sparrows flew away. It occurred to him that he should go home early to keep the sparrows out of the rice paddy near his house.

"Oh, that's funny."

The girl grabbed the rope and shook it. The scarecrow swaggered and danced. A dimple appeared in the girl's left cheek.

There was another scarecrow in the next field. The girl ran to it. The boy followed, trying to forget that he should go home early on a day like this and help with the chores.

The boy brushed past the girl and ran on. The grasshoppers struck his face as they flew into it. The clear indigo autumn sky set him into a spin. He was dizzy. It's that eagle up there, that eagle, that eagle. He's making me dizzy.

When he looked back, the girl was shaking the rope of the second scarecrow. It danced better than the first.

There was a creek at the end of the paddies. The girl jumped across first.

From there to the foot of the the hill were dry fields. They passed one field where some sorghum shocks stood.

"What's that?"

"A field watchman's hut."

"Are the yellow melons good here?"

"They're good, but the watermelons are better."

"I'd sure like to eat one."

The boy went over to a patch of radishes growing among the melons. He pulled up two radishes. They were still small. He twisted off the tops, tossed them away, and handed one radish to the girl. As if to show her how to eat them, he bit off the end, scraped the skin off in a circle with his fingernail, and took a bite.

The girl followed his example. But before she had eaten three bites, she tossed it away. "It's hot."

"It *isn't* good. I can't eat it." The boy threw his even farther away.

They drew near the hill. The autumn maples were brilliant.

The girl shouted as she ran toward the mountain. This time the boy didn't run after her. Soon he had picked a large bunch of flowers.

"These are wild asters, these are bush clovers, these are bell-flowers . . ."

"I didn't know bellflowers were so pretty. I like purple . . . What's this yellow flower shaped like an umbrella?"

"A mountain parsley flower."

She held up the flower like an umbrella. The dimple appeared in her slightly flushed cheek.

The boy picked another handful of flowers. He chose the freshest ones and handed them to the girl. "Don't throw any of them away."

They climbed up to the ridge. There were several thatched houses in the valley on the other side.

Though neither suggested it, they sat side by side on a rock. It had grown quiet around them. The tingling autumn sun dispersed the scent of drying grass.

"What kind of flower is that over there?"

The slope was covered with arrowroot vines, and among the tangles some flowers bloomed long past their season.

"They look like wisteria," the girl went on. "There was a big wisteria vine at my school in Seoul. Those flowers make me think of playing with my friends under the wisteria."

The girl stood up quietly and walked to the slope. She grabbed the vine from which the cluster of flowers hung and began to pull, but the flowers would not break off easily. She slipped and grabbed the arrowroot vines.

Alarmed, the boy ran to her. The girl put out her hand. As the boy took hold and pulled her up the slope, he regretted not offering to get the flowers for her.

A drop of blood appeared on the girl's right knee. Without thinking, the boy put his lips on the wound and began to suck.

Then, as if something had occurred to him, he jumped and ran off.

He returned in a moment, out of breath. "If you put some of this on, it'll make it better."

He rubbed some pine resin on the scratch, then went down where the arrowroot vines were growing. He bit the stems in two and brought the flowers back up to the girl.

"There's a calf over there. Let's go look at it."

The calf was light brown, so young it didn't have a ring in its nose yet.

The boy took hold of the calf's halter up close, as if he wanted to scratch its back. Then he sprang onto its back. The calf jumped and ran in circles.

The girl's white face, her pink sweater, her navy blue skirt, and the flowers she held all whirled about like a giant bouquet of flowers. He was dizzy, but he didn't want to get off. He was proud of himself; only he could do this—the girl couldn't copy him.

"What are you kids doing?" A farmer came up from the reed patch.

The boy jumped down off the calf's back. He was sure he would get a scolding. What am I supposed to do if you injure my calf's back by riding it when it's so young?

But the long-bearded farmer just looked the boy over once, untied the calf's halter, and said, "Hurry on home, before you're caught in the cloudburst."

Clouds dark as india ink had gathered over their heads. Suddenly there was a commotion all around them. The wind gusted, and instantly everything turned a dark violet.

As they came down the hill, they heard the rain striking the leaves of the oak trees. They were great, heavy drops—cold on the backs of their necks. All at once, a wall of rain cut off the way before them.

They spotted the watchman's hut through the rain and mist. There was nothing to do but take cover there.

But the hut, which had no walls, was leaning, and the reed thatch was sparse. Finding a place where the roof wasn't leaking so freely, the boy had the girl stand inside. Her lips were blue, and her shoulders kept shaking.

The boy took off his cotton jacket and put it around the girl's shoulders. The girl lifted her eyes, wet from the rain, and looked at the boy. He just stood there silently. The girl pulled the torn and broken flowers from the bunch she had carried with her and threw them at her feet.

The rain began to pour through where the girl was standing. The hut would no longer provide them shelter.

Once outside, the boy thought of something and ran toward the sorghum field. He forced apart the inside of a shock of sheaves, then carried over more sheaves from nearby to add to it. Then he forced apart the inside again. He motioned for the girl to come.

The rain didn't leak inside the shock. But it was unpleasantly dark and close. The boy squatted in front of the shock in the rain. Steam rose from his shoulders.

The girl told him, almost in a whisper, to come inside and sit down. He said he was all right where he was. The girl told him again to come inside and sit down. The boy had no choice. He backed inside the sheaves. The flowers the girl was holding were crushed, but she didn't care. The smell of the boy's body, wet with rain, rushed into her nostrils. But she didn't turn her head away. Rather, the warmth of the boy's body made the trembling of her own body subside.

The clamor of rain on the sorghum leaves stopped abruptly. Outside it grew lighter.

They came out of their shelter. Not far away dazzling sunlight shone down.

When they came to the creek, they found the water was now turbulent and a deep red muddy color. They couldn't jump over it. The boy turned back to the girl. She meekly let him carry her across. The water came up to his rolled-up trousers. The girl cried out and held onto the boy's neck.

Before they reached the other side, the autumn sky was clear, as never before, not a trace of cloud in the deep expanse.

The boy didn't see the girl the next day, or the next, or the next. He ran to the stream every day, but she wasn't there.

He looked into the playground at her school during recess and even glanced into the fifth grade girls' classroom. But he didn't see her.

One day he went out to the stream, fingering the white pebble in his pocket. And wasn't that her sitting up on the bank?

The boy's chest throbbed.

"I've been sick for a while."

Her face looked pasty.

"Because you were caught in the cloudburst?"

She nodded silently.

"Are you all better now?"

"I'm still . . ."

"Then you should be home in bed."

"It's so boring, I came outside . . . It was fun that day . . . but somehow I got a stain here. It won't come out." The girl held out her sweater. On the front hem was a dark red spot, the color of muddy water.

The girl quietly showed her dimple.

"What kind of stain do you think it is?"

The boy just stared at the hem of the sweater.

"I figured it out. You carried me on your back across the stream, right? The stain came from your back."

The boy felt his face grow hot.

"I snitched some jujubes from home this morning. They're supposed to be for ancestral rites for the Harvest Moon Festival that's coming . . ." She held out a handful of jujubes.

The boy hesitated.

"Taste one. They say that my great-grandfather planted the tree. They're really sweet . . . After the ancestral rites are over, we're going to move out of our house."

The boy had overheard the grown-ups talking about the girl's family before they moved here: Yun's grandson had failed in business in Seoul and had to move back to his ancestral home. It seemed that now they had to give up their family's old home, too.

"I don't know why. I hate to move. But the grown-ups decided, so I can't do anything about it."

A lonely light he had never seen before appeared in the girl's dark eyes.

On his way home after parting with the girl, the boy turned the words over in his mind: the girl was moving away. There was nothing for him to be so upset or sad about. Even so, the boy couldn't taste the sweetness of the jujube he was chewing.

That night the boy sneaked over to the walnut grove that belonged to old man Tŏk-soe.

He climbed a tree he had spotted in the daylight and headed for a branch he had noticed. He hit the branch with a stick. The din of the walnuts falling was so loud! His chest quickened. But in the next instant he struck the limb violently. Fall down, you big walnuts! Lots of you, fall down! Driven by a power he didn't understand, he thrashed the branch with the stick.

On the way home he stayed in the shadows, away from the light of the moon, almost full. For the first time he felt grateful for shadows.

He put his hand on his bulging pocket. He didn't worry about what they say—that you can get a rash from husking walnuts with your bare hands. His only thought was that he should give the walnuts to the girl soon. Then he suddenly realized he had not asked the girl to come out to the stream one more time if she got well before she moved. Silly fool. Silly fool.

Two days later on the eve of the Harvest Moon Festival, when the boy came home from school, he found his father had changed into his best clothes and was carrying a chicken.

The boy asked where he was going.

Without answering, the boy's father held the chicken up to check its weight. "Is this one heavy enough?"

The boy's mother brought out a net bag. "She's already been cackling for several days now, looking for a place to nest. She's not that big, but she's fat."

This time the boy asked his mother where his father was going.

"Well, he's going over to Yun's in the valley where the school is. It's for their ancestral rites . . ."

"Then he should take a big one—the speckled rooster . . ."

The boy's father laughed, "You little blockhead, this one has more meat on it."

The boy felt awkward. He threw down his bundle of school books, ran to the barn, and gave the cow a slap on the back as if to kill a fly.

As the days went by, the water in the stream turned colder.

The boy took the lower path at the fork in the road. The village in the valley with the school appeared close as he gazed down on it beneath the indigo sky.

He had heard the adults saying that the girl's family would move to Yangp'yŏng tomorrow. They were planning to open a small store there.

The boy unconsciously fingered a walnut in his pocket, and with his other hand he broke off reed tufts.

That night as he lay in bed, the same questions kept running through his head. Should I go see them off when they leave tomorrow? If I go, I wonder if I'll get to see her?

The boy wasn't really sure if he had been asleep.

"Really . . . the things that happen in this world . . ." His father had come back from the village. "I mean over at Yun's. They had to sell all their fields, then that house that's been in the family for generations, and on top of that to have a death in the family . . ."

The boy's mother was sewing by lamplight. "Was that girl their only great-grandchild?"

"Yes. They lost two boys when they were just babies."

"I wonder why they haven't had any luck with children."

"I do, too. This girl was sick a long, long time. They couldn't get the proper medicine . . . That means the end of the Yun family line . . . This girl sure was precocious. Before she died, you know what she said? She asked to be buried in the same clothes she was wearing."

tr. J. MARTIN HOLMAN

SNOW

눈

Snow began to fall as night set in. I glanced out the door, and what at first had resembled swirling white ashes changed into large downy flakes before I knew it. A villager stepped up onto the stone veranda, shaking the snow off his shoes and brushing it from his shoulders. As he entered the room, the great flakes of snow came tumbling down in a flurry behind him.

I was out again this evening to visit the home of Yuk-son's grandfather in the lower part of the village. I had come back to my native village in autumn of last year, and during my two winters here, it has become something of a habit for me to go out to the lower part of the village to visit this old man's house whenever I have the time.

The men who gather there are people I have known intimately since my youth—that is, except for Sam-bong's father, who moved here some time ago from Hamgyŏng Province.

Whenever we get together, our talk is limited to ordinary subjects. The season being what it is, our conversations tonight concerned production quotas of rice. The men all talked as if everyone else's worries were their own and their own worries were everyone else's business.

As I stirred up the embers of the dying fire in the earthen brazier, I found, still left somewhere deep within my body, the breath of my grandfather, who was a farmer, and of my father, who had farmed for part of his life. I saw my own life with these people of my home village, and I bowed my head.

Outside, the big flakes of snow were falling as before. As the door was opened and closed, someone said we must surely have had a foot of snow already. Then the men talked of how it had rained quite a bit in May and the snow had come early this year, how the spell of cold weather last winter had frozen the wheat and barley, but how this year it seemed that grain production would be good since the snow would cover everything. At the end of these various discussions someone asked Sam-bong's father if it snowed hard where he was from. Answering that it did, he began to talk with his friends in the Hamgyŏng dialect.

Indeed it was true; it does snow heavily in Samsu and Kapsan counties. In winter they tie a rope from the house to the privy in the back. Then when the snow piles up in deep drifts they shake the rope to form a tunnel so they can make their way to and from the outhouse. It was said that a man once lost his straw sandal while walking on top of the deep snow only to find it hanging from the limb of a pine tree behind his house after the spring thaw. Here such a snowfall was unheard of, but the story was true.

It was also true that one winter there had been so much snow that there was no communication with the outside until the spring thaw the next year. Once, the master of an isolated home in the mountains, having run out of provisions, went out to get some food. But while he was gone it began to snow heavily. That evening a passing traveler, unable to get any farther through the snow, arranged to stay at this house. The master's wife stocked the kitchen with wood and even filled the inner rooms. She stacked them full, leaving only enough room for one straw mat to be spread out on the heated floor. She placed a pot with holes in the bottom into an earthenware vessel. Then the woman put a dipper of beans into the pot from the half bushel that was all she had left and poured in water to grow bean sprouts.

The snow continued for several days, and finally the two of them were unable to go out at all. The master's wife and the traveler passed the winter on broth made from bean sprouts boiled in water flavored with soy sauce. The next spring, after the snow had melted and the roads were clear, the traveler continued on the path he had been following before he stopped at the house. He traveled some distance before night fell and finally reached an inn. It happened that the master who had gone out to get food before the snowstorm had come also stopped there. The master had also been caught by the storm and was only now on his way home. That evening the two men stayed in the same room, and as they talked of various things, the master realized that the place where the traveler had spent the winter was surely his own house. When the master asked if the woman had starved to death, the traveler told him how they had survived the winter together on bean sprouts. "Is that so?" the master said. Telling the traveler that the house where he had spent the winter was indeed his own, he thanked the traveler heartily. The master seemed to be unable to express enough appreciation to the traveler. Then, the next morning, having shared even their wine, they parted, bidding each other farewell.

The great flakes of snow continued to tumble down outside. The men who had gathered here earlier had quit talking and were sitting quietly, as if contemplating how they might survive the winter, piecing together threads of hope for the coming year's unrewarding crop. Once again I stirred up the dying embers in the earthen brazier.

tr. J. MARTIN HOLMAN

MERRY CHRISTMAS

메리크리스마스

By the time I got off the train that went from downtown Pusan to the west side, it was already almost three o'clock. I couldn't get a truck going from Pusan to Taegu, so I got a ride on one going as far as the village. Since it was on the way, I thought I could at least get a little closer to Taegu.

I wasn't able to catch a truck to Taegu from the village either. Since it was already late, I resigned myself to the possibility that I would have to sleep there and get up early in the morning if I didn't get one tonight. Even so I stood for a little longer, and, fortunately, two covered military trucks came by. I asked the clerk, and he told me they were going as far as Seoul. "Just in time," I thought, and climbed aboard.

The truck had plenty of room inside. It was fast, too. Although it was after four o'clock when we left the village, we passed Ulsan while the sun was still shining. The truck had a roof that kept out the cold. But it didn't keep out the dust, which was thick inside the truck. I covered my nose and mouth with a towel. And as the interior became dark, I had to remind myself to close my eyes.

When I heard we had passed Kyŏngju I opened my eyes and

looked around. Here and there electric lights were scattered across the lonely landscape.

Someone looked at his watch and said that at this rate we would reach Taegu before nine o'clock. Because of Christmas, curfew had been extended to ten o'clock, so I was happy I would be able to get home before it. Besides myself, there were three or four others in the truck who planned to get off at Taegu.

The truck stopped at Yŏngch'ŏn. They said they were waiting for the other truck that was with us. We were in the place where a fierce battle had erupted in the war going on now. Since it was the middle of the night I could not tell where I was. On the main road, the flames of the guards' fire licked the darkness in an unusually beautiful way.

A few minutes later the rear truck arrived. The drivers spoke among themselves, then told us we would have dinner here before moving on. They had left today without having any lunch. The passengers followed the drivers, and we all entered a roadside inn to get something to eat.

It took us a full forty or fifty minutes to eat. Still, though, it would be possible to reach Taegu before curfew.

When we reached Hayang the truck stopped again. Again the drivers conferred among themselves. They told us that they had intended to stay in Taegu, but since they didn't know if or where they could find a place to stay there, they had decided it was better to sleep here and continue the trip in the morning. I had no choice. So I joined the others, and we went to a small inn. Two people had to share a blanket that reached only to the waist.

We were to leave at four in the morning. After sleeping fitfully, we got up and went over to where the truck was parked. It was a frozen dawn.

In no time we were in Taegu. The truck stopped at the railroad station, and those of us bound for Taegu got off. It was still before five o'clock. The place I was looking for was called Kongp'yŏng-dong. That was where I first sent my wife and children as refugees from Seoul; we had planned to meet in Pusan, but my wife had decided to stay in Taegu because prices in Pusan were so much higher. A few days later, I went to Pusan by train and learned of my wife's decision to stay in Taegu from my brother-in-law in Pusan, who had traveled south in a truck with my wife.

I had never been here before, so I asked the riders who got off with me where Kongp'yŏng-dong was, but they said they didn't know. And, one by one, they hurried off and disappeared around the still dim street corners; they knew where they were going. Not knowing what else to do, I decided to go to the station building to ask an employee or porter for directions.

I went over to the station and beneath a dim electric light I saw refugees scrambling for places to sit along the station wall. I had watched refugees sleeping under the open sky in front of the busy station in Pusan, too. I was one of them.

Cutting across the public square, I hesitated, then stopped short. Unwittingly, I cried out.

What a queer sight! It was only a decorated Christmas tree in the middle of the square. It wasn't that I hadn't known that yesterday was Christmas Eve or that today was Christmas. And it wasn't that this Christmas tree was so brilliantly decorated. Perhaps it was the silence that made me cry out when I suddenly saw the Christmas tree in the square in front of the station.

I walked closer to it as though drawn. Cottony snow covered the tree and the ground underneath it. As I gazed at the electric lights silently illuminating the fluffy snow, I thought in my heart of a desolate, wind-blown plain, the ground frozen from the cold, a small snow-covered village sleeping, while the unspeakable, peaceful glow of fire shone from the windows of silent homes . . . This touching scene was a reminder of the past. I wept. For some reason, I wept.

Maybe it was because of trudging and shivering through the cold. And more than that, maybe it was because I had shivered as I sat on top of a freight car full of empty gasoline drums for five days and nights, exposed to the sleet from Seoul to Pusan.

I saw this and wondered if this shivering was something that had started not yesterday or today but before — maybe it had been going on since I was born.

I don't know how long I stood there like that. Suddenly, I saw something move behind the tree. A piece of a straw mat was raised, and a black head appeared. It was a woman. I had thought it was the ground, but it was someone lying down covered by a straw mat. Probably she hadn't been able to find a place in the station and had come here.

The woman didn't get up, just turned over on her side and put her ear to the ground. So cautiously . . . then she turned her head the other way and lay there. Yes, at that moment I knew everything. She had just given birth to a child. And lying next to her was her newborn baby. In fact, it seemed reasonable that right after the birth a warm foglike vapor should still remain.

Shortly, the woman raised the child's head as if to check its breathing and stretched out her hand. It was a peculiarly long hand. With her hand she swept up the snow lying at the base of the tree. What was she up to? She heaped up all the snow within her reach and pushed it under the straw mat where the baby lay.

The woman then removed herself from the straw mat and gathered snow from underneath the tree a bit farther away. Then, as though something had occurred to her, she stretched to remove the snow on the tree, and reaching up, she turned her head and gave a startled look. It was as though she had been caught in a forbidden act. Her face, which at first seemed attractive, became pale. Although she appeared to be middle-aged, she also looked very young.

Suddenly, she started to shake from her lower body, and in a moment her whole body shivered. The snow she held in her hands also trembled. Illuminated obliquely by the electric lights, it gave off a milky white light.

Only then did I wonder why I was still standing there. I felt that I was making a mistake. I left that spot no longer feeling the silent peace in my heart I had felt moments earlier. All I felt was the cold of a morning before daybreak. It was not at all accidental that the cold was like the snow the woman was using to insulate her newborn child.

I muttered as if fighting off that cold. "Merry Christmas."

tr. DOUGLAS A. CLARK

OLD MAN HWANG

黃老人

The next day would be old man Hwang's sixtieth birthday. But, for some reason, he only wished that today and tomorrow would pass quickly. In the past two or three years Hwang had come to particularly detest events where people gathered in crowds. He had decided not to allow a huge feast, even though it was for his sixtieth birthday. It wasn't just because a diligent farmer like old Hwang feared the expense, but also because he hated the commotion.

Nevertheless, that evening a number of old men flocked to the guest room at Hwang's house and began to trade stories in spirited voices. Feeling as he had earlier in the day, Hwang had no intention of talking with the men. He went outside to walk around the inner courtyard, as if to avoid them, his hands clasped behind his back. He had acquired this habit many years ago – not because he had nothing to do; rather, it was the posture he adopted whenever he was looking for some task to take up.

When he reached the kitchen door, he could hear the clatter of dishes and the voices of the village women. Regardless of his wishes, tomorrow morning he would have to treat the old men to a cup of liquor. The women were making snacks to go with it.

Listening to the voices, he could tell whose mother or grandmother each was. And, in spite of himself, he felt an emptiness in a corner of his heart: there was a voice he should have heard among the others that he could not. Hwang started toward the front gate, but seeing some empty bean pods lying scattered about, he said to himself, "These shouldn't be wasted. They can be burned." He began to pick them up, all the while wishing today and tomorrow would soon be over.

Then his daughter, who had married and moved to Kinjae, came in through the gate with a sleeping baby on her back and a bundle in her hand. Her husband was holding the hands of an older girl and boy. She discovered her father picking up bean pods. My same old father. Still, I wish he would take it easy these couple of days.

Hwang lifted his head to acknowledge his daughter and her family. "Oh, so you came?" He bent over and went back to picking up bean pods.

"Father, please accept our regards." His daughter bowed formally in respect for such an occasion.

Old man Hwang stood up straight. "Oh, stop it." He received his son-in-law's bow. Then his daughter told her son to bow to his grandfather. Hwang received his bow, all along saying, "Stop it, won't you. Just stop." When the boy finished, Hwang began again meticulously picking up the bean pods. "What do they mean making such a fuss over me."

Hwang's daughter went inside. She felt disappointed that her father had not mentioned how the children had grown. He may act that way now, but when the children cry, he will surely pick them up and carry them on his back. Just wait and see. Still, whenever she came back to her parents' home, she could not help feeling a hollowness as though the house were empty. The thought that it was because her mother was no longer here pierced her heart.

When she took her sleeping child off her back and laid her down, the kitchen door opened. Wŏn-dang's wife welcomed her in her gravelly voice. "Well, look who's here." The women in the kitchen chattered their greetings, asking about her children.

Old man Hwang came to the kitchen door with the bean pods he had gathered and heard his daughter telling her sister-in-law that she had changed into an old blouse that she'd found hanging on a nail. He realized that she had gone into the kitchen. He could hear the women telling her that she needn't be working now; she should rest and come in later.

Hwang tossed the bean pods into the kitchen and told the women to burn them sparingly for fuel. He hasn't changed a bit. His daughter dispelled the sad thoughts of her mother by busying herself as the head of the kitchen, which she had now become.

Hwang went to the shed to feed the chickens. There were things he had to take care of with his own hands. The lid to the millet crock had been left open, and the stones had come out from under an empty crock that was now leaning over. He first propped up the leaning crock and shook it to make sure it was steady, then put the lid on the millet crock. Picking up a handful of sorghum, he came out of the shed. If I don't keep an eye on everything, it gets like this.

Next he decided he should put some straw in the pigpen.

On the way back, Hwang saw his son standing at the front gate, talking with two people. His grandson Tang-son was also there carrying a net bag full of skewers of mushrooms. The two strangers—an old man and a younger one—were itinerant minstrels, he could tell at a glance by their appearance.

Hwang's son told them to look around and see for themselves. This was no big sixtieth birthday celebration. They weren't preparing a feast of rice cakes or vegetable pancakes.

As Hwang passed near them, he spoke as if to himself. "What's the use of a big banquet?"

Then he walked toward the kitchen. "Don't forget to cook up some slop for the pigs."

"All right!" his daughter-in-law answered.

"We have to make certain the sow that's about to farrow eats well."

Inside the kitchen he could hear Wŏn-dang's wife trying to stifle a giggle. "Of all things. 'Cook up some slop for the pigs.' He certainly is insistent."

Wŏn-dang's wife was so flippant about everything. Old Hwang hoped she wouldn't break any of the dishes they had borrowed from all over the village.

Hwang happened to glance back at the gate, and his eyes met those of the old minstrel, who was standing there importuning Hwang's son. Who is that? he thought to himself, and his heart began to throb. He drew closer to get a better look. Ch'a-son? It's Ch'a-son! The old minstrel seemed to recognize Hwang, and he pulled at the younger minstrel's sleeve as if to tell him they should leave. The younger man hesitated, wondering what was going on, then, muttering in a dissatisfied tone, turned to follow the older man.

Hwang watched as they walked away. Then he called out to Tang-son. "Get those two to come back."

This time it was Hwang's son who did not understand what was happening. He looked back at this father.

"Hurry up and go get them."

At his grandfather's command, Tang-son dropped the net bag he had been carrying and dashed off after the entertainers.

When Tang-son called them, the two stopped and the older man looked back at Hwang. He spoke to the younger man for some time, then to Tang-son. He seemed unwilling to do as Tang-son had asked.

It occurred to Hwang that the old minstrel might feel awkward as long as he was there, so he started toward the house.

"We'll have to give them some money," Hwang's son said, as if to get his father's attention as well as to ask his opinion.

Hwang stopped walking and was about to say something else, but he simply told his son, "Have them stay here tonight."

He went into the main room where his son-in-law was sitting.

"Is everything well with your family?"

"Yes."

"How many children do you have now?"

"Three."

"Two boys and a girl, right?"

"No, we have two girls and a boy." The last time we were here he turned the numbers around, and here he is doing it again,

Hwang's son-in-law thought. He didn't understand why Hwang kept getting this mixed up, unlike other matters. He wished that his wife's nephew Tang-son, who was like a brother-in-law, would return and this difficult old man would go back outside. He glanced at the old man's face and saw in his eyes that his last remark had not registered. His gaze was focused on a spot somewhere before him. As he stared off, oblivious, his hand stroked the yellowed ends of his beard.

Hwang was thinking about the old minstrel.

The old minstrel—no, Ch'a-son—the last time he saw him was at the sixtieth birthday celebration for Mr. Pak in the upper part of the village. Ch'a-son had aged, and the clothes draped over him were almost rags. But what Hwang saw before his eyes now was not the old wandering minstrel, but Ch'a-son, the boy he had known—Ch'a-son, naked beside a stream. This was the image that came to mind whenever Hwang saw the minstrel at birthday celebrations around about.

Ch'a-son had played the bamboo flute well since he was a child. Whenever they went swimming, he would pluck blades of grass and blow on them to make music. If any kind of grass just touched Ch'a-son's lips, he could make a sound. Hwang would sing ballads in his yet unchanged boyish voice, accompanied by Ch'a-son's grass flute.

But when he was twelve years old, Hwang's family moved from Namch'on to the place where he now lived, and the two boys were separated. Some years later, when Hwang had gone with his father to the sixty-first birthday celebration of a Mr. Wi in a village over the mountain, he discovered Ch'a-son among the entertainers there. His old friend was playing the Korean fiddle. Hwang left his father's side and joined the crowd that surrounded the entertainers. At first he felt inexpressible pride that the boy who played so well and received such applause was his old friend. But when he realized that these people looked down on the musicians as playthings for their entertainment, he became afraid that the villagers would realize that he knew Ch'a-son. He worried that his old fiddling friend might notice him in the crowd and call out to him. He slipped away through the crowd. After that, Hwang occasionally saw Ch'a-son among the entertainers here and there, but he always tried to keep Ch'a-son from noticing him. After he turned forty, however, he began to think that there was nothing embarrassing about having been boyhood friends, but now it was Ch'a-son who avoided Hwang, in respect for Hwang's feelings. Hwang felt a kind of sorrow. And he felt it every time Ch'a-son avoided him. If Ch'a-son left today, Hwang thought he would feel a sorrow greater than he had ever experienced before.

Hwang heard someone in the courtyard. He stopped fingering the ends of his beard. He heard the sound of the door to the storeroom being opened. Hwang absentmindedly lit his pipe and drew in deeply. A long sigh of relief flowed from his chest along with the smoke.

He heard his daughter come out of the kitchen when she realized her brother had come. His daughter and son and grandson Tang-son all greeted each other. His son asked if his brother-in-law had come, and Hwang's daughter answered that he was in the main room. Hwang heard footsteps approaching. The door opened. Knowing who was going to enter, his son-in-law was already standing. He was about to make a formal greeting to his wife's brother, who was old enough to be his father, but the older man said, "Don't bother with that kind of thing. Sit back down."

Tang-son came in.

Hwang's son-in-law and Tang-son just smiled. That seemed to be all they needed to do to greet each other.

"You keep your uncle company," Hwang said as he left the room, his son still holding the door. He went to the kitchen door. "We have two guests staying in the storeroom."

"All right," his daughter-in-law answered.

He started to leave but thought of something. "Be sure to give the pigs their feed when it's ready."

"All right."

Just after his daughter-in-law answered, the kitchen door opened and his daughter stuck her head out. "Shouldn't you have your supper now, Father?"

"Yes, I will." For the first time in a long while, Hwang felt something like an appetite.

But as he lay in bed that night, as always, Hwang could not sleep. It had been this way since he had begun to grow old. But tonight he kept waking up just as he began to drift off to sleep. When he was small, his mother would tell him that it would be just a few more days until his birthday. He counted the nights. Finally, the night before, he couldn't sleep for the excitement of thinking that it would be here if only he could sleep one more night. But his sleeplessness tonight was not because of that kind of excitement. It was because of an inexpressible sense of emptiness that occupied a portion of his heart. In the midst of such feelings, old Hwang turned over in his bed, wishing that tonight and tomorrow would pass quickly.

The next morning, Hwang got up early, as usual. Today he was carrying his granddaughter on his back and sweeping the courtyard.

He had swept half the courtyard when his son came flying out. "I'll do the sweeping." He snatched the broom from his father's hands.

Even if it's just for today, why should they keep me from doing the sweeping? It's my sixtieth birthday, so I'm not supposed to do that. Who says I can't? Hwang thought to himself.

His daughter opened the door. "Give me the baby, Father, and you change your clothes."

"I don't need to. You mean what I've got on is so dirty I should change? I could wear these another month."

As if frustrated by his father's response, Hwang's son turned toward him. "Please go ahead and change. She went to a lot of trouble to bring something special for you."

Old Hwang went inside. His daughter had brought a white silk outfit with a gray serge vest.

"I had thought about making it wider through the chest, but if I had, it probably would have been too big," she said as she tied his coat string.

His dark face looked even darker in contrast with his white beard and white shirt. Hwang gave himself up to his daughter as she fussed over his clothes. Recalling how his mother had dressed him in a black cotton vest for his birthday when he was a child, he felt a lump rise in his throat. Then he thought perhaps the emptiness he had felt since yesterday always came on days like this, when his mother should have been here but was not. His mother's face, tanned dark, with countless wrinkles at the corners of her eyes. A face even darker and more wrinkled than his was now. He could not conjure up her face at a younger age. Old Hwang was now gazing on his aged mother's face. Mother, Mother, Mother, he cried inside.

Hwang's daughter thought that he was standing there staring off as if he wanted her to check the clothes to make certain everything was in place. She walked around behind, tugging at the hem of the jacket and pulling down the vest, arranging them just right. She seemed pleased when the women peeked in through the side door from the kitchen, admiring how well the suit fit.

"I was worried whether it would fit just right." How much better it would have been if she could have made the whole outfit, including a top coat, out of silk. No matter what, she planned to make that for his seventieth birthday, she said, so she wanted to ask her father to please live a long time.

Hwang noticed it had suddenly become quiet; he realized his daughter was looking at him and must have said she was worried about something. He awoke from his thoughts of his mother. He had his hand in his vest pocket, and when he found nothing there, he realized that he was inadvertently looking for his tobacco. He took his tobacco pouch and pipe from the vest he had taken off, put his pipe in his mouth, and lit it.

"What does she mean making nice things like this for me?" He muttered to himself and went outside.

He clasped his hands behind his back. His big, dark hands, with their rough knuckles, looked all the darker and bigger appearing from the white silk sleeves.

The courtyard had all been swept. But Tang-son had taken over from Hwang's son, so the patterns left on the ground by the broom were completely different—Tang-son had left only a few half-hearted tracks. Hwang thought how he had to do the work with his own hands, but he couldn't sweep the courtyard the way he wanted to wearing a new suit of silk clothes. And they weren't comfortable, either. How he wished this day could be done with.

Looking across the courtyard, Hwang found a button that had fallen and picked it up. It was a white porcelain button. He glanced down at the buttons on his vest, but none of the gray buttons there were missing. He wondered why this button would be lying here. Maybe it was his grandson's. He blew the dust off the button in his hand and put it in his pocket.

Hwang's son thought his father's new clothes made him look older. He felt as though his father had appeared from the house wearing a shroud. But instantly, he thought how inappropriate such thoughts were on such a day as this and shook his head vigorously to dispel them.

When Hwang noticed his grandson Chŭng-son marveling at his grandfather's new clothes, he thought of the button in his pocket. "Let me see. Are you missing a button off your vest?" He approached the boy.

Before his grandfather could check, Chŭng-son looked down at his vest. "No." He shook his head. "They're all here."

Tang-son came looking for his grandfather. "Grandfather, could you come to the guest room?"

"All right."

He walked toward the guest room, but when he heard the old men's boisterous singing and inebriated talk of their burial plots, he thought how much he would rather be alone outside than to go in and gab with them.

As soon as he entered, he was offered cups of wine from all sides to wish him a long life. Every time he took a cup, old man O Mok-nyŏ from the other village would tell him in a drunken voice to drink up, drink a cup of wine, then he would sing a drinking song. All Hwang wanted to do was to be by himself in some quiet place.

Outside, the wife of old henpecked Cho called out. "Is my husband in there?"

Before Cho could answer her, O Mok-nyŏ stopped singing. "No, he's not here." O grabbed the seat of Cho's pants when he tried to stand up.

"I'm leaving." Cho tried to get O to let go, but he was caught by the men next to him and almost tripped.

"Do you have to be so scared of her?" O Mok-nyŏ said, and the whole group burst out laughing.

As soon as Cho was outside, the men all started talking. That's the most henpecked man I've ever seen. What a sorry case—he just sits there when we ask him to have a few drinks. His old lady's so strict—she won't leave him be when he goes out. He's like a mouse before a cat. I couldn't live like that. They all rattled on.

Old man Hwang had never thought it was a pleasant sight to see Cho's wife following her husband wherever he went to keep him from drinking. But when he heard Cho's wife calling him today, he couldn't help but feel a catch in his throat at the thought of his own wife. No matter how unseemly it might be to have a wife go out looking for her husband, he envied Cho, who had someone beside him in his old age.

Before he realized what he was doing, Hwang had gone outside. He went near the kitchen. He could hear the voices of this woman and that old grandmother accompanied by the clatter of dishes. But he would never hear one voice that should be there. He couldn't help but feel an emptiness in his heart—an emptiness different from what he felt in regard to his mother.

The kitchen door opened. He gazed at his daughter's face, as if seeking the visage of his late wife. But his daughter's youthful face reflected only the vision of his wife in her younger days; somehow the face of the wife with whom he had grown old disappeared as if into a mist.

When she saw her father standing there staring at her, she assumed he wanted her to serve more food. "Should I bring out some more appetizers?"

"No." Hwang started to leave, but then something occurred to him. "Did you serve some wine in the storeroom?"

"I think someone did awhile ago."

"Good."

Hwang wondered why he had forgotten to share a cup of wine with Ch'a-son. It was as though the thought had been with him since the night before. He went to get a bottle of wine.

He came across Chŭng-son just as the boy was coming out of the storehouse with a chicken egg. "Look and see if you lost a button off your vest," he asked again.

This time Chŭng-son didn't even look down. "You just asked me a little while ago." He ran off thinking his grandfather had forgotten he had already asked about the button because it was his birthday and he was so happy to be wearing new clothes.

When Hwang came into the storeroom with the wine bottle, the two minstrels, who had been sitting across from each other at the low table, stood up in surprise and made room for him.

"Please, please. You don't need to stand up," he said, but it appeared the two would not sit down until Hwang had, so he sat beside the table.

They hesitated, then knelt very properly before the table.

"No. Make yourselves comfortable." Old man Hwang thought they would become relaxed once the wine had made a few rounds, so he offered a cup to the old minstrel. "Here you go."

"No. I shouldn't . . ." The old minstrel hesitated.

"Go ahead." Hwang passed the cup to the man, who, though reluctant, accepted it politely with both hands.

Hwang began to talk. "Do you . . ."

"Yes, sir."

"What do you mean 'yes, sir'? Aren't we the same age?"

"Yes, sir."

"There you go again with that 'yes, sir.' We're both sixty years old this year. Go ahead, drink up."

Hwang felt different from the way he had earlier in the guest room; he could drink cup after cup of wine if it were with this man of his own age.

After the wine had made several rounds, Hwang spoke, his heart contented. "Well, my same-age friend, why don't you play the fiddle now?"

For a second the old minstrel searched Hwang's face. This shrewd gaze had become a habit over his long years. But he could find no trace of condescension in Hwang's voice or face that indicated he regarded the minstrel as a plaything. The old minstrel quietly picked up his fiddle and tuned the strings.

"Play an old ballad."

Looking off at a spot in the distance for a moment, as though seeking something far, far away, the old minstrel closed his eyes and began to draw his bow across his fiddle.

Without realizing it, old man Hwang had closed his eyes, too.

A small stream appeared before the two men, on the bank stood two naked boys covered with mud – one blowing a tune on a grass flute and the other singing in a boy's voice that had not yet changed.

tr. J. MARTIN HOLMAN

A PEDDLER OF INK AND BRUSHES

筆墨장수

Old man Sŏ had not originally been a dealer in Chinese ink and brushes. When he was younger, he had studied calligraphy and ink painting for about twenty years.

Finally, a man like him could not make a name for himself in such an art. And now, close to thirty years had slipped by since he had taken up the trade of peddling ink and brushes.

Every year, old man Sŏ made one round each in spring and autumn by way of the steep mountain paths from which he could smell the ocean. He always stopped in tiny Saetkol Village, deep in a valley far from Uljin. When he arrived, he would visit the home of the village headman.

The old village headman always put him up in the guest room of his own home. And every time, Sŏ would sell him brushes and ink sticks.

The village headman had bought them thinking he would have his own sons and grandsons use them; however, with the winds of reform, the old-style Confucian schools were replaced by public schools, so he did not press his sons and grandsons to use them. Still, he could not give up his attachment to writing with brush and ink. In the beginning, he would doodle on a sheet with the brushes and ink he had bought from old man Sŏ. But as the years went by, he gradually lost his inclination to write with a brush himself. Now he was satisfied with merely collecting the paraphernalia of calligraphy, the brushes and ink that old man Sŏ peddled.

Every time he stayed at the village headman's house, Sŏ would write characters for scrolls and do paintings of the four gracious plants—the plum, orchid, chrysanthemum, and bamboo. Receiving the paintings Sŏ did on his spring and autumn rounds each year was one of the village headman's joys.

It wasn't that the headman considered these samples of calligraphy or ink paintings to be at all engaging. He merely felt a kind of pleasure or consolation in any work done with a brush.

After Sŏ had moved on, the old headman would unroll the calligraphy and ink paintings, repeating the same words: "These are so dull, and as he gets older, they'll get worse."

Everyone who saw old man Sŏ's calligraphy and painting found them unsatisfying.

Perhaps it was his own father's stubbornness that made old man Sŏ study calligraphy and painting. When Sŏ was young, his right leg was crippled by polio. Soon afterward, his father told the boy he would make arrangements for him to have an occupation he could pursue sitting down. What he chose for his son was calligraphy and painting.

In those days, teaching calligraphy and painting was considered an extremely pure occupation.

Sŏ's father was completely devoted to his son. He was not tempted by wine or tobacco, and even though he had lost his wife when Sŏ was five years old, he never tried to remarry.

He made a moderate living, so he was able to bring in a tutor to teach his son calligraphy and painting. From then on, his main pleasures became playing *paduk* with the teacher in his spare time and looking in on his son's studies.

But Sŏ made no progress at all; he had no innate artistic talent.

At first, when his father asked, "How is he? Does he show promise?" the teacher would reply, "We'll have to wait and see."

After several years had passed, his father said to the tutor, "He seems to show no sign of improvement. What do you think?"

The teacher said, "Well, even if he isn't very good now, sometimes natural gifts can manifest themselves later on."

Sŏ's father tried changing teachers, but it did not help. The new teacher was an impatient man who told Sŏ's father, "I have never seen such a stupid person. If I had spent this much time teaching calligraphy to a dog, it would have done better work with its paws." The tutor ended up going elsewhere.

Even after that incident, Sŏ's father continued to call in new teachers and compare them. And remarkably, all the while, his son never grew tired of his study of calligraphy and painting. He worked so assiduously that no one could keep up with him.

On the one hand, Sŏ's father tried to believe what the first teacher had said, that his genius might appear all of a sudden even though he showed no promise so far. In the end, however, the father's expectations ran up against reality. On his deathbed, Sŏ's father told his son, "Now, after thinking it over, I realize the only remarkable thing was my vain greed. Abandon the brush and do whatever you like from now on."

Sŏ's life became quite wretched. He did whatever he could to make a living.

At first, since it was all he knew how to do, he decided to try selling the hanging scrolls he had painted, pictures of plum blossoms, chrysanthemums, orchids, and bamboo. He traveled, seeking out large markets, but when he spread out his work for display, business did not go well.

Finally, after giving the situation some consideration, he became a seller of ink and brushes. By this time there were already private village schools in every region, so he would not be poor if he earned his living this way.

But as the enlightenment of modernization spread into these areas, the gates of the private schools began to close. Even the number of people in private homes who would buy brushes and ink decreased. Consequently, Sŏ suffered a succession of hardships in his later years.

Once Korea was liberated from Japanese rule in 1945, private schools appeared once again. Old man Sŏ wondered if he might be able to settle down somewhere and become a village schoolteacher, but no one would hire an old man like him, a shabby peddler of brushes and ink.

Lame in one leg, he had no choice but to live out his days traveling from district to district, carrying a knapsack full of brushes and ink.

One day in late autumn the year after the Liberation, old man Sŏ was caught in the rain on the way from Kangnŭng to Chumunjin at the foot of a mountain, where he seemed to be able to hear the ocean. The rain was cold. He finally managed to take refuge in a house in a small village nearby.

A middle-aged woman lived alone in the house. During the war her son had been conscripted to work and was taken off to Japan, but he had not yet returned.

The woman dried old man Sŏ's wet overcoat at the kitchen fireplace. After supper she told old man Sŏ about her son. He would be twenty-three years old next year. Before he had left, he had gotten engaged to a certain girl, but the woman said that she would not care if the girl disappeared and they never married, if only her son would come home.

At the end of her story the woman said that she had made it her habit not to turn away even a single beggar ever since her son had been taken away. She told old man Sŏ that he could drop in and stay at her house if he ever passed that way again.

As she spoke, her eyes rested on Sŏ's feet. One heel was visible, and the other sock left his toes exposed. Because he was lame in his right leg, that sock always wore out faster than the other, but when that happened, he would switch his socks to the opposite feet so they would wear evenly.

The woman told him that she would make him a pair of socks since the weather was getting colder. Old man Sŏ was very grateful and could not imagine on the spur of the moment how he could repay her.

The woman cast a glance at Sŏ's foot to measure it. Then she got out a roll of cotton cloth and began to cut.

"Isn't that the fabric you've been saving for your son's wedding? Why are you using it for socks for me?" old man Sŏ asked.

The woman answered softly, "If only my son would come home, what would this cloth mean to me?"

She worked late into the night to make the socks. When he pulled them on, his hands began to tremble. Perhaps the woman's making the socks sprang from her love for her son who had gone off to a distant country—a son who could be alive or dead. Nevertheless, this was the first time in his seventy years that old man Sŏ had tasted such warm friendship.

The next morning before Sŏ left this house, he did a painting of plum blossoms for the woman.

"Should I hang this on the wall?" she asked. "When my son returns I'll display it in the bridal room." She carefully rolled up the painting and placed it deep in a box.

Naturally, old man Sŏ treasured in his heart the woman's friendliness.

From then on, every time he passed the village, old man Sŏ inquired after the woman's health and asked about news of her son. He never visited the woman herself but always asked the neighborhood people he met. He did not want to call on the woman again, afraid that people would think that the generosity he enjoyed that day was the woman's bait to entice him to come back.

According to the villagers the woman was getting along well, but each time he asked, they told him that the woman's son had not yet returned. When he heard this, Sŏ wished that the young man would come home soon and be married and that the plum blossom painting Sŏ had done would be hung in the bridal room. Even so, he had made up his mind that if he ever succeeded in creating a fine painting after his own heart, he would give it to the woman in exchange for the earlier one.

One night when Sŏ was staying in Saetkol Village, he asked the old village headman, "Why don't the Japanese send back the men they took away to labor?"

"They *do* send them back. We even had two men go from our village. One came back just after the Liberation, and the other returned the spring of the following year."

"Don't they all go to the same area to work?"

"No, they go to some place called Kyushu or places near Tokyo. They get separated and end up scattered all over the country."

"Well, there must be someplace that hasn't sent them back yet."

"Why is that? The people who should have returned all did."

Sŏ did not have the heart to tell him that there were people who had not returned home. He could guess what the village headman's reply would be, and he did not have the heart to listen to the explanation either.

In June, about two or three days before the outbreak of the Korean War, the dogs in Saetkol Village barked as never before when old man Sŏ approached; he looked so shabby and wretched.

The village headman's granddaughter came outside when she heard the barking and told Sŏ to come back later, at dinnertime. Even though she had known Sŏ for years, she mistook him for a crippled beggar. The village headman recognized him, however, and led him into the guest room.

"Your color is bad."

Old man Sŏ rubbed his leg and said, "I've been sick for a while." The pallor of illness still lingered in the deep wrinkles of his face.

"So that's why you're so late this year."

As usual the headman bought one brush and one stick of ink.

Old man Sŏ dissolved some ink in water. As always, he was about to do an ink painting for the headman. But, this time, as if to repay a debt of gratitude, the headman tried to dissuade Sŏ from painting. He was concerned that Sŏ, in his sickly condition, would not be able to bear even the strain of holding a brush. Sŏ, however, had already begun to paint some plum blossoms, moving as if by a kind of inertia.

The headman was startled at the way old man Sŏ's appearance began to change. His dark yellow face was flushed, and his eyes grew bloodshot as if touched with fever. His hand trembled delicately as he held his brush. Thinking the old man was still sick, the headman asked him to stop painting for the day, but, as he spoke, he happened to look down at the painting. Once more he was startled; the blossoms hanging on the ancient gnarled plum branch twitched as if alive.

However, when he brought his face nearer to examine the work more closely, it turned into a commonplace painting, neither better nor worse than the others Sŏ had done. The headman blamed his eyes for the strange experience.

Sŏ had finished the work, touching the brush to one or two final spots, when all of a sudden he grabbed the painting and dashed outside. Stuffing it into the waist of his trousers, he muttered to himself like a madman, "This is it, this is it. This is what I've been trying to paint for all these years. This is it."

The headman did not understand why Sŏ was behaving so strangely. He ran out after him and found old man Sŏ at a tavern just outside the village.

"I thought you didn't drink," the headman said.

Actually, Sŏ was like his father; he did not use wine or tobacco. But somehow, just this once, his emotions would not allow him to go without a drink.

"You're still not quite well. I think you have a fever."

But the feverish look in Sŏ's face sprang from a hidden vitality.

"What did you do with the painting?"

"I tore it up and threw it away."

"Tore it up and threw it away? Why?"

"It was a terrible painting." The white whiskers under old man Sŏ's chin trembled slightly.

"It wasn't that bad."

"No, it was terrible. I'll paint another one for you." Sŏ felt guilty that he had lied to his friend of almost thirty years, but he knew that the painting already had an owner elsewhere.

The next day, old man Sŏ set out on the road toward Chumunjin. The headman had asked him to stay and rest another day before he left, thinking that the old man was not well. But Sŏ answered that he was all right and set out. His lame leg and his gait, which had once looked so heavy, now appeared brisk and light.

Before he could reach Samch'ŏk he learned of the invasion by North Korean forces on June 25. He was told that people could not travel on to Kangnŭng and Samch'ŏk. He stayed where he was for several days, unable to do anything else. He saw unfamiliar soldiers heading south. On the fifth day, he could no longer endure the waiting and set out on the road again. His age—a full seventy years—and his tattered, shabby appearance were now a help to him, unlike before; no one would bother to stop a beggarly old man to ask him what he was doing.

Three days later he arrived at the foot of the mountain from which he could hear the familiar sound of the ocean in the distance. As he rounded the foot of the mountain, hobbling on his bad leg, his feet suddenly seemed stuck firm to the earth.

At first he doubted his eyes. This could not be the village he had been searching for. The village had been small with a few houses, but now there was not a single house left standing. Even the willows outside the village gate were yellowed and half-burned.

As one might guess, the village had been bombed. Two damaged cargo trucks lay tumbled indifferently on the roadside.

As soon as he took in this scene, he collapsed on the spot, raising a small cloud of dust.

Old man Sŏ never showed himself in Saetkol Village again. During that time, the headman of the village, who suffered the ravages of war himself, stopped wondering whether Sŏ would ever come again.

One spring day, when the weather was balmy, a villager

returning from the market discovered a beggar who had fallen dead along the road through the back mountain pass.

The headman came out to look. Indeed, an old beggar had fallen dead on the spot. But somehow the knapsack he was carrying looked familiar. When the village headman drew closer, he realized that the man was none other than old man Sŏ.

The headman had a villager open the knapsack. Inside, where Sŏ kept the brushes and ink left over from his sales, lay a parcel meticulously wrapped in white mulberry paper.

When the villager opened the package, he found some money and one pair of finely made socks that had never been worn, as well as a scrap of paper with these words written on it: "Please use the money in the packet for my funeral. And, I know it will be difficult, but please put the enclosed socks on my feet."

One of the villagers picked up the white socks. They did not befit old man Sŏ's shabby appearance. He looked them over, then pulled out a beautifully folded sheet of paper from inside.

When he opened it, he saw a plum blossom painting—the one old man Sŏ had painted at the village headman's house, the one he had carried outside, running like a madman.

tr. J. MARTIN HOLMAN

WRITING ON A FINGERNAIL

손톱에 쓰다

I. THE MODEL

They wound up exhausted. Despite all their bustling around the streets, they had been unable to find any face that they particularly liked. Ordinarily in that amount of time several potential subjects would have attracted their attention. It appeared that they would have to give up and coax their teacher into hiring a model.

The two female art students, more than a bit disappointed, decided to look for a teahouse nearby in which to sit and rest their legs. But as they came around a street corner, the two stopped dead in their tracks as though they had an appointment to meet at that spot.

There stood a load carrier, his arms folded. He looked about forty years old and was wearing a worn-out jacket over shabby clothes. The abundant whiskers, the sunburnt face, that mustache – unconsciously the two women exchanged glances as if to say this was precisely the model they had been searching for.

They arranged to give the man a thousand hwan for two hours and took him to the studio. The "studio" was a wooden-floored room, barely ten feet square, attached to a dormitory.

They had a rather difficult time getting the man to pose naturally, but the two, feeling a new enthusiasm and sense of accomplishment at employing a model for the first time, sketched his features with the whiskers as a focus and asked him to return the following day.

The man took the money and went outside, quite satisfied. Not bad, earning a thousand hwan by sitting still for two hours. Even though he sweated constantly when he hauled loads, he never ended up with more than a couple of hundred hwan – and that was after wrangling with women who wanted to knock the price down forty or fifty hwan.

Although there was still time to carry another load or two today, he headed straight home.

He slid open the room door, which also served as a front gate, and put the money down; his wife started in surprise. Her husband had almost never come home at this hour, and with so much money. In one breath, her husband told her the story of what had happened to him that day.

The wife, in disbelief, said, "Now I've heard everything. Why on earth would they want to draw a mug like yours?"

"That's just what I mean. Tomorrow I should probably wear my overcoat, too. And change this filthy old collar for me, would you? I'm going down to the stalls under the bridge and get my hair cut. And it's been a long time since I've had a shave."

II. COMPASSION

Ah, he felt good. First rice wine at a tavern, then another drink at a snack house, and after that, scotch at a bar. Because he had been mixing his liquor, he was even more intoxicated. Damn, it had been quite a while, but tonight he was going to take it easy and get good and drunk. He had received a bonus, and since it was New Year's Eve, the curfew was off. Not only that, today the head of accounting had made himself quite clear. There was a good chance he would be installed as a chief clerk, in a position that was supposed to open up after the new year. At any rate, he felt good.

His rather inebriated steps took him into a cake shop, and he bought a box of expensive candies. Just the kind that would be lying around in piles at the house of a nitpicking head accountant, he thought.

He sang a popular song to himself. "What's the use of complaining? What's the use of sighing? . . ."

As usual, the old beggar who sat at the entrance to the alley that led to his house thrust forth his hand. In the dim light coming from the shop next door, he could see that the beggar's hand was shaking. Although he normally walked past him indifferently, tonight he was in a good mood, so he dipped into his pocket for money. Drunk as he was, he could see it was a five hundred hwan note. But rather than reach into his pocket again to find some small change, he thought "oh, well" and surrendered the money. He started to go but then turned around and called out, "Old man, on a night like tonight, go have a drink and cheer yourself up."

At home the bedding that had been spread out in advance was warm and snug. "Yes, that's why it's so nice to have the little woman around." He drifted into a peaceful sleep immediately.

The next day he got up earlier than usual, took the box of candy, and left his house. When he came to the main street after passing through the alley, he saw a number of people standing about as if something had happened. The old beggar lay in a heap, his tattered blanket clutched to his body. He was dead. The owner of the nearby shop stood in front of his door, his face clouded over. He could not help asking the shopkeeper what had happened.

"Well, it seems that at night he would usually go over to the soup shop and sleep on his mattress by the corner of the chimney, but last night I was up quite late folding bags, and for some reason he kept going back and forth in front of here muttering nonsense to himself the whole time. In the morning when I came out, that's what I found. You know, he really was smashed. I wonder how he was able to get so drunk . . ."

tr. STEPHEN J. EPSTEIN

THE OLD POTTER

독 짓는 늙은이

"Bitch! You deserve to die a hundred times over for this! It's bad enough leaving a sick husband, but how could you leave the child, too, and just run off? And with a hired hand young enough to be your own son! You say you're in the best years of your life? Well then, you old hag, do you think I'm only fit to beg just because I'm getting old too and I got sick? You bitch!"

His little son lying next to him cried out, "Father! Fa-a-ther!" but as the boy called out, Song, who was still dreaming, imagined that he was already holding him in his arms. The old man answered him in his sleep, "Hey, what do you want, anyway, I'm not your damned mother!" The boy, lying beside his father, kept crying until he finally woke old man Song from his sleep.

The old man's head felt even heavier and more uncomfortable now than it had before he went to sleep. Again, the little boy began to sniffle and cry. As though still talking in his sleep, Song said, "Now, now," and pulled the child over and held him the way he had in his dream. The child's body felt cold compared with Song's feverish temperature. He held the child tightly against him. "Really now, how did you get so cold? I think you're going to freeze."

While the old man was embracing the sobbing six-year-old, his feelings of resentment toward his wife began to rise again, for running off and leaving him, not so much him, but this young one. He thought about the pimply-faced young apprentice who had gone with her. A feeling something like the rivalry between two young men of the same age suddenly swept through old man Song's aching body—rivalry toward a boy young enough to be his own son.

Because Song had been sick with an ailment no one could seem to diagnose, the young helper had thrown and prepared the last firing of the fall almost all by himself. Old man Song thought how the large, medium-sized, and small earthen jars and crocks, which looked like a group of large and small gangly figures in the nearly full September moonlight, all seemed to be shadows of the helper who had run away. The old man felt like jumping up, grabbing a shaping stick, and smashing every one of them, but it occurred to him right away that tomorrow was not too late, he could make some more jars, fill the kiln, and fire it. This was the only way he and his little son could survive now; really, he would just have to do it. His heavy eyelids closed gently.

As soon as it was light, old man Song tied a towel around his head, which had swollen from the fever, and sat down to begin work. He had sent the boy to go and call Waeng-son, his helper, to come and knead the clay, but he was in such a hurry that he went ahead and kneaded a batch of clay with his own hands and put it on the wheel. Old man Song's hands kept trembling, and yet when he had thrown a jar about halfway up, he was able to support the inside with a "fist" block while tapping the outside with a mallet, at the same time keeping the wheel turning with his feet. His sure skill, anyway, seemed to be the same as before he had gotten sick. He quickly made several medium-sized jars.

But gradually his skill began to show lapses. It got so that when he was tapping the sides of the jar with the block and mallet, he would suddenly see before him the image of his wife and the apprentice. Then he could not distinguish whether he was striking the jar or his wife and that young man, so the jars came out so thin that they had to be thrown away. And his hands trembled so much that when he tried to shape the rim, after he had formed the rest, this most difficult part would not come out right. The fever was part of the problem. Finally old man Song, looking as if he would collapse, lay down beside the jars he had formed.

It was evening before the old man regained consciousness. Waeng-son had made up several lumps of clay and left. The child had come out of the house and was squatting in the evening shadows, looking south at the road to the marketplace. Perhaps he was still thinking that his mother would return, for he was sitting there just as he always used to in the evening when she had gone to market, waiting for her to return with the helper, who would be carrying the day's purchases.

Old man Song stopped looking outside, and calling on a strength that was not his own, he rose and began to throw jars again, but this time he had barely finished forming one when he nearly collapsed and had to lie down again.

When he came to, it was completely dark and the child was shaking him. The boy had been sobbing, but he finally seemed reassured when his father woke up. He brought over a bowl of rice and put it down in front of his father. When he asked the boy what this was all about, the child said the old lady at the house with the cherry tree had given it to him.

Old man Song's anger rose. "Who told you to go begging for our food?" he shouted, and knocked the bowl out of his son's hand. The boy began to sniffle and cry. The old man recalled that he had eaten only a few spoonfuls of leftover rice that morning and hadn't had a thing to eat all day. Then it occurred to him that the boy probably hadn't had his supper yet, so he pulled back the bowl and put a spoonful in his son's mouth, saying, "It's good, so you eat, too, now." But the old man himself couldn't swallow a thing; it was not so much that his illness had taken away his appetite, but somehow his throat rebelled and wouldn't let anything go down.

The next morning old man Song cooked rice that was so soft it was almost like paste. His appetite had been poor all along, but yesterday had been the first time he had been so choked that he could not swallow. That day the old man made a charcoal fire to help dry the earthen jars as he formed them. He would set the fire beside the jar until it was about half thrown, and then suspend it inside while he worked. The fumes from the fire made his head feel heavier than ever. It was the first time in forty years' experience that the charcoal fumes had bothered him like this.

Old man Song collapsed more times than he had the day before. The laborer who had been kneading clay tried several times to persuade Song that he could never finish off a kiln in time this fall and should wait and do it first thing in the spring. The old man would get up, fall over, get up again and keep collapsing, yet he showed no sign of giving up.

One time when old man Song had collapsed and stopped, the old woman who peddled notions and lived over in the house with the cherry tree, came to call. "You've been sick and really ought to take care of yourself," she said. Then she put a bowl of millet gruel down near his head.

Old man Song remembered how he had shouted at his little boy the day before, scolding him for having begged for their food. He felt sorry about the trouble this woman had gone to, this old grandmother who was always so friendly to everyone. He told her she had given a lot of rice to the boy yesterday, and now here she'd gone and fixed this special gruel and brought it for him. She'd really gone, he said, to too much trouble.

The "cherry tree house grandmother," as she was called, simply said, "Try some now, before it gets cold." The old man sipped a few swallows from the bowl, but soon gave up and weakly put the bowl aside.

When she saw this, the old woman appeared to be thinking that this time his sickness had just about killed the old man off. She spoke to him: "If you could find a good place for him, wouldn't it be a good idea to find another home for Tang-son?"

Old man Song's eyes opened wide as he stared intently at the grandmother from the cherry tree house. He no longer looked like a man who had just been in a state of collapse. And then somehow his hand was pushing the bowl of gruel away toward the old woman. "You brought this stuff just so you could say that kind of thing? Get out of my sight!" the old man shouted with the strength of a man who could not have been so weak a moment ago. The old woman was familiar with old man Song's stubbornness and said nothing.

As soon as the old woman had gone, Song began wondering where his little boy could have wandered off to this time; he called "Tang-son!" at the top of his voice, to get him to come in. When the little child appeared at the door of the shed, old man Song stared hard at his face this time, as if he were afraid he might forget it, but his strength soon failed and he lay back and closed his eyes. The boy was frightened by the strange way his father stared at him. He did not go any nearer, he merely stood still. When his father closed his eyes, he was overcome with fear and began to heave with sobs.

As time went by old man Song spent more time incapacitated in front of his work than he did throwing jars. There were still fewer than a hundred jars ready, which meant that he needed over twenty more for a full kiln. The old man was anxious and kept renewing his resolution to fill the kiln, but the flesh was weak, and, try as he might, he faltered again and again. He would try to raise his body, only to fall back. His mouth, surrounded by yellowed white whiskers, would drop open and his shoulders would heave as he panted for breath.

On one of these bad days the grandmother from the cherry tree house came over as she was returning from her rounds, selling fabric and needles. She said there just happened to be a good place for Tang-son right now, so how about sending him there. The people she had heard about were well off, but even more important, they were good, kind people. They had already raised the child of a young couple who had separated and given up their baby. Recently the father had come and gotten the child, who was then a little over ten years old. The older couple had just sat looking at each other and weeping endlessly after they gave up his belongings and turned him over. And now since they were looking for a fatherless child that they could raise, she urged him to send Tang-son.

Old man Song allowed that even after what had happened a few days ago, he knew the old woman had been sending things to eat by giving them to the boy. He knew this kind of adoption arrangement was often done through this sort of old woman, who usually earned something from doing it, but he knew she wouldn't covet that kind of reward.

He thought it was really just that she was a kindly old woman offering to help out, but old man Song again summoned a strength he did not know he possessed and said that if she was going to talk like this she needn't come back to his house. He said he wouldn't give up the child until his eyes were filled with earth.

The old woman from the cherry tree house replied that he needn't be so stubborn, he should think about how he could put his mind at ease about the child while he was still alive. It's a fact, you know, she went on, that even a healthy person never knows when he's going to die, and who knows what tomorrow will bring for a person who is sick already? She then added that winter was coming on, so he'd better think it over.

Old man Song told her not to worry. He would find a way to make a living and feed the child, even if it might mean resorting to begging.

After the old woman had left, the old man thought that even though he had just claimed he would beg for a living to support the child, and even though his wife had probably run away because she was afraid of having to beg if she stayed with him, when he was over this sickness and up and around again, he was determined to earn a reputation as a first-rate potter and make all the jars he wanted. He also thought that if he could just finish one firing and have it turn out as well as usual, there was hope of getting enough food ready for winter, and even of starting next year's work. As he thought, he again became anxious to be back at finishing up the jars for this firing.

Old man Song chose a good day for drying the formed jars; finally he set them outdoors to cure. He still did not have enough to fill the kiln, but he had decided to go ahead and fire anyway with the jars he had.

Drying the jars? Better to call it airing them in the wind than drying. It has to be sunny, but wind is essential. A day that is foggy or misty will not do. If a mist should rise, and then the sun suddenly beat down hot with no wind blowing, before you know it more than a hundred jars will break crosswise and lengthwise and the lot is ruined. But this day the wind was blowing about right; it was a fine day for drying.

After putting the jars out in the yard, he got the beggars to come out of the kiln. They emerged carrying their tattered possessions and muttering, "This is no time to be firing jars anyway." The beggars would come around each fall to find a kiln to stay in for the winter. In the early fall they would live in the lower forward section, then as winter deepened and the kiln grew colder, they would move farther up the hill into the long kiln where the air was warmer and pass the cold winter there.

Song was about to tell the beggars that his shed was empty and that they could stay there while he was doing the firing, but he said nothing, because for the first time he felt that he would also seem like a beggar if he let them come into the house where he was living. Some of the beggars who came out of the kiln went off looking for other houses where they could beg, others found a sunny spot to lie down, and some of the rest just sat down anywhere they could and did things like hunt for lice on their bodies.

Old man Song also sat down on the sunny slope and watched the way the jars were whitening as they dried. When the time came to place them in the kiln he went inside himself. Ordinarily he would have tried to arrange as many jars as possible within the space, but this time he tried to place both his own and the runaway apprentice's jars, according to their height, at equal distances from the firing place. It looked like a contest to see who had made the best-formed jars.

Toward late evening old man Song began the firing. Firing—in the end it was the firing that would decide whether these earthen jars were going to be any good or not. The firing method depended upon how the jars were made. It would not work if you fired gently when an intense heat was needed, and when you had to go easy it was no good if you gave it too much, and then it was also wrong to fire too long or stop too soon.

At first he started burning the fire gently, then gradually more and more intensely, and after some three or four hours the jars that had started out white turned black. After another three to five hours the jars turned back to their original white, then they became a red color, which turned to a bright crimson that resembled molten iron or the way the sun looks if you stare directly at it.

The next day brought a true autumn sky, with clear sunlight streaming down. Song began to lay the lateral fires. He put wood in the openings spaced along both sides of the long kiln that stretched up the hillside.

Now he began to feed bundles of pine branches onto the fires. The flames from the lower firebox and side openings would roil and shoot out with loud reports. This column of flame had etched itself into old man Song's vision and seemed to be burning within him, for he had been tending the fires continuously since late the previous evening, sitting and rising, lying and then rising again in a spot not far from the firebox.

He continued firing until the day ended and it had grown dark. But then one of the men tending the fires with him looked into one of the side openings where they had been firing and came running toward old Song. The old man already knew from the location of the opening where the man had been firing that his jars were in there. He anticipated what the man would say and asked first whether the jars had collapsed. The fireman said they had and suggested that even though the jars weren't quite finished, it would be better to stop firing through the sides and to seal up the firebox. But old man Song said to keep on firing until he said to stop.

Now that it was night, the beggars were returning to be near the kiln.

Old man Song was uneasy as he was saying, "All right, just a little more now," and just then, they began to hear the sound "Dang, dang" from within the kiln as the earthen jars and crocks began to crack. At first the old man started, and half stood up, but then he sat back down on his heels, fixed his blazing eyes on one spot and remained motionless there, listening. Looking toward the places where he had put the jars, he was saying, "That's one I made," and then, "That's one of mine, too." The ones that were cracking were almost all jars that the old man had thrown himself.

From the cracking sounds old man Song also knew that the jars he had made had all split except for the first few he had thrown when he began working after he fell ill. In the fading light of evening, listening to the distant sound of the firemen scolding the beggars for being in the way, old man Song finally just collapsed.

The next day when old man Song regained consciousness, he found himself lying in the shed of his house. His son had been lying there sobbing with his little body curled up next to him, and when the boy saw his father wake up he began to cry all the louder. When the old man saw the child, without intending to he began to speak. "I'm not going to die . . . no, not going to die." Yet at the same time he was screaming inwardly that the end had come and he was really dying after all.

The next day old man Song sent the child over to get the grandmother from the cherry tree house. As soon as the old woman arrived, Song told the boy to go out and play, and looked intently at his face before he went out. It was as though he were trying to make sure he would not forget his son's face.

As soon as the two of them were alone, old man Song closed his eyes and asked if it would still be possible to send the boy to the place the grandmother had mentioned. The old woman said that it would. He asked how far away the place was. She answered that it was a good distance, some five miles or so. Song asked if the boy could be sent immediately. She said it would even be all right to take the child there that very moment. As she spoke she took out a few bills and pressed them into Song's hand. He kept his eyes shut. She said she had promised to give him the money whenever he might be willing to send the child.

Old man Song suddenly opened his eyes and handed the money back to the old woman. He said money would be of no use to him, so she should give it to the person who would carry the child on his back. After he said this he closed his eyes again. The old woman said there was also money to give the person who carried the child. Old man Song said to give the money to him anyway and to ask him to take good care of the child on the way. Then he told her to hurry and go tell the boy his father had died. The old woman acted as though she was about to say something, but then just wiped her eyes with the end of the bow on her blouse and went outside.

Old man Song lay with his eyes closed and stifled his heavy breathing. He made up his mind that he was not going to cry or carry on like that, no matter what happened.

When the old grandmother from the cherry tree house came in with the boy, however, and told him to look and see that his father was dead, there was no way the old man could stop the tears from flowing out of his closed eyes. The old woman was so overcome she could barely control her voice, but said to the boy, "See, he's already beginning to decay, so water is running out of his eyes." Then, not wanting him to go any nearer his father, she pulled the boy by the hand and left.

The old man did not open his eyes, and once again fresh tears began to flow, like water seeping from decay, but these tears were still hot. Then from somewhere it seemed as though he heard the sound of a child sobbing. He opened his eyes. There was no reason for anyone else to be there. Yet if only something, even one of the earthen jars he had made, could have been there! In that moment the whole interior of the shed was a void that pressed down upon Song's gaunt chest. Old man Song felt his whole body shrivel and grow cold.

It was then that he noticed that the kiln stood before him. Suddenly he was overcome by a desire to go over to the kiln, so he arose. If only he could reach the kiln he would be warm. Half crawling, half walking, he emerged from the shed.

The beggars were lying at the kiln entrance, but they moved aside and made a place for him without even bothering to see who had crawled in to join them. Old man Song flopped down to one side of them. At least he felt warm now.

Old man Song got up and started to crawl again, toward the inside of the kiln. It was as though somehow he had not yet gotten warm enough. Soon he had reached a place that was hotter than most people could stand. Even so, old man Song did not stop crawling. But he was not just moving ahead aimlessly. As if he were now putting forth his last remaining spark of life, the old man's strangely shining eyes were searching out something in the darkness. Then, when he was bathed in the pale light of late autumn shining through one of the firing holes, old man Song stopped crawling. He seemed to have found what he was looking for. The broken pieces of the shattered jars he had made were lying there.

Old man Song quietly, slowly, raised himself up, and knelt correctly, very properly, at the spot—as if trying to put himself there in place of the jars that had shattered.

tr. EDWARD W. POITRAS

THE OLD WOMAN FROM MAENGSAN

孟山할머니

The tile-roofed house in the alley in front of Ssari Gate was not only one of the oldest houses in P'yŏngyang, it was without a doubt the shortest. The particularly wide-spreading rafters made the house look all the shorter, as if it were straining under the weight of the heavy, old tiles, seldom seen anymore. A glance at the short pillars by the small room beyond the kitchen would reveal that none of them was standing straight.

You would think that no one could enter this house without feeling some kind of uneasiness. But there were men—who might they be?—who did not appear to feel any such anxiety, going in and out every day. They had to duck and stoop to avoid bumping their foreheads on the low doorway. No one knew when these men had begun to frequent the house in such numbers. Only three people lived there. One was the mistress of the house, the old woman from Maengsan. There was also an old man whose gray head was shaved close with a razor. He had asthma, so he often coughed. And when he finished coughing, he always spit out frothy spittle. The third resident was an extremely tall young man who let his beard grow and always wore pants from a gray Western suit. The pants were covered with black grime, and his knees protruded from holes in them. The young man went about in shirt sleeves, wearing rubber shoes. Besides these three, there was also the array of men who came and went every day. Among these, two or three faces were familiar, men who came regularly, but most were new. Without exception, the men were all dressed in clean clothes.

An old man who lived in the neighborhood had come out to sit, seeking some shade, although summer had already passed. Wondering why all these men came and went, stooping to enter the old house, he asked the asthmatic old man, "What's with all those men?"

The asthmatic old man replied, as if he were spitting, "They're palm readers." From this short answer, the neighbor knew that these men were gamblers. He then asked, "Why does the old woman let them do that?"

The asthmatic man then said, "The old woman isn't doing it because she wants to. She's never been the sort who likes to talk. She doesn't care what they do."

It was true, the old woman from Maengsan was that kind of person.

This woman, whom the asthmatic man called "Mother," appeared well past seventy. Her wide mouth was always closed; she never spoke. Her heavy eyelids almost covered her eyes, which appeared small. And when those eyes noticed someone, the woman not only did not speak but seemed to dislike even looking at the person. Her face—her whole body in fact—manifested her disposition. She was always silent. But, it wasn't something the old woman did on purpose; rather, her temperament exuded from her like an odor.

The old woman was still healthy, despite her years. She did all the kitchen work by herself, effortlessly carrying the heavy dish-water container in and out. People in the neighborhood said the old woman had no sons, only a daughter who lived fairly close by. Some time ago, they said, her daughter had come, and though she had asked her mother to come live with her, the old woman had said nothing. Perhaps the old woman from Maengsan, having been alone since she reached middle age, intended to keep this lodging house until the day she died, though no new guests had come to stay in the house since she had gotten old.

The neighbors had seen a woman of about fifty visiting the house; she was said to be the daughter. When the two were about to part, the daughter cried her eyes red—but not the old woman from Maengsan.

One day, although he was the kind of man who hated talking to people more than anything, the asthmatic old man came out to sit and enjoy the shade. This time, after he spoke with another old man who lived in the neighborhood, the asthmatic old man said that his own son, who lived in a village not too far away, had told him he had gotten quite a little money together. Since he was doing so well, with no worries about food and such, the son had come some time ago to ask his father to let him take care of him, to live out his days eating his son's rice and drinking his son's wine. The old man went off with his son, but the arrangement had not set well with the old man. He ended up coming back, saying, "Living alone like this is best for me—making my own way with my own hands. It makes me feel most comfortable."

One old neighbor, hearing these words, said, "If it were me, I wouldn't have said anything. I'd have stayed at home watching the grandchildren and not gone anywhere."

But the asthmatic old man did not respond. He suddenly began coughing, and a long while later, when he finished, he merely spit his frothy spittle.

The asthmatic man worked at a brokerage business in the market. Every market day he would go out and buy and sell one thing and another. That's how he made his living. You might say it was a strange occupation for an old man who seemed particularly unwilling to talk to people.

But there was something even stranger than that. It was the relationship between the old woman from Maengsan and the asthmatic old man. Not a single word passed between these two lonely old people. Although it had been several years since the man had come to the house, the two behaved like total strangers, people who had just met. Even when it was time to eat, the

Maengsan woman never uttered a word to tell him. The asthmatic man knew that it was time to come into the house by looking at the woman's eyes as she worked in the kitchen.

The tall young man caught between the Maengsan woman and the asthmatic man also seemed to be rather quiet. According to the neighbors, he had been an errand boy for a soup shop. He had gotten into the habit of playing cards and had come to the old woman's house. At meals he sat at the far end of the table, and if one of the old people left some rice, he would pull it toward himself and eat. Occasionally he made a little money—a hundred won or so—in winnings, but he didn't even wear a decent set of clothes. They say he wasted all his money on cards until not a penny was left. Although someone had told him to go back to being an errand boy, he remained a fixture in the old woman's house.

Once someone had suggested to the old woman and man that if they left no rice in their bowls for several days, the young man would leave, perhaps even go back to the soup shop. The old Maengsan woman and the asthmatic man did not assent, nor did they wonder how they might do such a thing. They merely sat silently.

One autumn, when the nights and mornings were cool and invigorating, the asthmatic old man was not seen for a while; there was talk that he was probably in bed, ill. This seemed to be the case. Occasionally from the old house came the sound of the old man's cough mixed with spittle. Every time the neighbors heard him coughing, they would say that before the autumn got much later, they would have a task to do. They said that as the number of men who came to the house got larger, the old man's end grew closer.

One day it was noised from the village that the asthmatic old man's disease was typhoid. After this word got out, the number of men who came seemed to decrease, day by day, until finally not a single man was to be seen. Even the tall young man, who always let his beard grow, who had recently gone about in grimy pants from a gray Western suit with the knees out, had left and was nowhere to be seen.

Only the old woman from Maengsan and the sick man were left in the old house. The woman continued to do her kitchen work as always, without speaking. She easily carried the dishwater vessel in and out, but her eyelids drooped and her eyes had lost their vigor. More than a few villagers made quite a commotion about whether to notify the ward office at once and have the old woman take the man to the quarantine hospital or to leave them as they were. The old woman merely listened without a word to all the talk. According to what the neighbors said, the old woman sat at the sick man's bedside and put cold towels on his forehead. When the old man was delirious with fever, he looked at her as if he hated it when she fed him rice gruel, but when he realized it was the old Maengsan woman, he would meekly eat the food.

A week passed. The rumor went out that the old man had survived. He had seemed almost dead, but now he was eating. They said that the old woman even chewed up green chestnuts and put them in the old man's mouth as though she were feeding a baby. At such times, the stooping shadow of the Maengsan woman appeared on the paper windows late at night. On rare occasions the men who used to come would still open the door and duck their heads inside, in something like an inquiry after the old man's health. "What's up?" Just one sentence – then they would leave. No one stepped inside the house. But gradually the old man began to come outside, and as before, when he finished coughing, he would spit his frothy spittle.

One day, another rumor was spread in the village, that now the old woman was laid up with the same typhoid. One man said, "It's just like my senile parents. She didn't listen to anyone, so she got what she deserved." He promptly informed the ward office.

In fact, one morning when the frost was heavy, the old woman, without a groan, her feverish eyes closed, was tossed into the hand cart like a dead person and taken off to the quarantine hospital.

tr. J. MARTIN HOLMAN

A MAN

사
나
이

Kim stopped while removing his A-frame loaded with soybean sprouts and stood uncertainly, holding his breath. His wife was washing the upper half of her body in the kitchen. Propping herself against the deep, round earthenware water container, she scooped one gourdful of water after another and showered it over herself. The white of her armpit seemed to float before his eyes.

It was the first time he had seen his wife's body. Married more than two months, he had not yet been near her. His breathing quickened before he noticed it, and his temples were burning.

A month after their marriage she was still sleeping in her clothes. He was aware of that even though his mother slept between them.

Some time ago, though, she had begun to sleep without her skirt, he had sensed, and tonight she removed her jacket as well.

Kim could not get to sleep. He suspected that his mother, tossing this way and that between him and his wife, could not fall asleep either. From the day Kim took a wife, so to speak, at the age of twenty-nine, his mother had made her bed between them. And she was never the first to fall asleep. That may have been why she frequently took naps, something she had never done before.

That night his mother kept pulling his wife's sheet up to her nose. "What a way for a young woman to sleep, showing herself and all . . ." Then she would turn to him. "You'll have to get those sprouts to the stores early in the morning, just like always. Get some sleep."

His wife, lying beyond his mother, seemed ever so far away to Kim.

A middle-aged woman from the neighborhood came to visit. "Are you feeling all right?"

Kim's mother sat up, rubbing her sleepy eyes.

"Life was no picnic when I was a girl, and these days there isn't a joint in my body that doesn't ache."

"Why don't you take it easy? You have a daughter-in-law now, and everybody talks about what a good worker she is . . ."

Kim's mother listened intently to the sounds from the kitchen.

"That's no lie. When it comes to young women these days, no one works harder than she does." Her voice was deliberately loud.

From the kitchen came the sound of her daughter-in-law watering the potted sprouts.

"All she needs to do now is produce a handsome, strapping boy, and you'll be sitting pretty, Sister."

Kim's mother raised her voice a notch: "What sweethearts they are! Like a pair of doves."

The patter of water on the sprouts became more forceful.

Kim was in the yard fixing a strap on his A-frame. He stopped and looked vacantly at the sky.

Kim's wife went to visit her family and did not return. His mother dared not mention her to him. Three months later they heard she had remarried.

"I knew it," his mother said to him. "The way she wiggled her butt, even in front of her mother-in-law, I knew she was a loose woman. Don't you ever think about that slut again."

From that day on, Kim's mother seemed to rejoice in her housework. No longer did she take her naps.

One day his mother suddenly fell ill, and five days later she passed away. The night before her death, she clutched his wrist and said, "I've known only two men in my life—your father and you. And I don't want you trusting any woman besides your mother."

Kim went to work at a restaurant on the recommendation of the bean sprout wholesaler. His job was to clean the restaurant. He tenasciously swept the floor and wiped the tables all day long. He also cleaned up at night and first thing in the morning. There were women to take orders.

Ten days after he began work there, the owner softly called him to the living quarters at the back of the restaurant. With her hand on the sliding door, she beckoned him inside with her eyes.

Kim found someone sick in bed. A damp, fetid smell pierced his nostrils.

The woman whispered into his ear: "Could you move in here and look after her from now on? I'm asking you because I think you're such a nice man." Having said this, she left.

Kim suddenly heard sobbing. Feeble and faint, it sounded just as if it were coming from the next room. Kim silently looked down at the gentle trembling of the invalid's quilt.

"Would you scratch my back for me?"

It was a woman's voice.

"Please—I can't stand this itching."

He sat and lifted the quilt. Her back was that of a hag. Wrinkled, lifeless skin hung from her bones.

She was the daughter of the woman who kept the restaurant. Barely thirty and a mother three times over, she had been driven from her husband's family after developing a severe uterine cancer.

At first the kitchen maid had been asked to attend to her. But she ended up leaving before long. A girl was then hired to care for the woman round the clock. She endured a few days and then disappeared. Next the invalid was supplied with a middle-aged widow. This woman lasted the longest, but she eventually became ill herself.

Helping the sick woman with the chamberpot was no problem for Kim. But she was forever needing her arms and legs massaged and her back scratched, regardless of the hour. And she had a way of sobbing at the slightest opposition to her wishes.

Kim often lurched up in bed at the sound of her sobbing, even when he had nodded off. So sensitive was he to the feeble sound that he could only doze at night.

One night Kim heard a noise and bolted out of bed. He found the sick woman sitting up partway. He reached out to scratch her back, but she motioned to him to keep still. She was straining to listen to something. Her eyes were unusually sober. Whispers came from another room. They also heard restrained giggling. The room was where the waitresses slept.

"Screwing with some guy again. Don't listen, Mr. Kim."

The invalid's hand pulled his and made him scratch her lower back. She asked him to scratch harder and harder.

Another night Kim heard a sound and rose to find the woman pressed against the sliding door to the restaurant. She made a gesture of silence and beckoned him to come and look. The woman had wet her finger with saliva and poked a hole in the rice paper panel of the door.

Kim peeped through the hole, and in the light leaking from the adjoining room he saw two men rolling around fighting. He looked more closely and recognized them as the cooks.

"A new girl must have come," said the woman. "Whoever wins gets her for the night. Don't look anymore – it's disgusting!"

The next morning, on his way to clean the chamberpot, Kim ran into a young woman emerging from the outhouse. It was the new waitress. Eyelids a bit puffy, he told himself. But her face, which had a dark wart the size of a mung bean below her left nostril, showed no concern, as if nothing had happened the previous night.

Eventually, not a sob escaped from the sick woman. To that extent did Kim anticipate her wishes and attend to them.

One night Kim awoke to a strange noise. It was the woman, moaning in agony. Kim tried to massage her limbs. She asked him to hug her instead. Her emaciated chest was strangely cool. Alarmed, Kim decided to call the woman's mother, but the woman asked him to keep hugging her. Propping her chin on his shoulder, she whispered to him in a voice he barely understood: "My husband and kids deserted me, and even my mother wouldn't come near. You're the only one who's stayed with me. Here," she said, indicating her double-band ring and an ornamental hairpin, "keep these after I'm gone."

Kim bought a shack and started selling noodles.

Occasionally a customer would ask for a drink. So Kim decided to serve liquor, and he began frying mung-bean pancakes to go along with it. Appetizingly large, the cakes attracted throngs. During the evening crush it was impossible to find a seat.

One of the regulars happened to ask Kim if he was still getting along by himself.

Kim smiled sheepishly.

"Women are as common as dirt, but here you are living alone . . . This kind of business would be decent if you got a wife and ran it together. You could add a loft too . . ."

In fact, Kim was short-handed. At peak hours he often burned the cakes while tending the pots of noodles. He had to hire a helper.

One day an old peddler of knickknacks lingering over a piece of mung-bean cake asked Kim if he might like to hire someone. The woman she had in mind was presently working as a kitchen maid but had to find another job because her employer and his family happened to be moving to the countryside. An excellent kitchen worker, the woman would be well suited to Kim's shop.

Kim had a loft added to his shack.

The young woman brought by the peddler appeared to be in her midtwenties, if that.

That evening, the same regular customer whispered to Kim, "You ought to stand me to a few drinks. You can't keep a pretty wife like that a secret, you know."

"Now wait a minute. She's not my wife. She's just a helper," Kim said, his face immediately reddening.

"Come on. Who do you think you're fooling? This innocent stuff is just a big front. God only knows whose skirt you're sniffing under when nobody's looking."

"You've got it all wrong. You'll see."

In truth, Kim had no interest in the young woman. The days passed with scarcely a word between them. She would fry the cakes and boil the noodles, and Kim would deliver them to the tables and collect payment.

Hiring the woman proved enormously helpful. Kim was especially aware of this in the evening when grinding the next day's mung beans. Compared with before, business was a breeze.

One night Kim was lying in bed after grinding the mung beans. The young woman came down from the loft, went into the kitchen, and lit the lantern. Then she drew water in the wash-basin and briskly stripped to the waist.

Kim held his breath. The woman began washing her upper body. Her armpit floated dimly white in the lantern light. Kim was reminded of his former wife's whitish armpit. Instantly he flushed; his throat was parched.

Barely covering her chest with her jacket, the young woman extinguished the lantern and returned to the loft.

Kim suddenly had an urge to drink. This was unusual, for he neither drank nor smoked. At that moment, though, he felt he couldn't get by without a drink.

He poured himself a full glass but began retching before he had finished half of it.

Just then Kim was struck by the thought that this woman would end up disappearing like his former wife had. Before, his mother had placed herself between him and his wife, but now there was only the stairway to the loft between him and the woman. The stairs seemed much the lesser obstacle, he told himself.

A scene from his days at the restaurant rose before him – the two men fighting for the young woman with the dark wart beneath her nostril. He could understand now why they'd had to roll around like that.

Kim put a foot on the stairs, drawn to something. His legs wouldn't stop trembling.

After that Kim was aware only of embracing sleek flesh and presently being encoiled in it.

The young woman started sobbing.

It was still like a dream to Kim. Once again he could hear the sick woman sobbing in the living quarters behind the restaurant.

What could she want, this young woman lying beside him?

"What am I going to do? You've stolen my virginity, and now what?" She spoke rather clearly for one who was sobbing.

There was a change in Kim's life. The young woman still prepared bok choy kimchi and radish kimchi, but now and then Kim had to cook the mung-bean cakes and the noodles. The young woman often delivered the orders and collected payment.

The young woman bought a small vanity. The bottles of cosmetics increased one by one in front of the mirror. When the spirit moved her, she would stop whatever she was doing and go up to the loft to line her eyebrows and powder her face.

Increasingly Kim ground the next day's mung beans by himself.

Early one morning Kim awakened to find himself alone. The young woman had always been the second to rise; she should have been asleep next to him.

Kim went downstairs but she wasn't there. He returned to inspect the loft and found the vanity gone. The cosmetics had disappeared, too. And his money pouch was nowhere to be seen.

"What happened to your wife?" asked the regular customer that evening.

Kim tried in vain to smile.

"Aha, some guy snatched her. What an idiot you are!"

It was true. This was what happened when you were a poor excuse for a man. Kim had never felt so ashamed.

"All she did lately was paint her face . . . You should've latched onto that piece. I can't believe you let her loose."

Still, Kim felt he had been freed from something. Boiling the noodles and frying the mung-bean cakes by himself was relaxing. And he was grinding the beans by himself again – that was the way it should be. And taking payment directly from the customers was like regaining something he had lost.

That was not the whole story, though. As the days passed, Kim began to sense an empty space somewhere in his life. Something precious had slipped from his grasp. This was a sentiment he had never experienced before hiring the young woman. He got in the habit of having a nip every evening.

Any way he looked at it, it seemed he would have to hire someone else. He went to see the woman who sold trifles on a wooden tray at the street corner.

"Could you find me a woman to help out in the kitchen?" Kim asked. "Not a young one," he added as if he needed to justify his request, "but someone who's been around for a while."

A woman arrived. She was over thirty. Tagging along was a girl of five or so.

That evening, the waggish regular whispered to Kim, "This one comes with a bonus. What a nose you have for women! This time latch onto her and don't let go."

"Now hold on – she's just a helper."

Kim genuinely tried to be indifferent to her. The days passed with hardly a word between them. All he wanted from her was some help in the kitchen, he thought.

These days Kim's nightly drinking was nothing to scoff at.

Kim finished two bowls of liquor as usual.

As he and the woman were grinding mung beans, her hands pressed gently against his. Bit by bit his hands were pushed up the handle of the grinding stone, and finally he let go and grabbed the base of the handle. This time the woman gently pressed his hands down. Kim let go again and grabbed the top of the handle.

"My, it's hot," the woman said as soon as they were done with the grinding. She undid the ties of her jacket, then rose and went to the water pail.

Kim fanned his chest continuously.

The woman began washing her back. Something black was revealed in the woman's whitish armpit. Kim's eyes became riveted on it.

Kim felt part of his body ignite. No matter how he fanned himself, it didn't help. He rose and went upstairs to the loft.

At first he couldn't decide why he was there. The girl was sleeping. Only then did it dawn on him that he might have come up to see whether the girl was fast asleep. He left it at that and went back down, driven by something.

The woman went up to the loft, her jacket draped over her shoulder and her chest exposed.

Kim went out front and poured himself a bowl of liquor. It occurred to him that the next morning might see his life turned topsy-turvy by this woman too. Beads of sweat broke out on his forehead. He gulped the liquor in a breath. Let's think about tomorrow's problems tomorrow. He placed a trembling leg on the stairs.

tr. BRUCE AND JU-CHAN FULTON

DRIZZLE

가
랑
비

The drizzling rain that had started after midnight showed no sign of letting up. He was among the twenty combat policemen who formed a reconnaissance patrol that night. Dawn was still two or three hours away. Marching in the drizzle for hours, they were all wet to the skin. Though it was summer, the drizzle in the night and the wet uniforms were enough to make them shiver. But that part wasn't too bad; what really bothered them was the mud caking on their boots. It was no use shaking it off; you just had to wait until the mud got thick and heavy and fell off by itself.

The mud in that part of the country caked even without rain. Only a few days earlier he had buried his wife and baby son. The earth was muddy then, too. They had been killed by the Communist guerrillas, so-called mountain men, because they were members of a policeman's family. He had rushed home when he heard the news, but they had already been temporarily buried. He exhumed the bodies, put them in coffins, and buried them again properly. The mud caked on the shoes of the workers who were helping him make the mounds. Occasionally the workers shaved the mud off their boots with the blade of their shovels. But the mud seemed to cake back on in no time.

He was now silently marching among the men, fighting with the sticky mud that caked on the soles of his boots. Then suddenly he thought that someone else ought to be buried under this very mud, too. Who? Somehow he felt it had to be his own corpse.

The drizzling rain stopped as the dawn broke, although the sky was overcast. The village to which the group was traveling emerged from the fog and soon they could see the mountain behind the village, too. The village consisted of no more than ten houses altogether. The patrol approached with proper caution and alertness, but the mountain men had already fled, as they had expected. An old woman was kneeling in front of what used to be a house. It was in ruins. Smoke still rose from the ashes, and the air was filled with the pungent odor of burning straw and wood. A man's body lay nearby, and the woman was wailing, burying her face in the dead man's chest. He looked about twenty-two or twenty-three years old. With eyes closed, his face was ghastly pale, but his half-open mouth was filled with bloody rainwater. Two other old women stood by, looking down at the corpse as if they didn't know what else to do. The dense overcast changed to drizzle again.

One of the policemen tried to help the wailing woman stand up, but she wouldn't leave the body. Then, suddenly noticing the helping hands were not those of a villager, she sprang to her feet. Her mud-covered skirt slipped halfway down, revealing her waist. The front of her bedraggled blouse was stained with blood — a color redder than that of the mud. The woman looked up at the policeman, her unkempt hair stuck to her face. Her eyes were hollow and vacant. She took the arm of the policeman, gripped it, and started to tremble. She tried to say something but could not speak. Instead, her foamy lips merely twitched spasmodically. All of a sudden she shoved the man aside violently. Then she flopped down and began to scrape mud from the ground to throw at the policeman. He backed off a few steps in dismay. Others in the group nearby did the same. The woman threw herself on the man's body again. The bloody water that filled the mouth trickled down as she shook the corpse.

A middle-aged man wearing a straw cape and a ragged straw hat appeared at the scene. In one hand he carried a shovel all covered with red mud. Was it possible he, too, had been digging a grave? He first greeted the leader of the police patrol and then added seriously that their arrival was just a little late. He said the band of mountain men had come down from the hills twice to plunder the village, taking what livestock they had and raiding their scanty stores of grain. What's more, they had forced the young men of the village to go with them against their will. The patrol leader asked the man how many there were in the band. Five. And the man added in a low tone, as if he were talking to himself, that they had ransacked every house in the village and killed this young man who was hiding under the kitchen floor. Then he shouted to a man in a nearby house, telling him to come out. A man of around fifty shambled out of the house carrying a makeshift stretcher. The two of them, after a struggle with the old woman, picked up the body of the youth and put it on the stretcher. As they lifted it, the old woman rushed toward the stretcher, screaming unintelligbly. Then she flopped down in the mud again as if the pain inside her was more than she could bear. As if drawn to her, the other two old women crouched down beside her and placed their hands on her shoulders. The bloody water kept trickling from the mouth as they carried the body away. The steady drizzle wet the face. It did not wash away the bloody stain. Some of the pain of death still clung to the face of the young man, who had been killed with a bamboo spear.

When the policeman had dug up the bodies of his wife and son, they had already started to decay, and he could detect no sign of pain on their faces. They, too, had been killed with bamboo spears, and the blood and mud had clotted their wounds. One of the laborers scraped the clots off to reveal dark, ugly wounds; with a handful of crumpled straw he wiped the dirt from their eyes. How deep their eye sockets were! The policeman regretted his decision to give them a decent burial. The laborers then dug the dirt from the mouths of the corpses. The two front teeth of his son were red with mud. They looked so fragile. He told the workers to stop and place the bodies in the coffins as they were.

The patrol leader asked all the villagers to gather in the village square. There were only children and old men and women left in the village. The drizzle that had let up a while earlier began to fall again. The faces of the villagers were tense—frozen with fear and anxiety. The children, with cowed looks, instinctively cringed behind their elders. It was obvious that it would be impossible to get any information from them about the activities of the guerrillas. As in other similar instances, they merely searched one another's faces in silence. They feared retaliation. The leader ordered his men to search the houses to see if any of the mountain men had stayed behind and were in hiding.

While they were going through one of the houses, the middle-aged man wearing the straw cape joined them and said it was his house they were searching. Since he looked honest enough and seemed to act for the villagers, they decided not to go through his house as thoroughly as they would have ordinarily. But just as they were about to leave, one of the men searching the backyard reported that he had found something unusual. Going around the house, they found one end of a long bamboo spear dangling from the eaves. No doubt it had been securely tied there, but the straw rope had somehow become loose at one end. The middle-aged man blandly explained that the spear was for hunting rabbits, but it was obviously a pretense of innocence. So they went about a more thorough search. Indeed, they found a kerosene lantern hidden away under a haystack in the barn. Again the middle-aged man came up with an explanation, that he used it for crab hunting in the fall. One of the policeman loudly demanded why he had used the lantern the night before when the crab season was still so far off. Sure enough the lantern, half filled with oil, was wet. It must have been used by the guerrillas the night before. The policeman asked in a still louder voice: "The death of that young man is your doing, isn't it?" The middle-aged man turned white but kept repeating, "No, no!" There was nothing they could do but take him away for further questioning. Then he started to talk very rapidly. He rattled on without stopping, repeating over and over that he himself was innocent. The police learned from him that a certain woman in the village was the agent of the guerrillas, that her husband had joined the guerrillas voluntarily, that it was the husband who had come down yesterday and killed the young man and this time he had planned to take his family along with him, but, with the drizzling rain and unexpected arrival of the patrol, he had not had enough time to move his family to the mountain.

When it was all over, the police still insisted he go along with them. The middle-aged man asked if he might leave his cape at his house before he left. They wondered why he wanted to do that since it was still drizzling. The man walked a few steps toward the house, then suddenly he threw off the straw cape and ran toward the mountain. They shouted to him to halt, but he kept on running. One of the policemen let him have it with his carbine. The straw hat flew up in the air as the man reeled once and fell forward as if he had tripped on something. One of the policemen walked up to him to make sure he was dead.

It was easy enough to single out the woman agent. She was in a group of villagers suckling her baby. She turned deathly pale and trembled like a leaf when the police began to question her about her husband. Searching her house, they found that she had packed all her belongings. The police were authorized to shoot anybody in cooperation with the guerrillas once it was proven, as an object lesson to the people. He stepped up and volunteered to perform this duty.

The woman begged them to spare the life of the baby, but they flatly refused. She said nothing more.

He told the woman to walk ahead of him toward the ravine at the back of the village. As he followed, he felt a certain pleasure, a sense of satisfaction, at the thought of having his revenge. Tonight, you will come down to the village and see what you and your kind have been inflicting on us. I want to hurt you as much as you hurt me a few days ago, when I had to bury my wife and baby, only that and no more. No, I suppose you will suffer more because in this case you will still see agony on the dead faces of your wife and son.

The woman's pace slowed. He spoke sharply, ordering her to walk faster. She tried, but lost one of her rubber shoes in the mud. She kicked the other one off and walked on barefoot. Her garments were soaking wet, and the lower part of her dress was caked with mud.

When they had reached a spot he considered suitable, he ordered her to halt. He made her sit on the ground facing him. By now she seemed to be completely resigned and did exactly as she was told. He hooked his forefinger around the trigger of his carbine. The woman shivered once and closed her eyes. Raindrops trickled down her deathly pale face.

He told her to look straight at the muzzle. He thought it would make his task complete. He also told her to make the baby face him. I want to shoot right through the chest of the baby, too. The baby, thus forced to stop suckling, looked up at its mother with a scowl of disapproval. The man went ahead and aimed his carbine. Just then, noticing the policeman with his rifle, the infant broke into a broad baby smile and began to wave at him. He saw two shiny baby teeth in a smiling mouth. He pulled the trigger twice.

"I suppose at the time he was about the same age as my dead son, you know." The middle-aged real estate man I had been talking to concluded his story with this simple statement.

I glanced at his not-too-prosperous clothing.

"When did you quit the police force?"

"Just after the incident. You are not expected to stay on in the force when you miss something at such close range. Two of them in a row, too. I never was really qualified to be a policeman, you know."

tr. KIM CHONG-UN

MASKS

탈

Wounded in the leg by a bullet, the private tried to lift himself up after he collapsed, but a bayonet pierced his chest. In the instant he lost consciousness, the face of his opponent was imprinted in his eyes as though burned there. The blood flowing from the private's chest vanished into the yellow earth of this desolate battlefield. It was at the foot of a hill far from his home, yet it resembled the land around his own village.

His blood soaked into the ground and became earth. At first, this soil was a deeper shade than that surrounding it, but gradually it all became one color. The private was a man who had worked on a farm, so he considered soil to be life itself.

The roots of a purple eulalia reed furtively drew up the sap of the private's life, and he became a reed.

A jumble of combat boots trampled the reed and moved on. Then, in winter, boots heavier than before trod upon the snow-covered reed. Time after time they trampled it and left, but the reed did not die. After the boots moved on, the reed was blown by the breezes in spring, bathed in sunbeams, washed by the rain and dew, covered with snow, and blown once again by the spring breezes. In the late spring the reed was cut down by a farmer's scythe and carried to a stable.

Here, the reed became a bull. As the private had done when he was a farmer, the man who owned the bull cared for it as if it were the most important member of his family. Now the private worked hard alongside the farmer. He worked until his skin was perpetually bruised and swollen, but making a living from one year to the next was seldom easy. One year, a flood swept away the fields, and on a night that autumn the farmer cried, stifling the sound of his sobbing as he stroked the scruff of the private's neck.

The private passed through the market, then went by train to the slaughterhouse and was hung up in a butcher shop in the city, where cuts of meat were sold off him. There he met a person he knew—the man who had pierced his chest with a bayonet at the foot of a hill. The man was begging food. He ate a piece of the private's meat from the scraps of food he had begged at a restaurant, and the private entered the man.

The man tossed away his empty begging tin and hoisted himself up, one sleeve of his worn-out work clothes dangling where he had no arm. The man reached the front of the iron foundry. He had worked here as a lathe operator before he lost an arm on the battlefield. He did not hesitate as he stepped inside. The man who had been in charge of the foundry for a long time was there.

"Good day."

The foundry master's displeasure showed in his face. He had been smoking, but he crushed the cigarette with the toe of his shoe.

"Sir, there's nothing to be displeased about. I haven't come here to badger you. You understand that, don't you? I came here to work as I did before."

The foundry master cast an uncomfortable glance at the armless sleeve.

"What are you looking at?" The man looked at the master

squarely and continued, "I was wounded in the leg by a bullet, but does that mean I can't operate a lathe?"

The man shifted his body as he spoke, his one empty sleeve dangling loosely at his side.

tr. J. MARTIN HOLMAN

CLOWNS

曲藝師

In Pusan, as in Taegu, we were beholden to a lawyer's family for our shelter.

I sent my family on ahead of me for refuge. Later, when I followed, I found that they had not gone all the way down to Pusan but had stopped in Taegu because it cost less to live in Taegu than in Pusan. So I went to Taegu on Christmas day. My wife and children were living in a rented room on the large property of a lawyer next to the skeleton of a burned-out courthouse. The nest of my beloved wife and darling children was a shed in a corner of the spacious garden surrounding this grand mansion.

The weather was much colder in Taegu than in Pusan. Since the room was built for storage, with the only door facing north, not a ray of sunshine strayed into it all day. It was chilly and sinister, so much so that the children all went out as soon as day broke, even though it was freezing cold outside. However, we deemed ourselves lucky. We were fortunate to have among our acquaintances a friend of this family, so we were able to obtain some kind of shelter—needless to say a great good fortune for refugees like us.

While we lived there, they had some rules we had to observe. By decree of the mother-in-law of the lawyer, we were forbidden to draw water from the well in the inner yard after dusk, or in the morning before they did, or to do laundry of any kind in the inner yard, where there was a well and also city water. The prohibition against drawing water in the morning was no inconvenience for us. As we ate only twice a day, we only needed to draw water late in the morning for a late breakfast, after the lawyer's family had finished theirs. It was the same with laundry. We only had to carry water to the outer yard and wash our things there. But on days when we had used up our water, if somebody got thirsty at night, especially if any of the children got thirsty, it was difficult not to have any water. But then, people don't die or get ill because of one night's thirst.

Another of the prohibitions decreed by this august old lady concerned the use of the lavatory. We were forbidden to use the one in the inner yard, so my wife had to build makeshift facilities in a corner of the garden behind the bushes. It was hidden from view by straw matting hung like a curtain. It was very embarrassing for grown-ups to use this crude latrine in the daytime, but we were not in a position to complain about such small inconveniences.

It did not take long for us to realize that the mother-in-law of the lawyer dominated the household. My wife was informed by the housemaid that, since the lawyer's wife was her only child, this old lady had come to live with her daughter and son-in-law when they got married; from the first she had governed the whole household. The couple had a separate room to themselves, and the old lady occupied a big room with a heated floor, from whence she reigned. Nobody in her family ate in the morning until after the old lady had finished her breakfast.

The old lady's hobby was playing cards with friends, and they met for that purpose in each of their homes in turn. They also went to Buddhist temples in a group to offer prayers every now and then. We often saw the old lady going out in a silk dress, and she looked so erect and trim that it was hard to believe that she was nearing sixty. Her friends, who frequently visited the house, were all well-dressed, well-groomed women who did not look as if they had ever known hardship in their lives. Maybe life is something that should be lived with at least that much decency.

About ten days after I joined my family, we woke up one morning to discover that one of the rubber shoes belonging to my eight-year-old daughter Sŏn-a had disappeared. We looked everywhere without finding it. The whole family covered every square inch of the spacious garden. It could not have been stolen, because if anybody meant to steal shoes, why should he have taken only Sŏn-a's, and only one shoe at that? We concluded that the shepherd dog of the house had carried it away and left it somewhere far off.

Although we were extremely short of money, we couldn't let our daughter go around barefoot in winter, so my wife went out to buy a pair of shoes. When she came back with a new pair, she recounted what she had heard at the shoe shop: sometimes someone who has a sick member in the family steals one shoe, in the belief that the sickness will be transferred to the owner of the shoe if he or she is of the same age as the sick person and the shoe is disposed of in a certain manner. Then my wife said that one of the lawyer's children, who was about Sŏn-a's age, had been sick in bed for several days. As she spoke she looked worried, and angry, and also sad.

I shook my head and told her that such could not be the case. But I, too, could not help feeling anxious and angry. Granted, it was a foolish superstition, and granted, we were people of no consequence at all; still, if one loves one's own child, one should realize that other people's children are just as dear to their parents. Moreover, Sŏn-a was the most fragile of our four children. If she fell ill, living as refugees like this we could never restore her health.

A few days of anxiety and uneasiness passed. We heard that the lawyer's sick child was well again. And our Sŏn-a did not take ill. The disappearance of the shoe must have been the dog's doing. The old lady, who spent many days praying to Buddha in the temple, could not have done anything so inhuman as that.

A few days later, when I got home, my wife was sitting alone in the cold, dark room. She told me in a voice full of anxiety that the old lady of the house had told her that we must vacate the room. The explanation she gave was that they needed the room (which was in fact a shed) to store coal. But my wife had heard a different story from the housemaid.

At midday, a large group of the old lady's friends had come to play cards, as often happened. One of the old women caught sight of the straw mat screen behind the bush in the corner of the garden. Why don't people's eyes grow dim with old age as they should? She went over to see what it was. When she discovered what was behind it, she spat with disgust and complained vehemently about the monstrosity of the thing. She ran to the old lady of the house immediately and railed at her for letting people defecate in the garden. So the old lady of the house herself began cursing the uncivilized paupers who looked like people but were not fit to be treated as human beings. She went on to declare that since her house was not a refugee asylum, she would throw them out at once. Then she went to my wife and ordered her to move out. But she could not very well tell my wife that we had to leave the house because we had made a latrine in the garden, so she gave a different excuse – that they needed our room to store coal. Well, that proved the truth of the old lady's saying that human beings should behave so as to be worthy of being regarded as human beings, since she was the one who had forbidden us to use the facilities of the house and thereby forced us to relieve ourselves in the garden behind the straw screen. After all, she could not have forgotten that as human beings we had to defecate and so would be forced to resort to this uncivilized method, however reluctantly. And moreover, she made it clear to us, our room was not a fit dwelling place for human beings, but a shed for storing things like coal.

So this was how the shabby Hwang Sun-wŏn family, evicted from the shed in the lawyer's mansion garden, drifted into Pusan at last around the end of March, after a few more attempts at securing shelter in Taegu.

We had planned to stay with my sister-in-law's family for a while in her rented room until we could rent a room for ourselves. I had seen that the room the family was living in had space to accommodate a few more people.

This house happened to belong to a lawyer, too. It was located at the rear of the Kyŏngnam Middle School. It was a fairly large house of mixed Japanese and Western style. My sister-in-law and her children were using a room that was about twelve square yards. There was an old cabinet and a small table to one side of the room, so the usable space consisted of about nine square yards. That was enough for my sister-in-law and her three children and the six members of our family.

But when we came to Pusan we found that another family, a mother and two children, was already living with my sister-in-law. The husband of this lady was an army judge advocate stationed at the front. Originally, the lawyer had promised to give this family a separate room, but later he said he needed to keep the other room for guests, so this lady and her children came to live in the room my sister-in-law was occupying. That had caused no inconvenience, as both families consisted of women and children (my brother-in-law had gone to the United States for technical training and was now staying in Tokyo because the war made it impossible for him to return home). Moreover, the acquaintance of my sister-in-law who had helped her rent this room from the lawyer and this lady's husband were both in the legal profession, so my sister-in-law and the lady quickly became good friends.

But the convenience did not last long. The landlord suddenly demanded that they vacate the room. They needed the room for the maid. The strange thing was that something else happened the same day. A transfer was approved, at least unofficially, for my sister-in-law's acquaintance, the one whose position had influenced the lawyer to rent her the room. My sister had learned of the transfer a few days later when it was officially made known, but the lawyer could easily have gotten the information through private channels in legal circles. It is rather extraordinary that the decision on the transfer and the order to move out were made on the same day, but I suppose I should regard it as a coincidence. A man of such prominent social position would not behave so hastily and impolitely from a calculation of immediate advantage. So that was the state of the room before we got to Pusan.

What could we do? Needless to say, we were not rich enough to stay at an inn. After a lengthy deliberation, we decided to take lodgings in separate groups. It was decided that I would sleep with my aged parents in their eighteen-square-yard room in Namp'odong, inhabited by nineteen people from three families. Our two eldest children would be sent away to where their maternal grandfather's family of six lived in a four-square-yard room, while the two younger children and my wife could do nothing but stay with my sister-in-law.

Every day I had to hear from my wife or from my older children who had been to see her how fiercely the landlord was demanding the evacuation of the room. In Taegu we had heard that many of the refugees had left Pusan, so we had supposed we would be able to rent a room if we tried hard enough. It was true that Pusan was not as crowded as when I had first come last winter, but there were still no rooms. My wife and I searched everywhere. We asked everybody we knew, but it was all in vain.

The demand for eviction was so insistent that the lady who had been sharing the room with my sister-in-law moved away to her husband's uncle's. And early the next morning a tempest broke out in the lawyer's residence.

While everybody was still in bed, the door of the room was thrust open and there stood the lawyer himself with fierce, glaring eyes. He thundered angrily, "How can you behave like this and still call yourselves human beings? Get out of my house at once. Go to an inn if you don't have anywhere else to go. Human beings should know how to behave. If you don't get out of this house today, I will settle the matter legally."

My wife and sister-in-law could no longer keep silent. They declared that they could not go out in the streets to live or go to an inn. The lawyer's two older daughters came to his support, and his wife and eldest son were also mobilized. The eldest son of the family, who was said to be attending law school in Seoul, threatened to use his fists, but the old lawyer dissuaded him and led him away, perhaps having determined that such violence would work to their disadvantage if the matter were brought to court.

I listened to this report from my wife in a corner of the room in Namp'odong in which nineteen people lived. That we were not worthy of being looked upon as human beings was no surprise, our worthlessness having been settled quite beyond a doubt by the old lady in Taegu; and that the landlord would deal with the matter legally was perhaps natural, since he was a lawyer. But we could not very well go stay at an inn. If we could have afforded such accommodations, we would have done it long before. As to the accusation that we did not behave properly, I know there may be truth in it, because refugees cannot very well afford to behave quite properly all the time. But we had not been all that barbarous. What my sister-in-law spent for mending the flooring of the room was as good as paying nearly twenty thousand won rent a month. Only the day before, we had told the lawyer's wife that we could give her some key money when we managed to sell all our remaining clothes. The lady of the house then said that it was not for lack of money that they wanted the room back, but because they needed the room to give to the maid. My wife then asked the lady to let her provide space in the room for the maid of the house, but she still refused. There was no way out. My wife had to ask for some time until she could rent a room. Since I mentioned the maid, I might as well set down here that the woman who was working as a maid there had told my wife and my sister-in-law that she was a not-too-distant relative of the family; she had come for a visit and was staying in the house to help with the household work; that no maid ever lasted in this house more than a couple of months; that the current servant was an old woman who was now away on a trip to the country to see her son; and that this room had never been used by people, but as a sort of storage room. Anyway, my sister-in-law already knew that an old woman worked as the maid.

Well, if we did not know how to behave, it all comes from our lack of ability to rent a room.

My wife then said solemnly, with a sad, tearful face, as if she had made a grave decision, that our whole family should live together in this room from that night on. She reasoned that, since our situation was at its worst, it might be better for the family to live together until we could rent a room. I hesitated to agree with her.

I thought of the law student. A young man who had threatened women with his fists would not let me alone. But how could a man with a weak constitution, nearing forty, confront a young man in his twenties? At the same time, how could I, as head of the family, leave my wife and children in such a plight, however much of a weakling I might be? Of course, it was not that my wife wanted protection from the brute force of the young man. On the contrary, if that were her concern, she would never have suggested that we live together in the room. My wife was only thinking of my poor old parents, who slept sitting up almost every night because of me. Thus she suggested that the family stay together until a room could be found, since things had gotten so bad they could not get worse.

I went to school. The school where I had been teaching in Seoul had moved down to Pusan and had begun to hold classes every other day in a park. This was one of the school days. I asked several colleagues who had come down to Pusan before me to look for a room for me. Although I knew it was not a very proper thing to do, I even asked some of my older students to keep their eyes open for a vacant room.

In the afternoon I sat in a tearoom without drinking any tea and asked some friends to help me out of this plight.

Toward evening I went out to drink cheap rice wine in one of the liquor stalls under awnings that stood in a row along the quay. I emptied one bowl. I happened to notice that a couple of sailing vessels were anchored beyond the bulwark. Oh, the sea was always good to behold. Right in front of my eyes, gulls kept darting up and down. Oh, they were nice to watch, too.

But in fact, I was not in a mood to appreciate the poetic beauty of the sea and the gulls. I felt as if a fishbone were stuck in my throat. That fishbone was the thought that from now on I had to go to the lawyer's house and, consequently, to confront the law student. I had never seen this young man, but I had once seen the lawyer himself when he was pruning trees in the garden. He looked past forty, but his well-groomed hair was as glossy and black as a young man's, and he was of a sturdy build. I thought that if the son took after his father, he must be well-built and strong. I was rather unwilling to meet him.

I gulped down another bowl of wine. I had had many a fistfight myself when in my twenties. My face had plenty of souvenirs of those battles. My nose had bled many a time, and I also made other noses bleed not a few times. Once I had broken two front teeth of a man and received in return a scar like a vaccination mark on the crown of my head. To be frank, at the height of my youth I had never lost an even battle. But after thirty, I had always avoided a confrontation of fists. Today, nearing forty, I began to have fears at the mere thought of a fight. I emptied another wine bowl. But if challenged, I could not just crouch in a corner. There is such a thing as self-defense. Yes. I will rise to the challenge. Even after this long interval, I will exhibit my old-time finesse. A fight cannot be won with physical strength alone. With the help of alcohol, I made plans about how to tackle the young man according to the various methods of attack he might use. I pictured a scene in which I was elated, having knocked my adversary down. Not before my pockets were empty and dusk covered the entire quay did I leave the liquor stall.

Nothing happened that night. Nothing happened the next day, or the day after that. In the meantime, the woman who had been working as maid went back to her home town and the servant woman of the house returned from the country. She was quite an old woman, her hair completely gray, her back bent. This old woman cooked, washed, and cleaned all day.

Once, when I saw my wife and my sister-in-law whispering in a corner and asked what it was about, I was told that the old servant woman wanted to sell secretly two bottles of soy sauce belonging to the lawyer's household. She needed money to settle an old debt for medicine to an herb doctor, and the lawyer's family would not pay her salary. I tried to figure out whether this kind of stealing would constitute a crime in the eyes of the law.

On the evening of the fourth day after I moved to this room, I talked it over with my wife and, in the hope that the landlord might accept a compromise, we concluded that my wife would go to the lady of the house to pay her one month's rent and plead for mercy. The problem was the amount of rent to take. We reckoned that twenty or thirty thousand won would never do, so we thought of offering forty thousand won, but at last, out of desperation, we decided on fifty thousand. We didn't know how we could pay fifty thousand won a month for the room and manage to live, but we had heard that the current price of rooms was ten thousand won per two square yards. We knew that some people demanded to have a room vacated so that they could raise the rent. Moreover, we thought anything would be better than having the matter brought to court, as the lawyer had threatened, and to be thrown out into the streets. So we decided to try to reach an agreement about the room by whatever means we could, and then go out with our minds at ease and work hard to earn a living. In fact we were already engaged in trade. My wife was taking what was left of our clothes to the Kukje Market, and the two older children were trading with the American troops. The fifty thousand won was taken out of my wife's business capital.

My wife went into the living room and returned after a short while. The money was not in her hands, so we thought a compromise had been reached. But my wife said no. They still insisted that we vacate the room. The master of the house and the eldest son slept in a sixteen-square-yard room; and in the main room the master's wife and the younger son slept; so I suppose they could not very well say they needed the room back because the house was too crowded. The lady of the house said that she had to have the room back for her grown-up daughters; they could hardly sleep because of the snoring of the old servant woman. When my wife suggested that we make space for the old servant woman to sleep in our room, the lady still insisted on taking the room back. She further said that a friend of her daughter had offered to make a present of a gold wristwatch if her family could rent the room, but they had said no.

I felt a chill in my liver. A gold wristwatch! That was certainly no trifle. I asked my wife what she had done with the money, and she said she just put it before the lady of the house, suggesting that she buy books for her daughters with it. Our ardent hope was that the money would not be returned. But the next day it was.

The following night, it happened. I always stayed away from the room in the daytime, spending much of my time in the room where my parents lived, except for teaching at school every other day. Most of the refugees in Pusan went out to the market to sell cigarettes, leaving only children in their places of shelter. My parents also sold cigarettes in the market. I waited in my parents' room for my older children to return, to go with them to the Kukje Market to pick up my wife so we could come back as a group. That's what we did that night.

When we got back in the evening, we found two strapping girls standing majestically in our room. They were the daughters of this family. We could not tell which was the elder of the two, but anyway, we had heard that the elder daughter was graduating from some girls' school in the city and the younger was in her fourth year. The two said they would sleep in our room that night. I wondered to myself which of the two girls was the one with a friend who had offered a gold wristwatch to rent the room. I felt I had to escape from the scene.

But before I had time to do so, the two big girls declared to no one in particular that the room would have to be vacated within a couple of days. They gave me a look, then went out. It does not matter whether it was a look of contempt, derision, or whatever. Anyway, I had to admit to myself these girls' tactics had a much greater effect on me than a few boxes on the ears from their elder brother would have.

When I left the house each morning, I always wished I wouldn't have to return.

The next day was a school day. When I opened the belled door of the entrance porch and stepped out, the lawyer was there stooping beside some flaming red camellia blossoms, pruning boxwood trees. With just a fleeting glance at him, one could perceive that he cherished the plants in his garden and carefully tended them. It was a cultured hobby. Maybe life should be lived with at least that much elegance and leisure. I escaped from the porch as if I were being pursued.

At school I again asked my colleagues to look for a room for me. I also asked some older students to help me out. After school I again sat in a tearoom without drinking any tea and begged my friends for help.

Then I waited in Namp'odong for my elder children to return. The children came back after dark. We were so late I thought my wife would have already gone home by herself. We decided to go straight home. The road from Namp'odong to the Kyŏngnam Middle School was dark.

We pushed at the iron gate. It was locked from inside. We peeped in and saw that our room was not lighted. I thought my wife must still be in the market waiting for us, and my sister-in-law had turned off the light to put her children to sleep. We decided to wait for my wife so we could all go in together. I led the children to the footbridge over a ditch that my wife had to cross on her way home. I crouched down.

My second son squatted beside me as did my eldest son. But my wife did not come for a long time. Nam-a, my second son, began to nod off although it was still early in the evening. What he did must be tiring for a boy his age. I turned my eyes to the ditch. I took out a cigarette. The match did not light. Rain began to fall.

Tong-a, my eldest son, stood up and walked to the house. In a little while he came running back, saying that his mother was already back home and the gate was open. He said he heard his mother's voice from our room when he drew near the gate.

When we went inside we learned that the light in our room was out for a reason we had not guessed. The electricity in this room was on a special separate line. The room could be disconnected while the house had power day and night; all the other rooms in the house were brightly lit even now. For a while we sat silently in the darkness.

My sister-in-law said, as if to herself, that she would leave the room tomorrow, even if she had to sleep under the bridge. She said that though the landlord's family had always been harsh to the children, of late it had become almost unbearable. If my sister-in-law's seven-year-old and my six-year-old began to sing or went out in the hall to go to the toilet, someone in the landlord's family never failed to shout at them to be quiet. If the children in our room joined in when the seven-year-old son of the lawyer marched in the hall singing a military song, they were reprimanded for making noise. Even more painful was to see the keen anguish of my girl, Sŏn-a, at the least sound her younger brother or cousin made, for fear they would be scolded by the landlord's family.

My sister-in-law wept in the darkness, stifling the sound. I felt fire burning in my chest. This was a different kind of anger from what I had felt when one of Sŏn-a's rubber shoes was stolen. But whatever tactics they adopted, we could only endure them and seek ways of minimizing the pain they produced.

The countermeasure we devised was to leave the room unoccupied during the daytime from the next day. My two younger children were to stay at Namp'odong, and my sister-in-law was to spend the day with her children where her parents were living and return alone in the evening to prepare dinner. Only after we had thus set up our plans did we swallow our cold food in the darkness.

I spent the whole next day in my parents' room in Namp'odong with Sŏn-a and Kyŏng-a. I was relieved that the day had brightened, although it had rained the night before.

My wife joined us before evening, but the elder children had not come back, even though it was already dark. Kyŏng-a said he was tired, then fell asleep in his mother's arms.

It was pitch dark when the two elder children came back. They said it was hard to get a ride on the tram lately. With nimble hands the two children excitedly took cigarettes and packages of chewing gum out of the secret pockets in their clothes and displayed them before their parents and grandparents. Their deft hands gave me sorrow. I averted my eyes.

We came out into the street. I was carrying the sleeping Kyŏng-a on my back, and my wife carried her bundle on her head. We walked up the wide street in front of the Tong'a Theatre. My elder son Tong-a walked close to me and showed off his conversational skill in English, telling me that he could easily make purchases if he walked up to GIs and said, "Please sall to me." I corrected him, saying that it was not "sall to me" but "sell to me." Tong-a is a third grader. I would have to send him to school soon so that he could graduate from primary school and enter middle school. Yet the boy had already begun to learn English conversation. And the father corrects him, too.

Nam-a caught up to me and began telling me about the clever boy he had met that day. When the lad was in danger of being caught, Nam-a said, he sprawled on his back in a nearby rice paddy, which was flooded. The lad, sunk in water up to his ears, kicked all four limbs, rolled his eyeballs, and moved his mouth wildly. The boy had a few GI bucks hidden in his shirt. The men who were going to nab him looked at the sight for some time with rather worried expressions, then poked his belly a few times. The boy pretended not to notice, but kept on rolling his eyes and moving his mouth wildly. Maybe they thought he was an epileptic. The men went away. Hearing this, I realized that my Nam-a, who was chattering away beside me, would also have to learn how to fake an epileptic fit to guard a few military bucks.

We turned to the right at the Pusŏng Bridge. The road along the ditch was dark, although stars twinkled in the sky.

Nam-a suddenly suggested that we all sing together. I was going to say no, but Sŏn-a, who was walking beside her mother, began singing as if she had been waiting for the opportunity. "Stepping over the dead bodies of our friends fallen in battle . . ." It was the military march the lawyer's son was allowed to sing, while our children were not. I recalled how Sŏn-a always tried to prevent her younger brother from singing and making noise in the lawyer's house. I did not have the heart to tell her not to sing. Nam-a and Tong-a added their voices to Sŏn-a's.

As soon as the march was over, Nam-a began to sing a cycling song, running in the dark, pretending to be riding a bicycle. Why so sprightly tonight, when he was so sleepy yesterday? Could it be that he had luck with his trade today? "Look out, you old fellow over there, or you'll get run over!" Nam-a's bicycle now turned toward us and swept past between his father and mother. This old fellow of a father had to dodge to avoid being run over.

That made Kyŏng-a on my back wake up. He joined his sister in singing "Come, sweet, pretty butterfly." Sŏn-a waved her arms, dancing to her song, like a butterfly fluttering in the dark.

When his sister's song was over, Kyŏng-a, now wide awake, began to sing "Beautiful Wild Rabbit." He began the wild rabbit hop, too. Not content with jumping on my back, he climbed onto my shoulders and bounced, sitting on my neck. "Whither are you hopping like that? I'm going over the hill by myself and I'll come back with lots and lots of chestnuts." Kyŏng-a continued bouncing until he finished the song.

Trying hard not to totter under Kyŏng-a's gyrations, I thought, if he is a rabbit, then his mother and father are rabbits, too. But his father rabbit, far from jumping over the hill and coming back with lots and lots of chestnuts, is staggering under his slight weight, as if walking straight were a great and formidable feat.

Then I suddenly thought of the word "clown." Oh yes, I am performing a circus act now with Kyŏng-a on my shoulders. Well then, Kyŏng-a on my shoulders is also performing a circus act. Sŏn-a was acting the part of the butterfly in this circus. Nam-a was the trick cyclist. It would be a sad circus if Nam-a had to put on an epileptic fit in order to guard a few military bucks, like the little boy he saw today. Tong-a's "please sall to me" is also a circus act, and their sleight of hand with the cigarette and chewing-gum packets are all polished circus routines. So they are the little clowns of the Hwang Sun-wŏn Circus Troupe, and I am their ringmaster. Our stage today is Pumindong Road beside the ditch.

Clown Tong-a began to sing "Sorrento." Yes, show off all your accomplishments. I do not know whether a long time from now, when you look back on today's circus performance, you will laugh or cry over it. And you don't have to know whether your father and mother watched your circus acts today with tears or laughter. I only wish, my dear little clowns, that when each of you has his own troupe, you will not have to repeat a circus such as this on this kind of stage with your own young clowns. Oh, excuse me, ladies and gentlemen, it was just the maundering of an old clown. Well then, shall we listen to Tong-a's solo?

My wife, who had been walking a few feet behind me, caught up and put her arm around my waist. This wife of the troupe leader must have thought her husband's circus act was in danger. I grasped my wife's hand to signal to her not to worry. At that moment, Clown Tong-a's solo stopped abruptly in the middle of the last bar. We were already at the entrance to the alley leading to the lawyer's house.

Well, ladies and gentlemen, that will have to conclude today's program. I am ashamed to have presented such a poor circus. We didn't have a chance to rehearse. Tomorrow we hope to show you something better. Thank you very much for your kind attention. I thank you on behalf of the entire troupe. Well then, a warm good night to you all.

tr. SUH JI-MOON

THE WHIP

매

The boy's mother was doing the wash just inside the backyard wall. The boy set his bookbag on the floor and quietly slid open the panel door to the room on the far side. As usual, the large collection of crystal stones was set out on the table beneath the window against the south wall. The stones had been collected by the boy's uncle, who was attending engineering college. The boy quickly singled out an amethyst and grabbed it. He knew that his friends at school would not have anything like it. This stone had a long sharp point at one end that stood out boldly.

The boy took the stone and went out into the yard. Once there, he buried the stone. He watered it with dishwater, thinking that he might get the point to grow larger and maybe even start some new ones.

The boy was fortunate that his uncle said nothing about the missing stone when he came home. His uncle did not seem to notice one stone missing, with so many others there.

In the evening the boy waited for the water in which the rice had been rinsed. He carried it outside and sprinkled it on the ground. His mother usually did this in the mornings and evenings to settle the dust. He sprinkled the water evenly over the yard, then went to where the stone was buried and watered it thoroughly. He did the same thing the next morning. He even took water from the washbasin and tossed it out over the yard. Then he folded his hands behind his back and strolled around the yard the way his grandfather did in the mornings and evenings during his frequent visits from Seoul. "C'mon rock, hurry and grow. Hurry up and grow."

His mother looked from the kitchen and said to herself, "Ch'ŏl is all grown up. He even knows how to water the yard."

How big has the stone gotten? The little boy wanted to dig it up to look at it. He finally did just that four days later. It looked as though the point had grown a little, but then again it looked the same as before. Once again he buried the stone. He waited a little longer before digging it up the next time. One day after supper the boy's uncle said, "I think I'll take little Ch'ŏl around town as a reward for working so hard watering the yard every day . . . The circus came in yesterday."

The boy knew about the circus, too. On the way back from school he had stood in front of the entrance for a while before coming home. Several horses were tied up outside the circus entrance. A monkey was sitting on one of them picking fleas. The monkey looked quite clever.

The boy sat with his uncle in the middle of the circus audience thinking only of the monkey. If that little guy comes out, he'll show us some really good tricks.

Two acrobats appeared. One grabbed the trapeze and started swinging back and forth, switching hands in midair. Applause rang out. The boy joined in, clapping his hands. Then came a clown, wearing a big nose stuck on his face and a baggy jumpsuit with big red polka-dots. The clown mimicked the trapeze artists for a moment, then fell down. Each time he fell, a cloud of white smoke came out of his pants. It was quite comical and entertaining.

Next were the horses. Their trainer shouted commands, and the horses knelt on their front legs and bowed. The clown tried to climb onto the horses' backs but kept slipping off. The crowd laughed. Once, when the trainer shouted, one of the horses jumped through a ring barely big enough for it to fit through. Then, the hoop was set on fire, and the horse turned around and jumped back through. Applause. The boy joined in and clapped his hands.

At last the monkey appeared, doing handsprings and flips around the ring. The clown imitated the monkey but often tripped and fell on his back, raising a cloud of smoke. When the monkey began riding a unicycle around the ring, the boy clapped as long as anyone.

Next, some girls came out and started to dance. Only their bosoms and bottoms were covered. Their hips were a little too big, and they wiggled them in a curious way. Whistles and shouts arose from the crowd.

The boy happened to glance at his uncle, who was leaning forward, blinking his eyes behind his glasses. The boy could not see what was so interesting.

After the girls finished their act, a muscleman came out carrying a large wooden pole over his shoulder. He tossed the pole up into the air and balanced it vertically, switching it from shoulder to shoulder, all without using his hands. Then a young girl in a bright red jumpsuit leapt into the ring and pranced up to the man. He picked her up with one hand and lifted her to his shoulder. As she rose, the girl began to climb the wooden pole. She climbed as if she had glue on her hands and feet. Below, the clown pretended to climb an invisible pole, but he slipped and fell each time. The girl reached the top. Fantastic. Without realizing it, the boy began to clap, but he was clapping alone. The rest of the crowd seemed to be anticipating something more. And, in fact, she was not coming down but was trying to balance on top of the pole on one foot. Then she extended her other leg and both arms out toward the crowd. Applause thundered. The boy was still clapping. Next she clasped her slender hands together around the top of the pole and started to turn over. She actually stood on her head. The boy unconsciously held his breath. Applause reverberated through the crowd, but the boy was too awestruck to clap.

After that, the tightrope walkers came out. They did several stunts on the trapeze as well. Once again the girls came out and did their strange dance. Even as the boy watched the later acts, the only thing he could see was the little girl way up on top of that pole.

On the way home the boy's uncle asked, "What did you like best about the circus?"

"I thought the girl upside down on top of the pole was best. How about you?" As he asked, the boy suddenly wondered if his uncle had liked the dancing girls.

His uncle walked on without speaking for a moment, then he said, "Years ago when I was a kid, the circus was a lot of fun, but lately it doesn't seem quite the same."

On the way home from school the next day, the boy stopped in front of the entrance to the circus. There were a few horses tied up outside, just like before. The monkey was riding one of the horses around. Today, however, it was the girl who had climbed the pole, rather than the monkey, who held the boy's imagination.

As soon as he got home, the boy approached his mother and quietly asked, "Could you give me a thousand won so I can buy a notebook and pencil?"

"You just bought a notebook and pencil a few days ago. What happened to them?"

"That was for arithmetic. What I need today is for social studies."

He took his money and went outside, his heart pounding. I just lied, he thought. Once he had bought the circus ticket and settled into the crowd, though, he had no other thoughts. As the boy waited to see the girl come out and climb the pole, he laughed even harder at the clown's antics than he had the day before. This time the boy's hands began to sweat as the girl started up the pole. He held his breath again as he watched her arms tremble slightly during her headstand. It was quite thrilling. Only after the girl finally slid down the pole, smiled, waved good-bye, and ran off did the boy heave a sigh of relief.

Two days later the boy went to his mother again. "Can I have some money for watering the yard?"

"What is this asking for money every day? Didn't your uncle just take you out as a reward for the yardwork?"

"That was my uncle. You're my mother. I'll water the yard every day."

"I see. You did the chores for money. Here, but if you think you're going to water the yard for money next time, you may as well not."

The next day the boy came home from school and was kicking a shuttlecock around in the yard when his uncle came over to him. "Hey, Ch'ŏl, go inside and get ten thousand won out of the desk drawer for me." It seemed his uncle did not want to take off his shoes to go inside for himself. There was a loose pile of seventy or eighty thousand won in the desk drawer next to a bundle of a hundred thousand. It was money that had come from his grandfather the day before. After his uncle left, the boy felt his heart pounding inexplicably. He could not kick the shuttlecock more than four or five times in a row, where moments ago he had reached twenty. No matter how he tried, it was no use.

He went inside to look at a book but continued to leaf through the same four or five pictures without seeing them. The sounds of the circus horns and drums drifted into the house. The boy went next door to play marbles with the neighbor children. The circus noises continued. His heart began to flutter. He tried to concentrate on the game, but he kept on losing until his pockets were empty.

Suddenly, without thinking, he ran back to his house. I'll only take one thousand won of his money. Today I'll go see it one last time.

This time there was something odd about the girl climbing the pole. Something was wrong from the beginning. The pole was so slippery that the girl could not even get halfway up before sliding back down. Incredible! Her arms and legs were trembling. Eventually she reached the top. As she stood there on one foot, she slipped somehow and almost fell. The boy was already holding his breath. The girl tried to do her headstand at the top but could not release her hands. Unlike before, she was not able to straighten out of her tuck. Each time she started to unfold, she could see her hands begin to slip and would go back to her original position. Unbelievable! Down below the clown who had imitated the girl the other times merely stood staring up at her. Finally, the girl stopped trying altogether and came down. Whistles and jeers sailed out of the crowd. She had quit. The performance was a failure. The girl ran across the ring, covering her face with one hand, and disappeared behind the curtain. The boy sprang up, unable to bear it, and slipped out the way the girl had gone. Following the footpath to the curtain, he ducked behind it.

"Hey, girl! What happened to you out there?" The burly acrobat's voice boomed out. The boy was peeking through a gap in the curtains in spite of himself.

The clown who had caused so much laughter before now glared at the tiny girl. She just stood there silently, choking back tears. There were also several other people standing nearby. "Who are you trying to ruin?" The girl sobbed something through her tears. "What's that? Are you sick?" The girl's face suddenly turned pale with fear. At that point a dreadful look crept into the face of the comical clown, the one who had brought only laughter from the crowd. Eyes glaring with anger and lips ferociously pressed closed, he looked horrifying. "Well, I'll have to cure you." Taking down a leather whip that was hanging nearby, he snapped it across the girl's thin shoulders with a crack. The girl let out a muffled scream but did not flinch. "Listen! Don't you know you've got to perform for the crowd, even if it means falling and dying?" The leather whip sang out again. Still again, and again . . . The boy was dumbfounded. Apparently this sort of behavior was not unusual. A man who was changing his clothes just continued to dress. A man moving equipment went on with his work. Another man was putting on his makeup. And the muscleman, who earlier had held the pole on his shoulders for the girl, merely gazed off into space, blowing puffs of smoke from a pipe.

The boy took in the entire scene and then left. Walking through the gate at home, he stopped for a moment and caught his breath. He seemed to be considering something. He went to the corner of the yard and dug up the crystal, not bothering to see if any new points had grown.

He slid the back door open. His uncle, who was sitting at the desk, turned toward him. The boy held out the stone, "You didn't know, but I took this."

His uncle quietly lifted his eyes behind his glasses and smiled. "So that's what you had buried in the ground and were watering."

"I even took some of your money. And I lied to Mama to get more." The boy took off his belt and held it out to his uncle. "You'd better beat me with this."

The uncle replied softly, "That's all right. You just took it so you could go to the circus . . . So, was the circus that neat? If it's that much fun, I should take you to see it once more before it leaves town."

"No. I've seen all I want of the circus. Quick, beat me with this . . . hard and fast."

tr. DAVID BRUNETTE

THE DIVING GIRL

비
바
리

When you first see Cheju Island from the sea, it appears to be just one huge mountain. On the ferry, when the indistinct mottled form rises on the distant horizon, outlined in pale purple, the people cry out, "Ah, there's Cheju!" In reality, its shape makes it seem not so much an island as an enormous mountain, with a high peak on the right and a lower peak continuous with it on the left. And of course what we call Cheju Island is actually formed by the volcanic peak Mount Halla.

Nearly all the island's villages are beside coves along the seashore at the foot of Mount Halla. Still, one has the impression that the town of Cheju is situated on a plain some distance from the foot of the mountain. But, if you think about it, this is all part of Mount Halla—the farthest point to which the base of the mountain has managed to stretch itself outward. The town is right on a backbonelike ridge, and this slope, with its lesser ridges, forms valleys that all become an integral part of the folds of land that make up the base of the great mountain itself.

Most days the peak is apt to be encircled by a wreath of clouds or fog. Ordinarily a mountain of this size and height would have water flowing down the folds of its sides, but Halla has little.

That is why water has become such a precious commodity on Cheju Island. You often see children walking with large bamboo baskets called *kudŏk* strapped over their shoulders, containing Cheju water jars known as *hŏbŏk*. They carry these around all the time so they can stop and collect water wherever they happen to find it.

The only exception is the town of Sŏgwip'o. Its only real similarity to other places, like Hallim or Mosŭlp'o, or the rest of the ports and villages, is that it is a part of the base of the mountain. It is actually more a part of the foot of the mountain itself than any of the other port towns, and yet water is more abundant there than in any other place. Clear, fresh water flows down from the mountain valleys, forming several streams. These course around behind the houses and along the borders of the courtyards, making the gurgling sounds you expect from mountain streams. Beneath the cliffs behind the villages, these streams form pools where people bathe, and when they reach the stone cliffs facing the sea, these streams become small waterfalls that raise clouds of mist.

Chun-i and his mother moved to Sŏgwip'o from the town of Cheju in the summer of 1951, the year of the January Fourth Retreat. Chun-i had always been a fussy eater. Whether or not that was the reason, the nape of his neck was still white like a little girl's, even though he was now over nineteen. Chun-i was also quite sensitive to drinking water. At the time of the January Fourth Retreat, they were told the easiest way out would be by sea, so Chun-i and his mother had gone by ship from Inch'ŏn. When the ship had sailed directly to Cheju Island without stopping at Pusan on the way, the problem that most bothered Chun-i was the water. He broke out in a rash several times, and it was necessary to rub on salt to remove the blistered skin.

Whenever his mother heard of good water to be found, she would go to any length to get some. After she had gotten it, though, she would boil it before giving a drop to Chun-i. She had heard from many people that the water was good in Sŏgwip'o. They ended up spending over half a year in the town of

Cheju, however, hesitating, thinking that they would return to the mainland as soon as they had news of Chun-i's uncle, who had evacuated earlier by truck. They spent that time trying to find some trace of him, but they never even managed to talk to anyone who had seen him. They were in no position to return to the mainland on their own, so after some uncertainty, Chun-i's mother decided that at least for the time being they should move to Sŏgwip'o and try to provide good water for him. She had heard stories that many hunchbacks and cripples were born on Cheju because there wasn't enough iron in the water, and this only made it harder for her to put up with the lack of good water. From the possessions they had brought along with them as they fled, she picked out the ones that would bring the best price and sold them.

The day Chun-i and his mother arrived in Sŏgwip'o, the weather had cleared after several days of rain and the wind had begun to rise. They had loaded everything on the bus; then, on the way, they had passed by a village that was encircled by a high fortress wall at least two or three times the height of a man. It had been built at the time of the April third guerrilla incident in 1948. On the bus they also had heard a rumor about an incident a couple of days earlier in which some guerrillas had appeared in a village on the eastern part of the island. To the accompaniment of vivid accounts of this incident they had reached Sŏgwip'o about noon.

It was such a sleepy-looking town that they wondered if this could be the Sŏgwip'o they had heard about. There was none of the bustle that they had seen from the bus window in the town of Mosŭlp'o. There was no imposing wall fortifying the town, either. Even though Chun-i felt for a moment the sense of bewilderment one feels when things do not turn out the way they were supposed to, he immediately decided that this was indeed the kind of place he could stay a long while before moving on.

This feeling grew even stronger when he found himself walking through rivulets of water that ran trickling beneath his feet. It had been a long time since he had felt such cool, refreshing water. The water had not been muddied even though there had been several days' rain, but remained pure and clean. Taking off his shoes and socks, he put his feet in the water and looked down toward the sea, which was now becoming a bit choppy. The sea was a deep indigo blue such as he had never seen before. He happened to turn his head and saw Mount Halla. On the north side the wind had blown in clouds that had snagged on the peak, while on the near southwest side the sky stood exposed like a great blue lake.

Chun-i began to go outside every day, wearing a straw sun hat, and got so that he practically lived outdoors. There was a button factory at the south end of the town. It was a one-story building, plastered white with a tin roof, where clam shells, conch, and abalone shells from the sea nearby were made into buttons. These Sŏgwip'o shells had the reputation of having the best texture of all the shells of Cheju Island. Right beside the factory was a pile of the broken pieces of shell that had been thrown away after the buttons had been made. For some reason the factory was not operating, so the place was unusually quiet. The oleanders that were planted as a hedge around the building were in full bloom, covered with red blossoms.

If you turned to the right beside this button factory, you came to a small breakwater. Beyond it was a little oval-shaped island that looked close enough to reach across and touch. It was called Sae Island. A few trees stood on its shore, but in the center it was bare. Just beyond this island was another called Mun Island. It was a bit larger and rose demurely out of the sea. This island was supposed to be one of the southernmost points in all Korea. It was the reverse of Sae Island, having a few trees standing in the center, with boulders at the shore on its circumference. The channel between Sae Island and Mun Island was so narrow and the current so swift that even the "underwater women," as the diving women of Cheju Island were called, had to stay away from the water there.

If you came back off the breakwater and followed the sea along the shore, which is strewn with volcanic rocks of all sizes, a little farther you could look across and see another small island, called Sup Island. It was about the size of Mun Island, and like Mun Island there were trees standing on top with boulders covering the shore all around the edge. The island was known for its white bellflower root and wild medicinal herbs. It was also known as the place where most diving women from the Sŏgwip'o area gathered to dive. When the seaweed harvesting season came in May, the diving women would converge on this island from all directions. They would come, of course, the short distance from villages like Pomok, but they also would come in droves from places twice as far away, like Tonghong or even Pŏphwan, to gather at Sup Island.

The time when Chun-i moved to Sŏgwip'o happened to be a busy season for farming, so there were not such large groups of diving women around. Yet each day you could see seven or eight of them out near Sup Island, bobbing on the surface and then plunging into the sea. You could hear the distinctive whistling sound their breathing made and see the form of their legs, which they called "masts," pointing skyward above the water as they dove.

Chun-i would sit on the shore trying to guess where the women would appear when they surfaced. Usually, though, the divers would shoot up out of the water in places other than the ones he had guessed, then make their whistling sounds. Then he tried counting the length of time the diving women would spend under the water during their dives. He tried holding his breath at the same time. But even after Chun-i had held his breath as long as he could three times, the women would still not have surfaced.

After this Chun-i would sometimes go to a place where there was a small waterfall and sit for a long while. Then if he began to feel too warm, he would go over to the *chaguri* bathing pool on the back side of the town. Chun-i didn't know where the local people had gotten the name *chaguri,* which they they used in referring to this pool. There were many other words, too, that he had heard for the first time since coming to Cheju Island. Some of the dialect was not hard to guess at, such as the unusual sentence endings with their guttural twang. But words were so completely different, that it was impossible at first to know what they meant. There were unrecognizable words for all sorts of things, from pigs and eggs to radishes and dust.

Among these words was the special term used for the young women of the island, often diving girls, whose local dialect name, *pibari,* suggested their association with the sea. When it came to the name used for the bathing pool behind the town, Chun-i had heard people repeat the word and thought it referred to a public bath of some sort, but eventually he discovered it just referred to a natural bathing pool behind the town.

It was a pond with an area of some sixty or more square yards. On the near side round, black boulders lay scattered on the bank, and there were small stones at the bottom of the water, and only in the deepest part did the water reach the level of an adult's waist. The thing that made this particular pool such a good place to bathe in the summer was its clear, cool water and the way the water always flowed into the pond over a stone ledge that stood like a folding screen at the far end. This fresh water was much colder than the water in the pool.

When Chun-i first went over under the stone ledge to try the water there, he felt the cold pierce right through him and ran straight out of the pool. The water was so cold that his whole body was covered with goose bumps and his teeth kept chattering for a long while after he had dashed out of the pool. Several times after that he tried clenching his teeth and getting into the water, but try as he might he could not count even to ten before rushing out of the water.

One day he washed himself in the pool, dunked himself in the water, and went over toward the place under the ledge. For the first time he counted to thirteen before rushing out of the pool. After that he climbed onto a boulder on the bank and sunned himself. His skin was very pale. He had been out in the sun like this for nearly a week, but his fair skin hadn't tanned a bit. It seemed that he must have skin that just wouldn't tan. His shoulders and back had turned a little pink, but under his arms and inside his thighs the skin was still pale and transparent.

The house where Chun-i and his mother were staying belonged to an older couple who had their grandson with them. Their son had gone off as one of the volunteer troops after the April Third Incident and had been killed. Chun-i's mother had heard from a neighbor's wife that the daughter-in-law had then given birth to the dead man's son, but immediately after his first birthday she had gone away and left no trace. Since then, rumors had it that she had become involved with a man in Sŏngsanp'o and had gone there to live with him. In spite of these rumors the old couple had never tried to locate the daughter-in-law, but had taken it upon themselves to raise the baby, who had not even been weaned before his mother left.

The old couple were always quiet and reserved. They supported themselves with a little garden and by raising a pig and ten or twelve chickens. Following Cheju custom, the wife would take five days' worth of eggs and take them in a basket to sell on market day. It looked as though she did most of the gardening, too. She even took care of gathering shells to give the chickens and greens to put in the pigsty. The old man's work seemed to consist of looking after their grandson. When it was time to put the baby down, the man would lay him in a basket in the shade of the cedar tree in the yard and rock him to sleep. The old man's rough rocking seemed more likely to keep the baby awake, but somehow it usually put him to sleep. The old man had a lot of time on his hands, and Chun-i began to go fishing with him. It wasn't so much with the idea of getting something to eat as it was of breaking the monotony.

If you went down to the shore after the tide had gone out you could look under the rocks and find sandcrawlers. They were a little thinner than the worms on land and more lively. Chun-i and the old man would put these worms in a jar, kill them with salt, and use them for bait. They had decided to fish at Sup Island. They borrowed a boat and went across to the island. They chose a spot on one of the spits on the island and put out their lines. This was Chun-i's first try at fishing, and the old landlord was such a poor fisherman that between them all they could manage was to gather a few snails and periwinkles along the shore. For Chun-i it was a change to pass the time seeing and hearing the diving women as they dove and made their whistling sound, pointing their "mast" legs into the air as they went under.

One day when it looked as though they weren't going to have much luck fishing, the two of them went up onto the top of the little island and dozed awhile in the thick grass where the white bellflowers were blooming. They were on their way down again and heading home when they noticed that someone was following them. They turned and discovered that one of the diving women was behind them. She had just come out of the water, had thrown a wet, yellowed cloth over her shoulder, and in one hand she carried a net bag with her catch of abalone and conch. She wanted to sell them. As she showed these abalone and conch to Chun-i she gave him a look that suggested it might be a good idea to take home something better than their usual meager catch. The abalone and conch in her bag were large and certainly did look as though they would be good to eat.

Chun-i had always liked fish better than meat anyway, but since moving to Cheju Island, he couldn't bring himself to buy anything that even suggested pork. On Cheju the pigsties are connected to the outhouses. At the slightest sign that someone may be approaching the privy, the pigs' eyes light up, and they put their heads close to the opening in anticipation of something to eat. Many times Chun-i couldn't pass a thing but just ran out of the toilet. He made up his mind that he would never eat pork again as long as he lived. The fish on Cheju were good, though, perhaps because the water was so clear. Fish at Sŏgwip'o had especially fresh and delicate flesh.

That day Chun-i had the young diving girl come home with him, and they bought some of her abalone and conch.

After that Chun-i and his mother never needed to go out to buy their fish. This young diving girl would always come by with seafood she had caught herself. Whenever she came, they would buy all the seafood they needed from her. This "underwater girl" would sometimes come every day, but at other times she would not appear for a day or two. Perhaps she was skipping the days when her catch was not very good. Besides the abalone and conch, she also brought a kind of fish called *pukbari*. It looked like a red snapper, but the mouth was a little bigger, and the body was speckled with reddish spots. They said this fish was caught with a spear. There was another kind of fish speared in the same way called a *tagŭmbari*. This also looked like a snapper, but its mouth was even larger than the *pukbari* and it had black spots on its body. Both these fish held onto life after they had been speared and often were still moving even when you had them on the chopping block.

Eventually, around Chun-i's household they began to refer to this young "underwater girl," who was such a regular caller, as the *pibari,* the pure Cheju Island dialect word, and stopped using other words like "the girl" or "the diving woman." They weren't sure of her age, but she was probably no more than nineteen or so.

One day when the diving girl called, she did something she had never done before. Just as she was leaving after selling them a *tagŭmbari,* she took a big abalone and quickly slipped it into Chun-i's hand. At the moment, Chun-i just took it, but afterward he began to feel uncertain about it somehow, wondering whether he had done the right thing. It was possible to think of it as a token of thanks for everything they had bought from her, but if that was what it meant, certainly it would have been proper to have given it to his mother while she was buying the fish. Chun-i turned quickly to get a look at the back of the girl as she left. The copper color of the skin on her firm figure made an impression that sank in as he looked. He was afraid everyone would notice how he was blushing.

The next day Chun-i and the landlord went fishing again at Sup Island. Chun-i wasn't getting any bites, and he was thinking of taking his line in, when at last the float shot down into the water. Chun-i was not paying any attention to his fishing, so he didn't notice a thing until the old man saw it and said something. The moment he took hold of the pole Chun-i could tell that he had caught something really big. The pole bent wildly. The old landlord ran over and held on with him. The two of them pulled upon the pole very cautiously. But as soon as Chun-i saw his catch emerging from the water, he threw down the fishing pole, fell back on the ground in surprise, and just sat there. It was a person's head.

When he looked more closely, he saw that it wasn't the head of a dead person, it was alive. After the head, the whole body appeared, then the person came out and stood on the shore. It was one of the diving women. Not just any diving woman, but the diving girl Chun-i knew. She had taken the fishhook in her mouth. Blood was trickling out between her lips. The diving girl looked straight at Chun-i as though it made no difference that someone else was there. The black eyes under her black eyelashes were not exactly dull-looking, but not glistening either. After a few moments she pulled the fishhook out of her mouth with her hand, a fleeting expression like a smile came across her blood-smeared lips, and then she turned around and jumped into the sea. After that she showed her lithe "mast" legs as she dove down into the water and disappeared.

Chun-i was stunned and didn't know what to think. It was upsetting enough to pull a person in on his fishing line, but while the diving girl stood looking at Chun-i, as if she were reprimanding him for his mistake, he had found himself doubling up and cowering before her. It was only after he had seen the girl give her half-smiling look and return to the water that he realized it was not his fault that she had been hooked in the mouth. She had come and taken his hook on purpose as a practical joke. He felt himself blushing involuntarily. When he turned his eyes toward the sea he saw that she had already come up some distance away near where the women were diving. The whistling sound of her breathing echoed across the surface of the water to him.

The old landlord picked up his fishing tackle and packed everything to leave. All the while he was frowning in disapproval at what he considered to be the insolent behavior of the diving girl. Chun-i also picked up his fishing gear. But for some reason he didn't altogether dislike what the diving girl had done. He found himself thinking of this diving girl, who had taken his hook, appeared out of the water with her wet, half-naked body, and then jumped back in the water, like a kind of giant fish. But even though she had jumped back in the water, it didn't seem like the feeling after a fish gets away. Chun-i still continued to feel the excitement of that moment when you are bringing in a fish that has been hooked.

That day on their way back home the old man told Chun-i a shocking and frightening story about this diving girl. Maybe it was because the diving girl's behavior had been so bold, but in any case the old man, who was by nature not given to saying much, started telling Chun-i the story as soon as they got in the boat. The story went that this girl had killed her own older brother. The diving girl's family had lived for many years in a village called Pŏlmok just over a mile east of Sŏgwip'o. It was the time of the April Third Incident. For some reason her older brother had joined the guerrillas and gone with them into the hills. A mission to search out and eliminate the guerrillas had been organized. Already her brother's wife had been found at the foot of Mount Halla, murdered by unknown persons, leaving behind only their small children.

One night, when the search mission had nearly ended, and there were only about thirty members left in the guerrilla band in the hills, the girl's brother came down out of hiding. The diving girl killed this brother of hers. She shot him with the rifle he had been carrying, after he set it down to go to the outhouse. People said she had shot her brother in a rage because their family had been ruined after the killing of her sister-in-law, who had left behind the two little children. Or because the brother had come down from the hills to loot in the village, and she was afraid that the family would really be ruined if that became known.

After he finished the story the old man added one more thing. He said that even though people had thought at first that the diving girl had done a courageous deed, they still recoiled from her inwardly and soon stopped having anything at all to do with her.

Now Chun-i understood. Even though this diving girl had been coming around to their house all this time, the old couple would never even exchange a word of greeting with her. A little while earlier, when this girl was playing her joke with the fishing line, the old man had made a face that showed that her behavior was more than he could stand. Now Chun-i knew why. When he had heard the whole story, for no apparent reason, Chun-i suddenly thought about the looks of the *pukbari* and the *tagŭmbari* and how those fish come to life and jump even while they bleed from being speared.

One afternoon, as the shadows were lengthening and he was returning from bathing at the *chaguri* pool, Chun-i came across the diving girl on the path. It seemed obvious that this was no accident; she had been waiting there for him. She appeared to be going home early that day. She had on faded cotton shorts and a jacket that left her elbows exposed. She held a gourd float with one hand, carrying in her other hand the net bag and the tools she used in the water.

She was just standing in one place, looking toward him. Her eyes were the same as always, not dull yet not bright, behind the black lashes. Chun-i thought he'd better act as though he knew her, and yet he avoided her gaze and wanted to slip past beside her. Since she looked as if she had been waiting for him, though, it occurred to him that he would have to answer if she should start a conversation.

The diving girl was not about to move aside. She stood where she was without saying a word. Quickly Chun-i walked away. He wondered if he was becoming afraid of the diving girl since the old landlord at his house had told him the story of how she had killed her own brother. But another part of him answered that this was not so.

When he reached home, his mother brought him raw abalone for his supper and said the diving girl had just been there and seemed to be looking for him. His mother smiled as she said she thought the girl may have wanted to give Chun-i something else when she came.

Chun-i's mother had been overjoyed at the improvement in his health since they had moved to Sŏgwip'o. But except for his mother's joking about it, thought Chun-i, why did he have to be so inhibited when he saw that diving girl a little while ago? And again he felt the color rising in his face.

Two or three days later, in the late afternoon, that time of day when it should have been cool, it had stayed hot. On Cheju Island, even in the hottest summer weather, a cool breeze comes in off the sea when the sun begins to go down, and the cool penetrates the body just the way it does in the autumn on the mainland.

Since it was still hot, late in the afternoon Chun-i went up to the *chaguri* bathing pool. It looked as though all the people who had come that day had already left, and in the stillness, the water spilling over the rock ledge sounded quite loud. In the evenings after supper the pool was usually taken over by the women of the town. As he always did, Chun-i went in the pool, washed his face, dunked himself in the water, and rubbed the perspiration off his body, then went over under the ledge. Today again, he had to come out of the cold part when he had barely counted to ten.

Just as he came out, he was surprised by someone jumping into the pool. When he looked, sure enough, he saw it was the diving girl. He was taken so completely by surprise that he crouched and headed for the water to get the lower part of his body covered, while the girl, without bothering to get used to the cold water, just went straight to the ledge and stood beneath it in the waterfall. During that moment Chun-i slipped up onto the bank and pulled on his outer clothes. While he was buttoning his shirt he stole a look over his shoulder and saw her standing in the falling water, wearing clothing that covered only her breasts and lower body. Without realizing it, Chun-i began to count, "One, two . . ." But he gave up counting when he had reached twenty because the very sight of her there sent such a chill through him.

He slipped between the big round boulders and was on his way to the path by the shore when the diving girl suddenly appeared. Apparently she had followed him. There she was, wringing out her wet hair and asking him whether he wouldn't like to go over and see their orange trees. She said there were lots of orange trees in her village. The orange trees of Cheju Island are famous, but Chun-i had been living in the towns of Cheju and Sŏgwip'o and hadn't seen any of them yet.

The idea came as such a surprise that he couldn't answer yes or no right away and just stood looking up at the western sky. The girl even said she would walk him back if it got too dark. Then without waiting for his answer, she just turned and began to lead the way.

The village of Pomok, where the diving girl lived, was one of the small hamlets at the foot of the mountain, facing the sea. When they had walked a mile or so, they reached a place on the shore from where a cluster of houses could be seen. The diving girl told him that this was the village where she lived. She pointed to a place in the shadow of the hill and said that the trees there were orange trees. On one side of the village stood rows of trees with dark green leaves and green fruit about the size of a newborn baby's fist. Chun-i wondered why the fruit was no larger than this when it was already summer.

Just then they saw a young girl of about five or six running toward them from the direction of the village. Her feet were bare. He marveled at how well this girl managed to avoid scratching the soles of her feet on the thorny plants growing along the ground. The girl came up and muttered something to the diving girl. It seemed this was her niece. By listening closely he could make out that she was saying the horse that was supposed to be sold tomorrow on the mainland was gone and couldn't be found anywhere. The diving girl told Chun-i to wait there for a bit, while she went toward the village with her niece. Chun-i had already heard that the horses on Cheju Island used to be allowed to run free and rounded up only once or twice a year. But since the April Third Incident and the Korean War, the people corralled their horses every evening. It looked as though this girl had been rounding up the horses that day when she discovered that one of them was missing.

Chun-i sat down. He could hear the sound of the sea, with its steady pulse coming from someplace not far off, but even without hearing its regular rhythm, Chun-i could tell which way the water was. You could tell by the direction the branches of the thornbushes bent. These water sage plants resembled flowering annuals, with their round, flat, waxy leaves sprouting white whiskers, and their profusion of little purple blossoms. The blowing of the wind from the sea had made every one of them, together with the other dwarfed plants along the shore, lie down as they grew, hug the ground, and point away from the sea.

After a while the young girl came running from the village, and then went running back after handing Chun-i two green fruit. They were oranges. They were so small that the two of them didn't make a handful, and yet they already looked like oranges. There was a light fuzz on the skin, which had the uneven surface of an orange peel. As Chun-i sat listening to the sound of the sea, holding one orange in each hand and smelling first one, then the other, the late afternoon around him turned to dusk, without his noticing it. The indistinct forms of people, houses, and orange trees in the direction of the village gradually disappeared into the dusk, leaving no trace. Then the sea and the land merged into one continuous color and the new moon appeared in the sky. The moon seemed very far away.

He heard the sound of someone approaching in the darkness from the direction of the village. At first Chun-i thought it was the sound of several people coming toward him. But by the light of the waxing silver moon he saw the diving girl emerge from the darkness leading two horses. She came up to the place where Chun-i was waiting, stroked the neck of one of the horses and said, "Tomorrow you're going to the mainland to be sold." She then led it over behind the other horse.

Even in the dim moonlight it was possible to see that this other horse was dappled and had a white patch on its back. Chun-i couldn't imagine what the diving girl could have had in mind in bringing these horses here. Suddenly the horse to the rear snorted, raised his front hooves, and mounted the other horse. Chun-i recoiled in surprise at this strange sight. In the shadowy, pale light of the slender moon the two great shapes merged into one.

The diving girl turned around, approached, and grasped Chun-i's wrist. She started to run, pulling him along, as if to flee from this monstrous sight. They came to the shore by the sea. There the diving girl took off and threw down all her clothes and jumped into the sea. She beckoned to Chun-i to hurry and get in the water, too.

Chun-i just stood there and felt his face grow flushed and hot. He didn't know what on earth could be going on and couldn't make up his mind what to do. The diving girl came out of the water and walked up to him. This time when she reached him, she grabbed hold of both sides of the front of his shirt, pulled them apart, and began to undress him. One after another the buttons tore off and dropped to the ground. The two oranges fell out of his hands.

Chun-i's fair, white body stood exposed in the dim moonlight. The girl's hands reached out and sought Chun-i's body covetously. These hands began to search and caress the entire area of his skin. Thinking all the while that he had to get away, he still could not resist her strange power and so submitted. He felt more strength come into her hands, and at that moment he thought he saw her eyes moisten and a smile flicker at the corners of her mouth. He felt her hot breath on his neck as she bit him. Then he felt something firm pressing against his chest. She pushed against him, and he tumbled to the ground.

The thorn branches beneath him scratched his body, but he did not notice any pain. The thin crescent moon toppled and fell against his eyes, but then returned to its place.

Chun-i met the diving girl at that spot every night while the moon grew into a full circle, then waned and once again became a thin crescent.

One night close to the time of the new moon, Chun-i returned from meeting the diving girl and went straight to bed. He had a slight fever and the joints of his limbs ached so he could hardly move.

His mother was the one who became upset about this. After they had moved to Sŏgwip'o and changed drinking water,

Chun-i had stopped breaking out in rashes and had become so healthy that his mother was happy and satisfied. Now he had come down so sick he had to stay in bed. Chun-i's mother had guessed why her son had been staying out every night, but she did not say anything. She could not bring it up with her son, afraid to do anything that might upset him. It had always been like that. When he was a little boy, Chun-i had been fond of eating dried squid. He had to have a couple of pieces under his pillow at night to be able to go to sleep. One time Chun-i became so sick from eating squid that he passed out. The doctor said the best thing to do would be to avoid squid altogether. But when Chun-i pestered his mother for squid, she would buy some and bring them home hidden in her skirt, even though she nearly cried as she did.

Being the sort of mother she was, she was not able to confront her sick son directly, but instead she tried to get back at the diving girl. What she did was to buy her seafood elsewhere and get nothing at all from the girl. She explained herself by saying that nowadays you would get saddled with inferior goods if you gave your business to one person all the time. This was, of course, just an excuse. It was not long before the mother completely stopped even mentioning the diving girl.

The diving girl, however, continued to stop at Chun-i's house, the same as before. She would bring the abalone, conch, or fish that she had caught that day. When she called, she never could sell anything but simply looked in from a distance at Chun-i in his sickbed, then went on her way. And those eyes of hers were always the same, neither dull nor bright.

At first after he fell ill, Chun-i didn't think about the diving girl at all. He had a slight fever, with aches and pains in his arms and legs. In fact he nearly forgot her, and the life he had been living with her recently seemed to belong to someone else. And even though she stopped by almost every day, he was not very interested in the diving girl's visits. As he took the medicine his mother brought all the way from the town of Cheju, though, his fever went down and he felt more rested. Now once again, like a vague longing, his relation with the diving girl began to gnaw at the center of his heart, and it would not let him go.

One day he had his mother buy a *pukbari* fish from the girl. His mother did not want to, but she could not contradict her son's wishes. Chun-i asked for some sea water. He put the fish in it. Even with the bloody spear wound in its back, the fish began to pump its gills. It waved its fins and tail and began to swim. What a remarkable performance! But soon the fish lost control of itself and turned over on its side. With great difficulty it righted itself again, then immediately rolled back onto its side. As the minutes went by the fish listed farther and farther. At that point Chun-i asked his mother to put the bowl with the fish outside. That day Chun-i didn't eat any of the fish at supper.

One day about two weeks later, when Chun-i was up again and could go outside in the fresh air, a letter came from his uncle on the mainland. Before they had moved to Sŏgwip'o and were still in the town of Cheju, Chun-i and his mother had asked everyone they knew who was going to the mainland to try to get some word of the uncle's whereabouts. Finally, after all this time, word had reached them. The letter said that at the time they had fled south, his plan had been to settle in Pusan, but things hadn't worked out and he had ended up putting down his roots in Taegu instead. The term had just started at the Federated National College there and he asked them to come right away so Chun-i could attend. Chun-i's mother had been eagerly awaiting news of this uncle all along, of course, always wondering whether it might come this day or the next. As soon as the letter arrived, she raced to get their belongings packed up and told Chun-i that they should leave on the first bus the next morning.

That day Chun-i put on his straw hat and went walking for the first time in a long while. He strolled down to the south end of town and looked at the button factory. As usual, it seemed to be closed, no one was working, and, as before, the oleanders were in full bloom.

He went out on the breakwater and gazed over toward Sae Island and Mun Island. Coming back along the shore he went to the beach covered with rocks and looked across at Sup Island. Four or five diving women were near the island, diving, bobbing in the water, and making their whistling sound.

Since the last time he had seen it, the trickling water in the rivulets was even clearer and looked even colder. The waterfall also had taken on a look of intense reality. He went and looked at the *chaguri* pool, but he felt no desire to bathe. Just looking at the water flowing over the rock ledge, spread like a folding screen across the back of the pool, chilled him to the bone. He lifted his head and saw the high peak of Mount Halla etching its vivid outline against the blue sky. The sun's rays beating down on the back of his neck felt hot and smooth. While Chun-i had been sick in bed, the season had begun to change, and fall was already setting in.

Chun-i began to follow the road toward Pŏlmok Village. He had been thinking of doing this since he left the house. He thought he should see the diving girl one last time. He walked slowly, and with the days becoming shorter, by the time he reached the shore where the village could be seen, it was already completely covered by the shadow of the mountain behind it. The one thing that stood out was the fruit on the orange trees near the village. The yellowish tinge was just beginning to show on the fruit, now the size of a man's fist, hanging there firm and abundant in the shadow cast by the mountain. Chun-i decided to sit there on the shore, carpeted with the low thorn plants, and wait for the diving girl to return home. The sound of the sea came to him from a place nearby, advancing, then receding with its regular rhythm.

Chun-i saw some of the village people rounding up and bringing in their horses. The horses were so tame that the people hardly had to exert themselves. He wondered if the diving girl's niece might be one of them. He strained his eyes to try to make her out. Then suddenly he noticed a woman with one hand on the back of the dappled horse, stroking its belly with her other hand as she brought it in. It was the diving girl. The horse she was stroking on the belly was the very animal he had seen on that night, once before. It looked as though the diving girl hadn't gone out diving that day or had come back early after a poor catch.

Chun-i stood up. The diving girl's niece was following behind with a long switch in her hand. She was the first to see Chun-i and let the diving girl know that someone was there. The diving girl snapped her head up, looked in Chun-i's direction, and immediately began to walk toward him. Chun-i sat back down.

Happy to see him again, the diving girl took his hand and squeezed it as she asked if he was better now. All the while her black eyes under their black eyelashes were the same as ever, not dull, yet not really bright, either. As he told her that he and his mother would be leaving for good on the first bus in the morning, he felt himself blush, but he couldn't help it.

Then the words just came out. He asked the diving girl if she would go with them. He hadn't intended to ask this; it had just slipped out at that moment. Once it had been spoken, though, he realized he felt as though he could not leave unless he could take this diving girl with him. Surely a little fussing would be enough to get his mother to agree. Squeezing the hands that were holding his, he said it again, as a promise that she could go. "Let's go to the mainland to live."

The diving girl looked at Chun-i for a moment with those eyes, neither dull nor bright, then shook her head. She finally spoke. No matter how much she might want to be with Chun-i, she couldn't possibly go to the mainland. She told him she had known there would be a day when he would leave for the mainland and that she had made up her mind to send him away without saying a word.

Then Chun-i heard from the diving girl something that he found very hard at first to comprehend. She said the reason she had killed her brother was not what people had assumed—that he had gone over to the guerrillas and that she feared he would make life miserable for the rest of the family. She said that from childhood she had loved her brother more than anyone else. After he had escaped to the hills, she was the one who had taken the risk of secretly bringing him food and clothing. Her brother had come down out of the hills one night and said that he had no choice now but to try to escape to Japan. He had already become very ill while in hiding, though, and was in such poor condition that he would hardly be able to travel. He could not possibly tolerate any exertion.

She tried to persuade him to turn himself in. He looked at her for a long while, then put down his rifle and went out to the toilet. It was then that she understood. She realized that it should be her hand and no other that should put him to rest in Cheju soil. And she knew then that this was what her brother wanted.

She said that from then on she knew she could never leave Cheju Island, no matter what might happen. As if to bring her story to its close, the diving girl told Chun-i that from now on whenever she saw any horses going to the mainland, she would think of him. Then with the same deft stroke she had used on the mare's belly earlier, she stroked her own abdomen, then drew near and with that hand embraced Chun-i's neck.

tr. EDWARD W. POITRAS

RINGWANDERUNG

링반데룽

I heard that my friend had contracted rabies and that he would probably not live through the day. It was almost evening by the time I hurried over to his home; the room where my friend lay was deep in the shadows cast by the house next door.

My friend's wife opened the door halfway for me to see him. He looked gruesome as he lay inside the room. In his dying hour, rather than panting, he was having convulsions. Every five or six seconds the sick man would grit his teeth and cry out. He threw his head back and spread his black, parched lips, revealing his gnashing teeth.

His eyes were the most unbearable thing to look at. With both the whites and the irises bloodshot, his eyes gave off a strange luster as they stared fixedly at one spot. This gaze made him look as though he were trying to focus but could not.

"He doesn't seem to recognize people anymore." My friend's wife spoke in a soft trembling voice.

I followed her to the lower room and listened as she spoke. I learned that his seizures had become quite severe since the previous night.

"I hadn't seen your husband at all, so I thought he had gone mountain climbing somewhere far away."

"It's been over two weeks since he fell ill."

Two weeks earlier, for no apparent reason, my friend had begun to feel uneasy. Everything had begun to annoy him. He went to the clinic and was examined, but they could not find out what was wrong. One doctor said it was general overexertion. Another said it was an early symptom of neurosis, a fashionable ailment at the time. Their diagnoses were diverse and conflicting.

My friend gradually lost more and more of his vitality. Finally, he asked a doctor to make a house call in the afternoon. He had had little appetite for some days, and a look of illness had appeared on his face, but the doctor could not determine what kind of disease it was.

After completing a detailed examination, the doctor was still unable to pinpoint the problem. But when the doctor was cleaning up at the washstand, my friend suddenly let out a weird scream. Turning his head, the doctor stared at him and asked if he had been bitten by a dog recently.

My friend could not recall anything immediately. But then he looked down at his right hand and said that a puppy had bitten him on the back of his hand.

About three or four months earlier, he and his wife had received a puppy from one of his wife's old classmates from her days at the girls' school. The puppy usually stayed close to people, but one day it left and was nowhere to be found. Several days later, when it finally came back, my friend, happy to see it, brought it some food. But the dog made no attempt to eat and ran away. Thinking he would lose the dog for good if it ran off another time, my friend chased it, but when he grabbed the dog around the middle, it jerked away and bit him. It was not a severe wound—just a slight reddening with a little blood appearing on the surface—so my friend just put some Mercurochrome on it.

The doctor asked what had become of the dog.

My friend had shut the dog up so it would not get away, but one day it escaped and never came back. The bite wound formed only a small scab, and when it came off, my friend could not even find a scar. But, in those three months, the disease had incubated in his body, and when the doctor was washing his hands that day and my friend saw the water, he had his first seizure.

"Just because of one good-for-nothing puppy he had to get a disease like this." My friend's wife turned pale as she lowered her head. She spoke hopelessly. "This is a wicked disease. He looks like a mad dog. Since last night he won't let other people near him. He said he wanted to bite them. He even told the family not to come into the room. He said I shouldn't even let our son come in beside him."

His wife stopped speaking for a moment and let out a sigh. "I've done all I can for him. I know he's beyond help, but I had to do it. I even went so far as to have a doctor of traditional Chinese medicine grind tiger bones to feed to him, but I couldn't get him to take it."

Her voice was severely fatigued. "Some families can't endure a sick family member's suffering, so they bring in a basin of water and put it in front of the victim's eyes to cause convulsions that will kill him. There's nothing so dreadful in the world as this disease. If a person is bitten by someone with the disease, he'll end up getting the disease, too."

I saw the reason for putting my friend alone in the room opposite the main part of the house.

"One time he kept grasping and pulling with his hands at a spot in front of his eyes, as if he saw something there or something were there obstructing his view and he couldn't see. I asked him why, but he didn't answer."

As soon as I heard these words, my chest was seized by the meaning in the look in my friend's eyes—those red, lustrous eyes that I had seen just a bit earlier as he strained to focus yet could not. The word *ringwanderung* came to mind.

Early that year in the spring, my friend had developed a passion for mountain climbing. Gathering all the tools used in mountain climbing—ropes, tents, compasses, and maps—he began to visit the nearby mountains. People who knew him were sure he was crazed with mountain climbing when they saw him dressed to go.

My friend had not been a very heavy drinker, but he did enjoy women. At drinking parties, whenever we noticed that he had left his seat, we would realize that a serving girl had disappeared, too. Eventually his close friends came to call him by the nickname "digger wasp."

His dissolute life was said to be the reason he had no other children after his son, who was now six years old.

Originally, my friend was not a woman chaser. His friends all knew it was no lie to say that he had never once kept company with a woman until he was married, at the age of twenty-seven. He had always been a bit eccentric. When he started high school, his poorest grades had been in English. Then he studied for six months; the following semester he not only received the highest English grades in his school, but he also participated in a national English oratory contest for high school students. He even won a prize.

In college he chose English as his major, but in his third year, all of a sudden, he bought some law books, and the next year he took the higher civil service examination, passing in both the executive and judicial categories.

After graduation, he taught English at a middle school for one year, after which he lectured at a law school for a year and a half. Then he resigned from teaching.

According to his own story, he had not wanted to leave. But, he said, he would be at the lectern in the middle of an eloquent speech, when he would suddenly become convinced that he did not really understand the materials he was teaching. Suddenly he would feel something like fog in front of his eyes, so he could not see his students' faces. I wonder if it wasn't after this time that he began his descent into debauchery.

My friend never had a long relationship with one woman. He did not seem to choose beautiful women or those who struck his fancy. Indeed, what seemed to attract him was debauchery itself. Some time later, after his descent, he began traveling around to mountains, absorbed in climbing.

One day, he was in a tearoom having a chat with several friends when the topic turned to mountain climbing. That was when my friend mentioned *ringwanderung*, saying it was something he had read about in a book on mountain climbing.

Mountain climbing is a sport that makes nature the opponent. With such an opponent, unpredictable calamities are inevitable. Even if the mountain climber were able to avoid disasters of which he himself is the cause, there is always the danger that a rock will suddenly tumble down or a boulder will give way. More dreadful than anything, however, is a sudden change in the weather. It is possible for a sudden shower to pour from skies that had earlier been clear and blue. When thunder begins to rumble it is easy for the climber, who is a solitary projection from the top of the mountain, to become a target for lightning.

Surely it is an abrupt change of weather due to a blizzard or fog that claims victims most frequently. When a climber meets a furious blizzard or dense fog, the safest thing is to stay put and wait until the weather takes a favorable turn; however, sometimes the climber is forced to move on because of unavoidable problems with food or schedule. But, traveling in a blizzard or fog, the mountain climber may think he is going straight toward his his destination, when, in reality, because of an optical illusion of which he is unaware, he is circling around a central point. In this so-called *ringwanderung,* some people turn right, while others curve to the left. A climber will wander in a circle in the blizzard or fog until he finally meets with disaster.

When my friend's wife told me that there seemed to be something obscuring her husband's vision—something in front of his eyes that he was trying to brush away with vain movements of his hands—the thing that struck me was that his eyes were straining to focus, yet they could not. From this grew the thought that my friend, after all his mountain climbing, had now reached a point of *ringwanderung* in his life.

Perhaps thinking he had been walking forward recklessly in this fog that is life, he finally realized he was wandering in a vain circle—in his life as a teacher, in his relations with women, and, finally, in his devotion to mountain climbing itself.

My thoughts of my friend led me to think of my experience with the woman Sŏl-hŭi.

The day I first held Sŏl-hŭi, she confessed that she was not a virgin.

It was under an aged pine tree in Samch'ŏng Park. I held her head and placed my lips on hers. Her cold lips gradually took on warmth, and the moment I felt her breath grow hot, she softly pushed at my chest. In a moment, she spoke, her eyes closed.

When she was thirteen, she had had this kind of experience with a man who was past thirty. It was a man in the neighborhood who had a wife and at least three children. He treated her affectionately, so she followed him as though he were an uncle.

"I couldn't even scream."

After making this confession to me, the woman Sŏl-hŭi disappeared.

Then I finally realized how important she was to me. The incident in her youth was something that could not be helped. It had nothing to do with her character. It was nothing for which she should take the least responsibility. After she confessed to me that day, I had put my lips on hers again. For a moment she kept her eyes closed. Between our lips, I must have erased the memory of her helpless mishap.

A full six months later a letter came from her. It was a short note asking that we meet again.

Her face, which I had not seen in a long time, was gaunt.

As we walked down a back alley with no particular destination in mind, she told me the story of how she had gotten married since we had last met and how the marriage had failed. She said her husband had been a young man who had just graduated from college. He was an extremely jovial fellow, so there had been no shadows in their married life. But, one day, while they were talking, her young husband told her about a girlfriend from his college days. It had been just a superficial exchange of affection. He said that they might want to get together with the girl and her husband as a family if both families were to have babies. He then asked Sŏl-hŭi to tell him about her old romances. What came to her lips was the story of when she was thirteen. This atrocious story now came out, even though she had intended to bury it deep in her heart now that she was married. Her husband stared silently into space for a while. He muttered to himself that it was as though he had been bitten by a mad dog. From then on, he came home drunk almost every night. Once he was home, he would mumble that she should not be blamed for the events of her past. Rather, she should receive sympathy. "But why should it be like this? After hearing your confession, why have I lost my desire for you? If in the past you had made love with someone in spirit only, I could forget it more easily, as a kind offer of love." Harping on this, he made her suffer.

"He no longer looked like a young man, the one who had been so cheerful and jovial. But I don't regret having confessed the past. At first I had intended to hide it all my life, but in spite of what has happened, I'm happy that I confessed before we had a baby and our married life became complicated."

After we parted that day on a back street, Sŏl-hŭi did not appear again for some time. But the way the woman appeared and disappeared caused me to have a self-awakening.

Why should she destroy her married life by showing her husband the wounds from the past that she had resolved to keep hidden all her life? Ultimately, wasn't it that she could not be satisfied with that marriage? But if so, why should such a cloudless married life with such a cheerful young man be unsatisfying? As soon as my thoughts reached that point, I could not help but realize that the affection that linked the woman with me was not yet resolved, that the pulse was still beating.

One day, three or four months later, another short note came from Sŏl-hŭi. She wanted to meet briefly, just as she had said in the previous note. She looked more haggard than she had before. Her eyes were bloodshot.

We strolled along the bank of the Han River as the sky grew darker. She told me what she had been doing during the time we had not seen each other, as if it were her responsibility to report to me. She had tried married life again. This time her husband had been a pilot.

He had been a rather strong-willed young man who had many flying hours behind him. He married Sŏl-hŭi, aware not only of the failure of her first marriage but also of the incident from her youth, as well as the experience she had had with me before her first marriage.

This young man had died a few days earlier in a plane crash. The cause of the accident had been determined to be engine failure, but Sŏl-hŭi thought there was more to it. The night before he had flown, her husband had spoken to her. He had looked very grave, unlike ever before. "Nowadays, when I hold you to my chest I don't have the feeling that I'm holding you completely. Even as you give your body to me, in your heart you're holding someone else. Who in the world is it? I know that it's not the man from the incident when you were young. If not, then is it the man you were married to first? If not, is it that man you were in love with? Somehow I've lost the confidence to control you as I would pilot a plane. At night I can't sleep."

"There seems to be a poison in my body that destroys men."

She did not say whether she had answered the young man who was her husband. So, I could not know whether it was true that she was holding someone besides her husband in her heart when she held her husband in her arms. But, if this is all true, I could guess who the man was she embraced in her heart.

I wrapped my arms around Sŏl-hŭi's shoulders, in spite of myself, and sought her lips. But she shook her head coldly, her face sallow in the dim light of dusk.

No words were spoken in the taxi on the way back.

The car passed Samgakji and arrived at the neighborhood of Namyŏngdong. The windshield suddenly lit up with a light like that of sunset. The driver muttered something about there being another fire. Not far ahead was a roadblock. We had to stop.

Gazing at the windshield as it turned a deeper red, Sŏl-hŭi suddenly spoke, as if to herself. "Over there homes will probably burn, and people will surely die. Those who must deal with the fire are probably wondering what to do—and don't know what to do. But it's all right for the bystanders to gawk to their hearts' content. They don't have to worry. In one corner of their hearts they're afraid and think it's horrible, but the stronger their feelings become, the more intense their interest grows in these events that touch others. They needn't hesitate to look all they want."

The car was about to turn down a side street, but Sŏl-hŭi told the driver to stop. She jumped out of the car.

Sŏl-hŭi dashed down an alley, heading toward the flames. Her emaciated body shone in the light of the fire, red like sunset; she looked different from before when she had shaken her head, her face pale. Now she possessed a kind of vitality.

Suddenly a thought came to me. She had always been a sufferer. Wasn't I a third-party spectator? I hurriedly paid the fare and ran down the alley where she had disappeared, but I could find no trace of her.

After that, I didn't know anything of her whereabouts until a couple of months later, when I received another short note from her.

Today on the way to the tearoom where we had planned to meet, I had learned that my friend had contracted rabies and was on the point of death. I left the tearoom early, before Sŏl-hŭi arrived, and went to see him.

I suddenly had the feeling that Sŏl-hŭi and I had a relationship that was nothing more than a kind of *ringwanderung*. This thought had begun with my friend's appearance and extended toward Sŏl-hŭi's image. But, if I think about it objectively, it may be that my relationship with Sŏl-hŭi had always had latent in it this circular wandering—even before I associated this circular wandering with my friend's condition. Rather, it may have been my recognition that I was in the same condition that made me think of *ringwanderung* when I saw my friend.

Surely Sŏl-hŭi and I had been wandering in circles without realizing it. In *ringwanderung,* some people go left, while others go right. Neither Sŏl-hŭi nor I could know in which direction the other was turning.

The number of occasions that our two circles intersected was determined by the length of the radius of each. It would seem a circumscription or inscription occurred once, and a tangential contact occurred twice. Even if it were impossible to know whether Sŏl-hŭi's circle and mine were inscribed or circumscribed or whether they were tangent, it is at least a fact that they came into contact.

But, in circular wandering, the most important thing – more than anything else – is the moment when the two circles meet. If you look at it that way, I reached a contact point with Sŏl-hŭi's circle each time she passed.

Before I left my friend's house, I opened the sliding door to the room where he lay and peered inside. Amid the vague shadows of the late autumn evening, my friend was still staring at one spot, his red, lustrous eyes unfocused. His convulsions recurred at intervals, each shorter than before.

What was happening in this room was something I could do nothing about. Even though he was my friend and still alive, I could do nothing but close the sliding door. Unable to say a single word to him, I turned to leave.

As I did, something came to mind. Indeed, this once, when it would have been so appropriate, perhaps I should not have missed my meeting with Sŏl-hŭi – even if, as she herself said, it may have meant my own destruction.

tr. J. MARTIN HOLMAN

MELONS

참외

"Grandmother!"

From the front yard I heard this cry of delight from our youngest boy.

"Well! How have you been?" It was my mother's voice.

Ogi's ringing voice followed, calling the boy's older sister.

My mother had moved with Ogi and other members of our family to the Kwangju area to escape the war.

"I saw Grandmother first," the five-year-old boy bragged to his sister as he led the visitors inside.

Here in Seoul, we never knew when to expect an air raid. But no matter how I scolded the boy for going outside, the little rascal would sneak out when my back was turned.

"The children are doing just fine there," Mother told my wife and me as she came inside.

"I want to go where my big brothers are," said the boy. "Grandmother, when you go back, I'll go with you. When are you going, Grandmother? Huh?"

"I'm going back tomorrow."

"Then, can I go with you?"

"All right."

Mother and the others were staying in the village of Ilwŏn, which you get to by ferrying across the Han River at Ttuksŏm and then going about four miles south. Young Pak lives there. He graduated last year from the high school where I teach, and now he's enrolled at a teacher's college.

Ilwŏn was the place my wife and I had decided on when we were trying to figure out where to shelter our family. Pak had visited us occasionally after graduation, and one evening early last June he had dropped by to invite us all there for a picnic. He said that plenty of *ch'amoe* melons and watermelons grew in the village, though he couldn't offer us much else in the way of fruit. But then the war broke out, and Pak's invitation got us thinking about Ilwŏn as a refugee site.

First we had to find out whether the location was suitable and, if so, whether we could find a decent room to live in. So Father decided to take a look at the area. He returned the same evening to report that the village was perfect for refugees, even though it was close to Seoul. It was a cozy place, away from the main road, tucked far back in the hills. Pak's father had said that his family had lived there for five hundred years – sixteen generations! And they had weathered all the major wars. Father told us it was a place of refuge in name as well as in fact; he cited the meaning of the Chinese characters in the name of the village – *il,* "peaceful," and *wŏn,* "house." As for a room, we couldn't stay at Pak's house, because a flock of his relatives from Seoul had already moved in. But if it wasn't too inconvenient, we could rent a room from someone else in the Pak clan. While listening to Father, we all tried the watermelon that Pak had sent along with him. It couldn't have been sweeter or more fragrant. It must have been ten years since I'd had a watermelon that tasty.

Most of my family went down to the village right away – my parents, my youngest brother, my other brother and his family, and Ogi. My wife and I also let our two oldest sons tag along. At the same time, we asked Pak to find an additional room for us. This was the situation when Mother arrived.

"Yesterday that student of yours said he got a room at his cousin's for you," Mother reported.

I could not put into words how grateful I felt. "In that case we might as well move tomorrow."

"Yes, it's high time we left," my wife said. She glanced at several bundles of our belongings, which she had packed a long time ago.

Our youngest boy had been poking around in a bundle that was sitting behind his grandmother. "Hey, look at this!" he whooped. "*Ch'amoe* melons!"

Mother looked back, leaning slightly to the side. The four corners of the wrapping cloth had been knotted in the middle, and the grinning boy was tugging at a melon through one of the openings. Part of it was sticking out, and I could see it was a green variety of *ch'amoe* melon.

"I want some too!" His sister dashed over and grabbed a corner of the bundle.

"Wait! I'll undo it," Mother said.

As soon as she had untied one of the knots, the boy and his sister each helped themselves to a melon. And in no time the boy had sneaked a second one and was clutching both to his chest.

"Now what kind of behavior is that? Let's peel one for Grandmother first," my wife said. She took the last melon, which looked the best.

"Just give them to the children," said Mother. She rose, sweat beading on her forehead, and stepped out on the veranda. Mother has never been physically strong, and she's particularly sensitive to the winter cold and summer heat.

Meanwhile, the boy had taken a bite of each of his melons, and now he stood, hesitating, glancing at his sister's. He wanted so much to savor his own melons, and yet he seemed to find them less than appealing.

"Somehow they don't look very sweet," said my wife. She was peeling the last one, and each cut she made revealed the drops of liquid that mark an unripe melon.

This fruit was from an area famous for watermelons and *ch'amoe* melons. Yet it still hadn't ripened when most *ch'amoe* melons were past their peak. I couldn't understand it. Was the food situation so bad that fruit such as this was being sold?

My wife turned to Ogi, who was sitting beside her. "How much did you pay for these?"

The girl smiled sheepishly, then said quietly, "We picked them from a field."

My heart jumped. So that's why there was mud on the melons. No wonder Mother had kept the bundle behind her back.

It's not uncommon for someone traveling in the countryside to pick a couple of *ch'amoe* melons or cucumbers from a wayside field to slake his thirst. There's nothing wrong with that. And it doesn't have to be limited to a couple; it could be three or four. But the traveler must eat them on the spot. He shouldn't touch a single one if he intends to take it with him.

Four melons—that was all Mother had taken. Still, she shouldn't have done it, not even for her little grandchildren here in Seoul. Maybe she had meant to buy them but couldn't find the owner. But that's no excuse. And if she had taken them because she had no money, that was even worse. If only she had come empty-handed . . . then she wouldn't have been forced to hide the bundle behind her back.

Mother doesn't have a greedy bone in her body. She enjoys giving her things away and never covets other people's things. She had a difficult time as a child but became rather well-to-do in her forties. Even so, because she is so generous, she is always short of clothes to dress up in. So, what Mother did that day, for whatever reason, was entirely out of character and therefore all the more unpleasant. I felt I was glimpsing a shabby side of her that she had kept hidden until then.

My wife called Mother to come in and have a slice of melon.

"Go ahead and give it to the kids," Mother replied from the direction of the faucet in the yard, as if she were busy washing her face.

"Then you have some first, dear." My wife offered me a slice of the melon, which she had finished peeling and quartering.

I couldn't help looking away.

"Come on! Have a taste. It's the first one we've had this year—" Suddenly my wife shouted, "What're you doing!"

The boy must have raced over and snatched a slice, I thought to myself.

"You kids!" my wife protested.

The boy's sister must have made off with a slice too.

My wife put one of the two remaining pieces on a plate and pushed it toward me. I decided not to eat it and lit a cigarette instead.

Mother came in. There were still some drops of water on her face.

"Mother, have a piece," said my wife.

"I'm fine. You all go ahead."

I didn't have to look at her to know she had sensed something. She glared at Ogi. Now what did you say this time, girl? her eyes seemed to be asking.

This girl Ogi had lost her mother and been abandoned by her father. Mother had raised her from early childhood. She was blessed with a cheerful disposition that was rare for a girl with such an unfortunate background. Mother had brought her up as her own granddaughter, and Ogi had become attached to Mother as if she were her real grandmother. If Ogi had a fault, it was that she chattered too much, though she was old enough to know better. This might have been because of her cheerful disposition. She had always been chided by grown-ups for this habit. But today Ogi had done nothing wrong, in my opinion.

I turned to Mother to protest. She looked back at me. I was about to yell at her, to say something nasty, but I managed to bite my lip. Mother's eyes were full of reproach all the same: You might just as well have yelled at me, they seemed to say.

My wife started peeling one of the melons the boy was holding. He stuck close to her, craning his neck toward the fruit.

"Was it sweet?" my wife asked.

The boy nodded.

I couldn't help being angry with my wife too, hearing her talk to the little ones as if nothing were wrong.

Mother could stand this no longer and turned to go outside again. I saw that there were fresh beads of sweat on her face and not just drops of water. Her face was unspeakably sad and haggard. At that instant I felt Mother was telling me something from the depths of her being: My son, I didn't get those melons without a price. I paid plenty for them, I'm still paying, and I'll pay even more – as much as I can, though they're not worth it.

A lump rose in my throat. Of all the crooked-minded bastards! How could you hurt your mother's feelings like that? Hurry up and apologize! I told myself.

But I shouted instead, as if I had become cross with her again, "You kids stop eating those green melons!"

tr. BRUCE AND JU-CHAN FULTON

TIME FOR YOU AND ME ALONE

너와 나만의 時間

It had already been two days.

The only view was of endlessly crooked rows of mountain ridges and gorges. Nothing seemed to stir, not even the wind.

Captain Chu's body began to sag though he was supported on both sides. Rather, he was being dragged along on the shoulders of his two companions. A bullet had torn through his leg two days earlier. With only a rag binding his thigh to stanch the flow of blood, he had managed to get through the encircling enemy lines with his companions. The bullet, mercifully, had missed both the bone and the nerves, but an awful numbing pain had set in since that morning—was the leg becoming gangrenous?

It wasn't a journey with a set distance or goal. They were merely heading southward. Captain Chu was well aware that a definite sense of distance and a goal could help the wounded a lot. Once he had seen a soldier with a bullet hole in his lower abdomen make it back to friendly lines over a distance that would normally have been a good half-hour walk, covering the wound with his shirttail, slumping down only when he knew he was in the hands of friends. The only reason he was able to struggle on with such a serious injury was that he had known the whereabouts of friendly lines. In other words, he had had an immediate goal to gain.

But they were denied a definite goal. Still the captain dared not tell Lieutenant Hyŏn and Private Kim that they should go ahead and leave him behind, though he could no longer walk and consequently was only a burden to them. To be left behind by himself meant sure death.

Thus when the private suggested carrying him on his back, the captain didn't hesitate a moment but let himself be carried without saying a word.

The private was seventeen years old, a mere stripling, but being a country boy, he showed considerable prowess in carrying the captain on his back. Then it was the lieutenant's turn to perform this duty.

Before he turned his back to the captain, however, the lieutenant gave a quick glance at the pistol which hung from the captain's side. The three had already cast aside their knapsacks, helmets, rifles, and, indeed, even their jackets, long ago. The only weapon left was the captain's pistol.

The captain could easily guess what the lieutenant meant by that glance. In all fairness he could not blame the lieutenant. Since he became incapable of going on alone, he had indeed become a mere burden to his companions. But the two had not had the heart to desert their superior. It boiled down to the fact that they were waiting for him to make good use of the pistol so as to expedite their own flight.

But the captain simply ignored the lieutenant's glance. He just took off his trousers and boots and entrusted his weight to the lieutenant's back.

Of course, Lieutenant Hyŏn was no match for Private Kim, but still he was heavier and stronger than Captain Chu and could carry a man on his back for a considerable distance. Both officers had originally been with the Student Volunteers Corps.

What they had eaten during the past two days was quite meager: mostly herb roots and occasional spring water to quench their thirst. Moreover, the scorching early summer sun did not help them any.

The streaming sweat flowed into the eyes and mouth of the carrier. Since he didn't have a free hand, however, the only thing he could do was close his eyelids tight to squeeze out the sweat, spit it out, or shake it off with quick, jerky movements of his head. Gradually, each step became shorter and each had to take a turn more and more frequently.

The captain could feel the unpleasant sensation of sticky and damp contact with the carrier's back through wet T-shirts, but oddly enough, it was now through this sensation that he felt assured of remaining alive.

The lieutenant, sweating profusely as he took his turn again carrying the captain on his back, was thinking of the same thing over and over. He was remembering a scene from a brief dream he'd had two nights earlier, just before the enemy began to make that horrible noise with tin pans and flutes.

The sun was burning down from a grayish sky, and under that, a brown and barren wasteland spread to the horizon. For no reason at all, he was standing in the middle of this wasteland, and the dust was so deep it buried his legs halfway up to his naked knees.

He was very troubled. There was something on his calves that he cherished. The night before he joined the army his sweetheart had seen his naked and hairy legs and had asked him to take good care of the longest hair on each shin since she would like to think those were her own. And now those two hairs were in danger of being buried under the brown dust.

But now that was not his only problem. There was an anthill just in front of him in the dust. For some strange reason he felt that he had to watch that anthill though no one had ordered him to do so. An endless line of brownish ants crawled out of the hole. Just outside the hole, however, stood a huge brown ant that was biting off the heads of the ants crawling out of the hole. In no time at all the place was filled with the bodies of ants. In the next instant they were no longer the bodies of ants; they had turned into brownish dust. This vast barren wasteland might well be made up of their bodies, he thought. The jaundiced sun was still burning in the grayish sky, and he was still doomed to watch the anthill without budging.

This scene from his dream kept coming back to him. He was painfully conscious of the weight of the captain pressing him down. There was one way, only one way, to get rid of this unpleasant burden if only the captain would face reality. If only he would realize . . . Otherwise, all three of them would surely meet their deaths on a nameless mountain.

He felt a burning thirst.

Then he thought of the letter he had received about five days earlier from his sweetheart. She had written, "The blooming flower of my lips never withers, for the joyous memory of the past that you have made for me waters them constantly." Once he had whispered into her ear after a particularly long kiss that her lips were a flower not of a single petal but of many layers of petals, for there was no end to the joy of exploring them.

There was a noticeable change in the letter, too. She used the familiar "you" form along with his first name; previously she had always used "Mr. Hyŏn." This change could mean only closer ties between them. He now remembered that while reading the letter, he had looked down at his hairy shins and had been conscious of a girl's smiling eyes fondly gazing down on him.

Carrying this man on his back in the scorching heat, he now tried to quench his thirst with memories of the past and of the touch of his sweetheart's lips. He also tried to see her loving, smiling eyes directed toward him, and in following after her imaginary eyes, his own sweat-filled eyes seemed to brighten up considerably.

They came to a crest in the ridge. It was the private's turn to carry the captain.

The terrain was such that they could either take a shortcut by going down into the gully and making the steep climb on the other side or make a detour by following the long but easy ridge line.

Lieutenant Hyŏn proposed crossing the gully, which was reasonable. They had to think about saving their strength even if it was a matter of only a few steps.

But the private had a different idea. If they lost their way in the thick brush down in the gully, they would only lose time and energy, he reasoned. While they were still hesitating, the captain spoke up. "Lieutenant, let's follow Private Kim's advice."

The lieutenant cast a glance toward the pistol at the captain's side. His dream flashed back into his mind.

The jaundiced sun was high in the grayish sky and the endlessly barren wasteland stretched out beneath it. He was standing in the middle of this scene, sweating profusely. The anthill just in front of him was still producing its endless line of brown ants, and the huge brown ant by the entrance to the hole was still biting off the heads of the emerging ants. It was as if the huge ant was mechanically working his mouth, and the ants in the line were automatically putting their heads into it one by one. The bodies of the ants were turning into brownish dust. The dust deepened accordingly, and the hairs on his shins were being buried under it.

He fretted, but there was nothing for him to do except to stand by the hole and watch.

Then, not far from the deadly hole, suddenly he found another fresh hole that was connected to it by a secret path. This new one, of course, had not been part of his dream. It was the result of a conscious plan. But the foolish ants kept on coming through the old hole and getting their heads cut off.

Then Lieutenant Hyŏn, though he wasn't carrying the captain on his back, felt a cold and sticky sweat cover his entire body.

Just before dusk they caught a snake, roasted it, and shared it. When they had finished eating, the lieutenant got up and left as if to go relieve himself. After a little while the captain spoke to the private: "You run along, too." It was the first time he had ever mentioned such a thing.

The private looked up at him as if he did not understand.

"Lieutenant Hyŏn's gone. Got tired of waiting, I suppose."

"Got tired of waiting?"

"Yes, got tired of waiting for me to kill myself."

Indeed, the lieutenant did not come back.

"I said, you run along, too," said the captain, avoiding the private's eyes.

Private Kim thought a little, but looking up once at the setting sun, he silently offered his back to the captain.

Now that there was nobody to relieve the private, they made very little progress. They had to rest frequently.

When night set in, they slumped down completely exhausted.

They thought of the packages of crackers in their knapsacks, which they had thrown away earlier to lighten their load, but they seemed to do so merely from habit; in fact, they had passed the point beyond which a person is no longer capable of feeling hunger.

They also thought of Lieutenant Hyŏn. How far had he gotten by now? Private Kim thought it was cruel of the lieutenant to desert them like that. But the captain had the vain hope that the lieutenant would reach friendly lines soon and arrange to have a rescue party sent for them. Of course, neither of them put what they were thinking in so many words.

The captain could not fall asleep until long after the private had done so. His wound no longer bothered him. He simply had the strange feeling that he might not wake up in the morning once he fell asleep.

Then, for no reason at all he began to think about the woman. It was quite odd that he should think about her at this particular moment.

It was the woman he had bought for a night in Pusan while he was on a three-day pass after a particularly hard battle in which he had played a key role in securing a hill.

Without being asked, she had narrated an experience she had had in Seoul around the time of the January Fourth Evacuation. She had been working as a hostess in a bar, and one day around dusk, a girl had run into her house chased by three foreign soldiers. She had let the girl escape through the back door, and she herself had borne the unpleasant and animal-like lust of the three soldiers. She wasn't even capable of distinguishing one soldier from another; she had fainted, and it was not until daybreak that she came to. Oddly enough she had run into the girl that day on a street in Pusan. Of course, it was the girl who stopped her and burst into tears of joy at the unexpected encounter. The girl wanted to know if there was anything she could do to help.

When she finished telling her story, she said she was very grateful to the girl and overwhelmed by her graciousness, because most girls like her would snub a woman such as herself under the circumstances.

While the captain was listening to her story, a laudable enough anecdote, he felt a sudden urge to twist her heart. So he asked if she would willingly do the same now and lie as in a faint till dawn just to experience such gratefulness and graciousness again if she had the chance.

The woman lit a cigarette in the dark and said quietly and simply that she didn't know, but she didn't think such things happened just because one wanted them that way, that she had stepped into the shoes of the girl without realizing what she was doing, that people often did things on the spur of the moment that they themselves might wonder about later, that she might or might not react in the same way if she were in the same situation again, and that it all depended on circumstances at the time.

And now lying on the ground in the darkness on a nameless hill, the captain was thinking over what the prostitute had said that night.

Now that he gave it a little thought, he could think of many instances in which he himself had acted in a similar way. Many times, due to the complexities arising from hard fighting, he had reacted unexpectedly in unforeseen situations.

Then a new thought flashed through his head. When he had asked her that spiteful question, had he not really taken it for granted that she could be expected to act the same way in a like situation? Had he not really expected her to do the same because she was a sullied woman?

Now with death just around the corner, lying flat on a nameless ridge in the darkness, he felt he had no right whatsoever to expect the woman to act one way or another. By the same token, he thought, no one had any right to pass judgment on his own conduct during the past fighting or to expect him to perform his duty one way or the other in the diverse situations engendered by the battlefield.

Suddenly he felt an urge to protest to somebody, anybody, but all around him he found nothing but ever-deepening darkness.

He, too, soon fell asleep.

They resumed their journey at the crack of dawn. They were forced to stop and rest more frequently. The private, too, shed his fatigue trousers and combat boots. He was well aware of the difficulty of treading rocky mountain paths barefoot but the weight of his boots had become quite unbearable.

Soon the soles of his feet were cut and bloody. It was impossible to carefully pick one's way and protect one's feet.

Nothing was in sight but endless peaks and still gullies and gorges. Hadn't this god-forsaken region ever been inhabited by humans? Instead of the sound of friendly artillery, which they had so anxiously awaited hearing, there was only a deep and endless quiet and the labored breathing of the private.

Nevertheless the captain was all ears. He could not afford to miss the sound of a pin dropping, he thought.

Once the captain suggested taking a rest and having a drink of water. The private did not know what the captain was talking about, but directed by the latter, they came upon clear spring water trickling from a crack in the rocks.

The entire distance they covered that day was less than three miles. During that time they had only eaten three or four raw frogs that they had caught.

The private's knees became more and more bent, and his back was so stooped that he now seemed to be crawling.

The captain felt death coming closer and closer as the private's back bent lower and lower.

Rounding a bend on the ridge late in the afternoon, they saw a crow overhead. The path ran out abruptly at a deadly cliff. They nearly stepped over the edge.

Drawing back from the edge, the private looked far down at the bottom of the cliff. There he saw several carrion crows eagerly pecking at something.

It was a human body; there was no mistaking it, it was the body of Lieutenant Hyŏn. It had the same T-shirt, fatigue trousers, and boots that the lieutenant had been wearing when he had deserted them the previous evening.

The crows were pecking at the face of the corpse. Then the ferocious birds looked up at the two men on the top of the cliff and flew off, but they soon returned to their repast.

The eyes were already gone from the face, and only two dark gaping holes remained. The two stepped back a few paces and slumped down on the ground. Seeing the body of the lieutenant, their last bit of strength seemed to drain out of their bodies.

After a while the private got to his feet and scrambled to the edge; from there he threw rocks down the cliff. Every time he threw a rock the crows fluttered up from the body, but they immediately settled back with a few dissatisfied and ominous caws.

The private came back and slumped down again. He gave a quick glance at the captain. The captain was lying down with his eyes closed.

The private could feel death closing in. It was odd to feel it now, for he had not felt it in the severest fighting on the battlefield. Tomorrow those carrion crows would peck out their eyes. Then he thought he would rather die first than see the body of the captain picked over by those crows.

He wanted to cry but he hadn't the strength to do so.

The private was awakened by the captain's voice. When he opened his eyes, he could see the starry sky above.

"Listen to that," said the captain in a hoarse whisper. "It's artillery."

Fully awake now, the private sat up to listen. Indeed faint rumblings of artillery like distant thunder could be heard.

"Whose guns are they?"

"Ours. 155s, I believe."

There couldn't be any mistake if the captain said so. Just as the private was going to ask, the captain spoke up. "But it's far. A good fifteen miles."

If that was the case, it was no use. Private Kim lay back down, disappointed.

Captain Chu could now feel that he was slowly dying. He could feel it with absolute lucidity of mind. Then he squarely faced the idea he had so far carefully avoided. He would now put the pistol to good use. If he had killed his doomed self long ago, things would have turned out well for the others, he thought. Lieutenant Hyŏn might not have stolen away and fallen off the cliff to his death. At any rate it's not too late to help, he thought. For all his exhaustion, Private Kim still stood a chance of making it back to friendly lines if he were given a free hand. He turned to the private.

"The artillery is to the southeast. Go down the left side of the cliff. Run along. It's an order," he told the private. That said he slowly and limply pulled his pistol from its holster.

Then, just at that moment, he picked up another sound, quite distinct from the rumbling of guns. At first he doubted his ears.

"What's that sound?" he said to the private.

Private Kim cocked his head and listened. "What sound, sir?"

"It's stopped. I can't hear it now," said the captain. Then he heard the sound once more. "There it goes again. It's coming from that direction." But still the private could not hear anything. "It sounds like a dog barking," the captain said.

A dog! Despite his exhaustion, the private came to his knees and crawled to the edge of the cliff. If it was a dog barking, there had to be a house and people in the vicinity.

"It's over that ridge," said the captain.

But the private still could not hear anything. He backed down to the spot where he had lain before and slumped down.

The private is a good soldier and a real man, thought the captain. He wanted to do something for the boy now, and he wanted to do the same for himself if he could. But now the private was mumbling to himself.

"Tomorrow there will be more crows. Then we won't have any eyes."

But even before he finished saying that, he heard the cocking of the pistol right by one of his ears. Startled, he turned around to see the captain aiming the pistol straight at him in the darkness.

"Carry me," ordered the captain in a hoarse but strong voice.

The private did not know what was up, but at gunpoint he had no choice but to offer his back to the captain.

"Walk!"

The private felt the muzzle of the gun touch his right ear. They went over the ridge and descended into the woods.

"Halt!" The captain listened for a while.

"Go to the left a little!" Then after a while he said, "Wait!" Then, "Go ahead!"

The private blindly followed the captain's commands, to the right, to the left, halt, go ahead. All the while he was struggling, however, the private could hear nothing. The captain, at the point of death, might be losing his mind and hearing things, he thought. If so, what will happen to me now? He had never borne a grudge against the captain until this moment, but now a furious rage against this man began to well up in him.

But he had to keep on walking; the pressure of the gun behind his ear never slackened. His progress, weak and shambling as it was, seemed to be spurred by the muzzle of the gun.

Finally they reached the foot of the hill.

"To the right." Then, "Straight ahead."

Then the private began to hear something. He slowly realized it was a dog barking. But he could not guess the distance.

His throat was dry, and each step was like falling into an ever-deepening abyss. He felt like giving up and flopping down. But he couldn't afford to; the gun behind his ear pressed harder and harder. He could see nothing. He wasn't even aware of taking each step. Then, just as he became conscious of the silhouette of a house, a man, and a barking dog in the darkness, he felt the slackening of pressure at the back of his ear. He sagged to the ground under the dead weight of the captain.

tr. KIM CHONG-UN

A SHADOW SOLUTION

그림자풀이

He was wandering about looking for his shadow, which he had lost quite some time ago. He did not know when or where or how he had lost his shadow. That made finding it more difficult.

He began his search at the taverns because he went to taverns more than anywhere else. He was always forgetting things like umbrellas after he had a drink. Perhaps he had gotten drunk and gone home, leaving his shadow behind.

He only gave a quick glance into the beer halls, Japanese-style bars, and Western bars. He had never liked those kinds of drinks very much, so it was almost impossible that he could have left his shadow in one of those places. He also never drank *makkŏlli,* but there weren't any places that specialized in *makkŏlli* where he would have to search.

He dropped in at a tavern that sold mainly *soju*. It was a place he visited frequently.

When he looked inside, he saw a man sitting alone drinking, a friend he often drank with. He went in and sat down across from him.

His friend glanced at him, but showed no sign of recognition, casting his gaze back into his own glass.

Why would my friend behave like this? He cleared his throat so his friend would acknowledge that he had come in.

This time his friend lifted his glass without even looking up and drank from it. Then he picked up some fried octopus with his chopsticks, put it in his mouth, and began to chew.

Is he drunk? But if he were drunk, the tip of his nose would be white – and it's not.

His friend took out a cigarette and put it in his mouth. Pardon me, but might I trouble you for a light?

Why is he acting this way today? He knows I quit smoking. And why was he so formal?

Please forgive me. I'm afraid I don't smoke. He also adopted a formal tone to see how his friend would react.

But his expression did not change. He asked the young waiter for some matches and lit his cigarette.

Stop this ridiculous game!

As soon as he spoke, his friend looked across at him seriously.

Are you talking to me? Who on earth are you?

Me? I've known you for over thirty years. What do you mean asking my name? Should I tell you about how we drank here just a few days ago? Okay, fine. Should I tell you what we talked about that day? We were lamenting the fact that we couldn't drink as much as before, but we promised to stick to just one bottle of *soju*. Now do you remember?

His friend seemed dumbfounded, then called the waiter and asked for a seat somewhere else. His friend looked at him as if he were out of his mind.

There was nothing to do but leave. He slipped out of the tavern and realized for the first time that his friend did not recognize him because he did not have a shadow.

That day he was wandering the streets looking for his shadow when three laughing youths came walking toward him from the opposite direction. They were students at the university where he taught.

Good afternoon, Professor?

Good afternoon.

As they spoke, he realized the students recognized him even without his shadow.

What brings you this way? Actually, we were just looking for you, Professor.

I'm a little busy now . . .

What is it, Professor? If it's something we could help you with, we would . . .

No, you couldn't. You couldn't. He answered hurriedly.

The shadows of the three students were distinct on the sidewalk. He could not bring himself to tell them that he was searching for his shadow; he didn't want to reveal his own negligence in losing it.

But as long as I've run into the three of you here, shall we stop in at a tearoom?

When you're so busy?

A little while wouldn't hurt.

He thought perhaps the conversation with the students might lead him to where he had lost his shadow.

As soon as they went inside the tearoom and sat down, he began to talk.

Consider this. How would it be if we looked at the relationship between a teacher and students this way? It's the relationship of a flower to a bee. The students are the bees and the teacher is the flower.

Even if their conversation was missing its premise, neither speaker nor listener felt any particular awkwardness.

It's a realistic relationship.

Isn't it a beautiful relationship? It's good, anyway. It's good. But bees get honey from roses and plantain flowers as well.

What kind of flower are you, Professor?

Me? Well . . .

A balsam flower.

What? A balsam flower? "Balsam growing at the base of a fence, you look so sad . . ."

". . . on long summer days, when you were in bloom, lovely girls played and delighted in you . . ." The three students sang together.

"But summer is gone, autumn winds blow, tearing the blossoms and scattering the petals. You grow old and look melancholy and bleak." . . . just like me.

It's not that, Professor. The soul remains. It dreams a peaceful dream, desiring rebirth with the balmy spring breezes.

Sure, that's the way it should be. But I don't care if I am not a flower. I wouldn't mind if I were a ditch.

What do you mean by that?

It's like this. A little boy was looking down at a ditch beside his grandfather's well.

People rinse rice, rinse your vegetables, wash clothes, clean out the chamberpot—this ditch is where all the waste collects. It was just after the boy came inside from the field and rinsed his feet. When summer vacation came, the boy always went to his grandfather's house in the country.

Bees drink the water in the ditch. They calmly drink all they can hold, then fly away, and other bees come and drink it. If you see pollen sticking to a bee's leg, it looks like it's carrying honey back home to the hive.

The boy was amazed and for a while could not take his eyes off the bees.

So you see. Bees don't make honey just from sucking nectar from flowers. No, they make honey by drinking water from sewer ditches, too.

But you're going too far saying that you would be the sewer water in a ditch.

Maybe not the water in a ditch, but perhaps I might be the liquid that flows from a rotting corpse. There is something called rock honey. It is made by bees that build their hives in the clefts between boulders deep in the mountains. The honey from those hives has an excellent flavor, and it's an essential ingredient of Korean medicine. This honey is regarded as precious, not just because it is made from such rare flowers as mountain ginseng but also because bees make it by drinking the liquid that flows from the rotting corpses of mountain beasts. Did you know that? Whatever the bees suck up they make into honey.

I know bees must do that, but aren't you being a bit self-debasing to say that you are like the fluid from a rotting corpse?

What I just said is not meant to be self-debasing. I'm just exposing my feelings quite frankly.

Of course, aren't you being humble? "Be a leader in humility." That's a line from somewhere, isn't it?

There is also the saying that a fool will be regarded as wise if he holds his tongue. If you keep your mouth shut, you'll be considered a sage.

But we can't keep quiet. We just rattle on. Are those words of warning for us?

No.

The conversation went on for a long time, but no clue appeared as to how he might be able to find his shadow.

I have some pressing business, so I'll have to go now.

As he got up from the seat, he felt fortunate that these students had not caught on that his shadow had disappeared.

One day, when he reached the plaza in front of City Hall as he was looking for his shadow, throngs of people were standing together in anticipation, watching something in the air.

He understood what was going on. A moment ago the mass of people had been looking up at the sky. Turtle! Turtle! Put your head out! Quick. Quick. If you don't, we'll roast you on a charcoal fire and eat you, they had all shouted. And now they were waiting for a response.

A turtle was crawling on the seashore. Hanging its head, it lumbered along without stopping to rest, all the while dropping glossy white eggs that looked like a chicken's. It was the turtle he had once seen in a movie, one that had lost its sense of direction because of the effects of environmental pollution.

Before long, eggs came falling from the sky toward the crowd. Each was about the size of a soccer ball. There were ten in all.

The crowd raised a jubilant shout. Hurrah! Hurrah! Hurrah! A noble person from ancient times emerged from one of the eggs. Make the biggest child that comes out the king and make the others the leaders of the ten provinces. That is what we should do.

But chaos erupted. The crowd divided into two groups—those who wanted to open the eggs since they seemed to be damaged by environmental pollution and those who wanted to wait until they hatched because they thought the eggs looked sound. Each group advanced its own opinion. The numbers in the group that said they were rotten and those who said they were sound were about the same.

They scolded and wagged their fingers at each other. Intermingled with their exchanges were words they had borrowed from somewhere. I am absolutely opposed to your opinion, but I am prepared to defend with my life your freedom to express it. Nevertheless, they finally decided to ignore their opponents' freedom of speech and resorted to force. They struck each other, they kicked, and, in an instant, a great turmoil arose. As soon as people were struck in the head with fists, their heads vanished; when people were kicked in the trunk, their lower bodies disappeared. Not a drop of blood flowed. The people who had lost their heads and those who had lost their lower bodies just fell on their backs on the asphalt pavement, moving in circles.

With a whir of wings, a gold beetle fell to the ground and spun in a circle on its back.

The big boy from the house next door caught the beetle. He twisted the beetle's head and dropped the insect onto its back.

The beetle spun around in a circle for a moment, then slowed down. It struggled and kicked with its legs in the air. The big boy slapped the ground beside the beetle with his palm, trying to get it to spin again. Spin! As if it understood him, the beetle buzzed and spun.

The little boy had been watching the big boy and the beetle.

When the beetle stopped, the big boy struck the ground another time and the beetle spun again. After that, no matter how the big boy struck the ground, the beetle would not spin again. The big boy's face turned red and he beat the ground more fiercely, swearing at the beetle. Gradually the movement of the beetle's feet grew more feeble.

The little boy began to fret and worry. Was the angry boy going to kill the beetle?

The people who had been dismembered were spinning well though no one pushed them to.

And while this happened, the eggs began to rise to the sky, one after another. It would be more accurate to say that they fell to heaven rather than rose. There were far more than ten.

From the beginning he felt that his shadow was surely among that crowd. He entered the turbulent throng to meet his shadow. In that instant a fist flew out, struck him flush between the eyes, and his head fell off.

For the first time in a long while, he went into the woods on Mount Kohwang behind the school. He wasn't looking for his shadow, but trying to gain the strength to continue his search. As always, the Quiet Bird flew down from the nest it had built in the upper branches of a huge oak tree and landed on his shoulder. It rubbed its long neck against his as a sign of welcome.

The bird was quite small when he first brought it here to the woods on Mount Kohwang to raise it; now its body was about the size of a magpie's, but it still had the same jet-black bill and tail, pure white body, and scarlet legs. Even as a young bird, its neck and bill and legs were long. But its method of greeting had been different. When it was young, it would fly out of the house he had built for it at the base of the oak tree and land on his shoulder, but it would not rub its neck against his. It shook its wings and tail.

As it grew, the Quiet Bird built its own nest in the branches of the oak tree, higher than the house he had built for it. The bird no longer fit in that house.

The bird did well even if he did not look after it. It got by on insects in the spring and summer, and in autumn and winter it ate seeds. His only worry was that someone might want the bird for a taxidermy specimen, since it was such an extraordinary bird, and take it with a snare or a gun. But when he realized that his anxiety was groundless, how relieved he felt! Once when he was sitting in the classroom, the bird came and flew about outside the window. He was worried that other people might see it. Wasn't the bird pecking at the glass with its long bill, obviously asking him to open the window? But no one seemed to notice the existence of the bird. As soon as he got up and opened the window, as if for fresh air, the bird flew in, perched on his shoulder and sat quietly, rubbing its neck against his. The bird never sang. It was silent, but its heart communicated to him through its breast. You look tired. Rest for a while. You may be exhausted, but cheer up.

Today when he entered the woods on Mount Kohwang, the Quiet Bird recognized his melancholy mood and tried to raise his spirits by performing antics in the air for him.

With its long feet and bill stretched out, it flew straight up into the sky. It flew like a fish swimming through the water with a swish of its tail. It flew like a creature hopping along the mountain ridge.

His shadow's whereabouts still unknown, he went on hunting aimlessly.

In one spot he saw a sign with an arrow on it and turned his steps in the direction it pointed. He was wearing a mismatched pair of shoes. The right shoe was his own, but the left one was someone else's. As he followed the arrow, he felt in his heart that he would meet the owner of the left shoe and that the owner would be his own shadow.

The arrow signs were spaced a certain distance apart and finally led to a building. He went into a room.

It was a hospital mortuary.

The lights were on even though it was daylight, so the room was not at all gloomy but very bright. On one side of the room there was a coffin covered with a white cloth. In front of that stood a portrait that leaned backward somewhat. It was no one he recognized, and yet he felt somehow that he knew him. Smoke from the incense burner in front of the portrait rose silently.

He did not see the chief mourner or the bereaved family, but three old men sat in chairs away from the door; they appeared to be mourners. They seemed to be about his age. He sat in a chair near the entrance.

He did not bother to figure out what relationship he might have had with the deceased that would have brought him here. He did not pay much attention to his mismatched shoes. However, he did not regard it as the least bit unnatural that he should have come to this place. The chief mourner should have come in and made some sort of introduction, but he never appeared. The old men in the chairs exchanged words as though they knew each other, and among their words were stories of the deceased. The dead man had devoted himself to the cultivation of orchids. He took so much care, it was as though he were raising precious children.

He noticed that there were no other funeral flowers, just one potted orchid on either side of the coffin. One was a *cymbidium* and the other was a *dendrobidium*. Thinking how much the dead man loved orchids, he wondered if the old men had bought these instead of funeral flowers or if these were orchids the dead man had raised, which they had brought to place here.

He had gone to a friend's house.

His friend liked animals. Recently he had been keeping three cats and a dog in his house. The dog, a Russian wolfhound, was elegant with soft, beautiful fur, but it was remarkable that he kept such a big dog inside. Even so, he took pleasure in it.

His friend had no children. They had been unable to have any. No matter how much his wife begged him to adopt a child, his friend would never listen, all the while devoting himself to caring for his dog and cats. It seemed he could never develop a taste for alcohol and tobacco, so he devoted himself to his pets all the more.

That day his friend was sitting reading a book and stroking the back of his dog, who was lying beside him. The cats were jumping, chasing, and wrestling with each other. They jumped up on his lap and back down. His friend was reading, but the cats would scratch at the book he had placed in front of him. How annoying. He would put aside his reading, appearing to enjoy their antics. This behavior was in sharp contrast to the sour face his friend made when he visited his house and saw his grandchildren running about playing.

Hadn't the dead man here also departed this world after leading a life without alcohol and tobacco, and without children, devoting himself only to his orchids, his wife having passed on? Perhaps that was why he saw no members of the bereaved family.

Suddenly his mismatched shoes came to mind. A man like this dead man, who did not smoke or drink, who devoted himself to his orchids, a man of such integrity would never do anything like wearing another man's shoes, he thought. If that's true, haven't I come here in vain? I should get out of here quickly. He got up from the chair. He muttered that he would never be able to escape his fear of death.

The bookstore was packed. The bookshelves on the walls were crammed so full of books no space was left. Once again his heart was satisfied. There had been a period when he would make time to drop into this and that bookstore even when he was not looking for any particular book, just as a diversion of sorts. He did not even need to take down books and look at them. It was a pleasure simply to gaze at them. However, as he grew older, he no longer went to bookstores unless he wanted to buy a certain book.

Now, too, he had come into the bookstore for a particular purpose. He had a presentiment, perhaps there would be something about his shadow in one of the books.

After a while he selected a book from the shelf. He opened the cover, and when he did, a cavern appeared. The empty, pitch-black cave was vast and deep. He quickly closed the book. He carefully opened the next book, but it was the same. Then the next, and the next.

Every time he took a book from the shelf and opened it, it was transformed into a vast, deep, black cavern, and he imagined that this was exactly how Pandora felt when she opened the lid of the box.

As soon as Pandora opened the box, Hunger, Disease, Sorrow, Jealousy, Distrust, Deceit, Hatred, Greed—all the things that afflict humankind—swarmed out like poisonous insects and flew off in all directions. There was no time to close the lid; they all flew out at once. But in one corner in the bottom of the empty black box there was something wiggling. It was a tiny caterpillar, Hope.

As soon as he opened the cover, he groped with his eyes in the transformed depths. In this black cavern, too—although all sorts of evils had already escaped from it and spread through the human world, and it seemed empty—still there was obviously something left. Deep in the bottom of the vast cavern, in a corner, he saw something wiggling, a creature even smaller than the caterpillar of Hope, a creature so small he might have missed it. It was Love. Searching for his shadow, he knew what kind of clue he was being offered.

Out looking for his shadow, he had arrived at a place he could not have known.

He could not guess what season it was. It was a plain, but he could not tell whether it was in the spring before the grass had sprouted or autumn after the grass had withered and dried up. It was also hard to tell whether it was morning or evening. Heavy ash-colored clouds covered the sky. A violent wind occasionally raged across the desolate plain.

An old woman sat on a wooden bench. Her chalk-white hair was a tangled mass. The woman faced him, and, pointing to her swollen belly with her wrinkled finger, she said she was in her last month. She twisted up her face and smiled with a satisfied air.

He felt both loathing and fear. It seemed to him that the child in the woman's belly could be none other than the shadow he had been hunting for. Then it occurred to him that the child was surely from the milky white eggs dropped by the turtle that had lost its sense of direction. He fled from the place as if driven.

He wondered how far he had walked at such a rapid pace. When he thought he was a good distance from the old woman, the Quiet Bird suddenly flew to him and landed on his shoulder. It rubbed its neck against his, as always, and, even after it stopped rubbing, it left its neck against his. Why so sad? There had been a time once before when the Quiet Bird had shed tears in this position.

It was an evening when, all over the campus, everyone's eyes were sore and smarting—an evening when everyone shed tears. He went to look for the Quiet Bird in the woods. Although it was late, he wanted to make sure everything was all right.

As usual, the Quiet Bird flew down from its nest in the upper branches of the oak tree, landed on his shoulder, and rubbed his neck with its own. After it stopped, it did not move away but remained there. He felt something damp against his neck. He wondered if the tears were a sign that its eyes still stung and smarted. But that was not it. A sobbing sound emerged from the Quiet Bird's throat as it held its neck against his. He finally understood: the bird was grieving over people's turning away from the preciousness of what they could not see with their eyes or hold in their hands.

That day, the Quiet Bird's heart flowed into his without a sound, without shedding tears, and without sobbing. The bird's heart opened, as did his.

You still aren't able to find your shadow?

No, I'm not.

Haven't you been wandering around searching for a long time?

Yes.

Sometimes you feel anxious and sometimes you feel impatient, don't you?

That's right.

When you feel that way, remember this. You know about cosmic luminescence, don't you? Beautiful tiny particles that give off light as they fly past a spacecraft. The astronaut's urine is expelled from the spacecraft and is turned into cosmic luminescence. Quite interesting, don't you think? Think of that and try to feel calm.

All right. I'll try.

I suppose you'll keep looking for your shadow.

I think so. But first it seems I need to understand whether the true form seeks the shadow or the shadow seeks the true form.

I think both happen.

The Quiet Bird rubbed its neck against his in the manner he liked so much he could hardly stand it.

tr. J. MARTIN HOLMAN

WIDOWS

寡

婦

It was Mrs. Han's pride that not a lock of her hair, much less any part of her body, had ever been touched by the hand of a man.

When she was betrothed at the age of fourteen to the eldest son of the scholar Mr. Kim, she was still too young to know what modesty was, but before the final marriage ceremony took place, the groom-to-be fell from a tree and died. Her father, the scholar Mr. Han, observed that just as a high government official could not serve two kings, a wife could not serve two husbands, so after the required three years of mourning, Mrs. Han moved to the house of her in-laws, and continued to live there as a crystal-pure widow, until she was nearly seventy years old.

No one knew how long Mrs. Han had looked upon the male sex as something dirty. Even now that she was nearly seventy, she could still detect the odor of a man well enough to wrinkle up her nose at it. She could not abide the scent of male perspiration for even a moment.

Mrs. Han did not like children either, being used to the freedom of a single person. Her in-laws once talked about having her raise her nephew's son as her own, but she declined. It was just as well, for the boy would quickly realize she was displeased, so he probably wouldn't like her.

Once, one of her nieces begged, "Aunty, please tell me a story about the old days."

Mrs. Han replied, "There were many frightening things in the old days."

"Like what?"

"Widows were heartlessly carried off in the middle of the night."

"Oh! Who carried them off?"

"Gangs of robbers."

"Why?"

"To disgrace them."

"What do you mean, 'disgrace them'?"

"It's better that you don't know . . . you shouldn't know how your old aunt trembled with fear every night."

"Why, Aunty?"

"Because they just carried pretty women away."

"Old women like you, Aunty?"

"Even I was quite pretty then. Why, I had to put soot on my face to fool them!"

"Really?"

Later, Mrs. Han told this same story to her other nieces. The first few times they were fascinated, but after hearing the same story again and again, they began to get tired of it. Soon, they would sneak away as soon as she began to tell it. Mrs. Han would declare that young girls these days were so self-important that they were not good for anything; then she would go lie down in her room. Mrs. Han's room was always sparkling clean. She would sweep it herself, over and over. It wasn't that she had no one to clean it for her; she was just keeping up her unblemished reputation in the neighborhood.

The oldest people respected her the most. She was not only the oldest person in her immediate family, she was the oldest in the entire clan. Mrs. Han had aged gracefully. She was large boned, and although she described herself as "doll-like," she had never been pretty. She was now an old widow, yet her back was unbent, her eyes were undimmed, and her ears and nose were still keen. Her face was gently lined and her hands were soft.

Whenever Mrs. Han felt lonely, she would visit her third cousin's wife, who lived in the lower village. Mrs. Pak was also a widow, but not a virgin widow like Mrs. Han. At sixteen she had gone as a bride to the house of Mrs. Han's third cousin, when the groom was eleven, but the boy died only two years later, when an epidemic swept the country. Mrs. Pak served her husband's family from that time until the death of her father-in-law, more than twenty years later. Then she moved to a thatched house in the lower village and began an independent life of farming. Mrs. Pak was some four years younger than Mrs. Han, but she looked older. Deep lines had been etched in her scorched face, and her hands were gnarled like a man's.

When Mrs. Han visited Mrs. Pak, they often worked together splitting gourds. Or if Mrs. Pak happened to be spinning thread, Mrs. Han would while away the hours rolling up the cotton at her side. If Mrs. Pak was tired and lying down, Mrs. Han would come in and lie down beside her. At such times especially, Mrs. Han wondered how anyone could live in such disorder.

On a day that was not particularly chilly, Mrs. Han went down to visit Mrs. Pak. She stayed there for a while, but when she got home, she came down with a cold. She had her nephew get some medicine from a clinic a couple of miles away.

When her nephew brought the earthenware bowl with the medicine, Mrs. Han said abruptly, "If I die, bury me in the family cemetery."

"Why are you talking like that? If you'll just take this medicine, you'll recover." But he was thinking, "She may be right. Someone her age is like a lamp that is flickering and running out of oil. If so, this may be a good time to clear up one problem."

"Well, Aunty, how would it be if we buried you next to Uncle? They say that Uncle's grave is in a very auspicious location."

"Mrs. Han glared up at him. "That's disgusting. To be next to my husband. After seventy years of virginity, to put me alongside a man now! True, his bones have decayed and he's rotted away.

But still, a man *was* buried there. Don't you ever say such an indecent thing again!"

Mrs. Han's cheeks were flushed like a girl's, and not merely with fever. Then something startled her. "Get away from me! What is that smell? You male bastards all give off that wicked stench . . ." Wrinkling her nose, she quickly waved him away and rolled over.

Three days later, Mrs. Han arose from her bed. It was a warm day but she wrapped an overcoat tightly around herself before going down to Mrs. Pak's house. After building a fire, Mrs. Pak swept the warmer part of the room and had Mrs. Han lie there.

"You've been feeling poorly lately, haven't you?"

"I was sick for a few days since the last time I came."

"Even so, you look quite healthy."

"Goodness, no! It won't be long before I leave this world!"

"Still, you'll be here longer than I will."

"What would I do if I lived so long? There is no longer anything to bring joy to life. Death is not sad . . ."

"But you've lived your whole life without worries, haven't you?"

"Indeed, I've lived my life cleanly and without shame."

Mrs. Pak wound a skein of thread for a moment and then spoke. "It's quite unusual for a young widow to live the way you have." She stopped winding her thread. She seemed to be thinking. She looked at Mrs. Han and said, "There are other kinds of widows in the world."

Mrs. Han blew the dust away from the pillow Mrs. Pak had dusted off only a moment earlier, as if she felt uneasy. She glanced toward the gourds and pumpkins and dust cloths spread around the colder part of the room. How could a person living alone make such a mess of a house?

Mrs. Pak hesitated a little, as though she were broaching a difficult subject. "I know about another kind of young widow . . ."

A young lady married and went to live with her in-laws. Her young husband was still attending the village school. He wrote

Chinese characters very well. She was more attracted to his handwriting than she was to him. She found meaning in her life by collecting and carefully arranging his papers.

Two summers after she came to her husband's home, there was an outbreak of typhoid fever that killed many people in the village. Her young husband breathed his last only ten days after he fell ill. On the orders of the family elders, she cut off a finger to give her husband blood, but it was no use. She observed the prescribed three years of mourning for him. Occasionally, she would pull out the papers her husband had written and look at them, thinking it was fate that she lived the way she did.

Her in-laws had a very large farm. She helped them both inside and outside the house.

One year there was a severe drought, and everyone in the house had to join in the noisy task of carrying water from the stream to the rice paddies during the night.

The young widow awoke one night, thinking she had heard someone come into her room. Lying still in the darkness, she heard someone breathing by her side. As she started with fright, something grabbed her breast. It was a strong male hand. She tried to cry out, but something prevented her—an odor of earth and water. The smell clearly came from a body that had been working in the mud. The young widow felt her strength dissolve.

It had to be him. He had been working as a hired hand at her in-laws' house since spring. The young man was a distant relative of her husband who had lost his parents early. After wandering about for some years, he had come back home. Eventually he was taken in by her husband's family, who needed another hand.

The young man had a well-developed physique and a strong, straight nose. By nature, he was not one to complain. It was said that once, after several years of work as a farmhand for a man he couldn't get along with, he had thrown his employer to the ground in a rice paddy and simply walked away from his job.

Sometimes while she was out in the yard, the young widow's eyes would meet his. They were a man's eyes—eyes she could not have seen in her young husband. The young widow's heart would begin to pound of its own accord, and her face would turn red.

The young man had been busy carrying water with her father-in-law. He was almost always in the fields—except for tonight.

Lying beneath this man, whose skin smelled of mud, the young widow thought that her problems would disappear if she were dead. "Shall I jump into the stream? Shall I hang myself? I'll drink some lye."

The following morning she went to the shed in the yard. She picked up the jar, but it was empty. Only then did she remember that her mother-in-law had lent out the rest of the lye several days earlier. She would have to wait until the next market day.

That night the young widow locked the door to her room, but sleep would not come. She listened constantly, in spite of herself. Even the night birds moving in their roosts under the eaves would startle her. Finally she unlatched the door. If someone were to come and tug at the locked door, the sound would reach the inner room, and then there would be trouble.

The next market day, as soon as she got the lye, the young widow used it all up boiling the laundry. And before long, she had begun awaiting the darkness of the night.

About the time the sap began to rise again in the willows that stood by the stream in front of the house, the young widow's body began to grow noticeably heavy. She would often tie her sash tightly around her waist.

One night, the man whispered in the darkness. "Let's go away from here, live somewhere else. Someplace with an irrigation system would be much better than the floods and droughts here."

The young widow was silent in the darkness, but her heart kept pressing her for an answer. Already, what seemed good to the man seemed good to her, and what seemed bad to him seemed bad to her.

They chose the last night of the month, when there would be no moon. He would leave the town first and wait on the bank of the stream.

She waited for the rooster to crow twice, then crept out of her room. Muffling her footsteps while going down the stone stairs, she headed toward the gate. Suddenly she stopped.

From the inner room, the stern, quiet voice of her father-in-law struck her ears. "Hush, my dear. I have been aware of the problem for some time."

After answering a murmured question from his wife, the father-in-law continued. "Silence! If you wag your tongue I'll chop it off with an axe! Just keep quiet, I'll take care of everything."

The young widow came to her senses. Instead of running away for the illusion of happiness, she should wait and see what her father-in-law would do.

After she returned to her room, the young widow's heart became calmer than it had ever been before. Let the man leave. Since he was the one who could not wait, she wished he would go away alone.

Before dawn, the man came back. "What happened?" he asked, gasping for breath. He set down the rock with which he had intended to kill her father-in-law if the old man had chanced to catch her. He was terrifying. She threw herself on the floor without a word and cried.

The next day, the father-in-law took advantage of a quiet moment to tell the young widow that from now on she should not go out any farther than the well. As always, his voice was soft, but the young widow could not help but be frightened. She wished he would quickly take care of the situation, as he had said the night before.

One evening as summer was approaching, the young widow finally gave birth. Fortunately, it happened in the middle of the night, though a crescent moon shone outside.

The young widow spread out a straw sack and after a short labor, delivered on it. She cut the umbilical cord herself.

The man came in. In the dim light of the oil lamp he reached toward this wiggling little "clot of blood," but the young widow's quick movement pushed his hand away. This baby would have to be tossed into a stream or left deep in some secluded mountains—that had been their understanding. But now the woman wanted to let the baby breathe, even if just for a moment.

The man began to roll the baby up in the straw sack. The young woman thought a moment, then opened up the dresser and pulled out a package of papers. They were her dead husband's compositions. She didn't think of their value—she was only grateful she could protect the baby's young skin.

The man wrapped the baby in the papers and left the room. She sensed someone else nearby, below the steps. It was her father-in-law. The blade of an axe flashed before her mind's eye.

Flustered, the young widow thought that she was the one who deserved the axe. In a flurry, she kicked open the door and ran out, jumping in between the man and her father-in-law.

Her father-in-law quietly thrust a scrap of paper toward the man. "Go find the place spoken of in this letter. I hear my niece just gave birth to a child and lost it. Commit the child to her care."

He spoke in his usual quiet manner. But his hand trembled in the light of the crescent moon as he held out the scrap of paper.

The man's eyes shone as he took the paper. Then he turned without a word, as was his nature.

"Child, hurry in and lie down."

One night, she heard her father-in-law building a fire in the fireplace. The frogs croaked all night long in the field in front of the house. The father-in-law told the young widow that the baby had been getting enough milk and was growing up healthy.

A year later, however, her father-in-law told her that the young man later returned to the house where the child had been left and took it away with him. That night, too, a crescent moon hung in the sky, and the frogs croaked all night in the field.

More than twenty years later, the widow's mother-in-law passed away, followed two years later by her father-in-law. Several days before her father-in-law passed away, he quietly called the young widow to his side.

"I have sinned against you. Back then, I was thinking only of the reputation of our family. Afterwards, I realized my error and tried to find out where the baby's father had gone, but couldn't. How your heart will ache throughout your life!"

Drops, like dew, came from the gently closed, sunken eyes of her father-in-law.

"Father, Father."

The widow buried her head in the old man's side at the thought of causing him so much sorrow.

She went so far as to cut off the fourth finger of her right hand to draw out her blood to try to save him. If only it would have helped, she would have drawn out all the blood in her body for him.

After the death of her father-in-law, she entrusted the family house to her husband's younger brother and built herself a thatch-roofed house in the lower village.

One summer day, many years later, as she was preparing supper after gathering potatoes that had been left in the field, she heard someone calling for the owner of the house. Outside the gate made of woven branches, a middle-aged man stood in the evening shadows, asking if he could trouble her to put him up for the night. Her house was near the entrance of the village, so travelers often stopped there.

When the evening table had been taken away, the visitor commented how especially delicious the potato soup had been. He lit a cigarette and asked if there was a Mrs. So-and-So living in this village. The old widow's heart fluttered. With a trembling hand she turned up the lamp. Ah, that strong, straight nose! She quickly extinguished the light, in spite of herself.

Thinking that the old woman was somewhat deaf and had not heard him, the visitor asked again if Mrs. So-and-So lived in the village.

"She died long ago." The widow's voice trembled.

"When?"

"Long ago – it's been forty years."

Just as I thought. Right after . . ." The visitor blew out a long puff of smoke. "It wasn't a natural death, was it?"

"What else could it have been? A terrible epidemic was going around that year, and then . . ." The widow broke off.

The visitor hastily put the cigarette to his lips.

The widow suddenly regretted having put out the lamp, but she did not have the courage to light it again. She regretted having said that the woman had died forty years ago. That single sentence had robbed her of what would have been most precious, but the next moment, she decided she had done well, after all. The image of her long-dead father-in-law arose before her eyes. "I have sinned against you. I was thinking only of the reputation of our family. How your heart will ache throughout your life!"

"No, Father, no."

The widow went outside. A crescent moon hung in the sky, and the frogs croaked all night in the field.

Unable to sleep, the visitor also came outside. After sitting silently for a moment at the widow's side, he said, "Sitting here like this makes me think about my father. When the frogs croaked at night like this, Father used to go out to sit in the garden. He sat there not realizing how late it got. For a long time, it's been my habit, too."

"When did your father leave this world?"

"Seven days ago. The day before he died, he told me for the first time that my mother was still alive. Until then, I'd thought that I had lost her while very young. He told me her name and where she lived. After the funeral ceremony, I rushed here . . . but you tell me my mother has already left this world." He paused. "You knew my mother well."

"Yes, I knew her."

"I would like to see her grave . . ."

"Her grave?" The widow caught her breath. "There's no way to find it now. She wasn't even buried in this village . . . and I'm probably the only one left who remembers her. It all happened forty years ago. As I remember . . ."

"What?"

"She was kindhearted. . . . And tell me, how many children do you have?" She managed to change the subject.

"Three boys and two girls. My eldest son started to help out in the business this year, so I thought that Father would finally be able to relax. But he passed away. Father suffered so much for me."

Near dawn, the sleeping widow dreamed. There were grandchildren gathered around her, jumping about—as numerous as the frogs that croaked in the field in front of the house. The widow-turned-grandmother ran away, even though she had resolved not to. Heartbroken that things had turned out this way, she cried all alone.

The next day as she was preparing breakfast, she saw the visitor outside sweeping the courtyard. She told him not to bother, but, saying that he had done it every day at his own home, he silently continued.

After asking if he might sack the potatoes in the courtyard, the visitor brushed the dirt from them one by one, placing them in a straw sack. Then he carried them into the shed. The widow could not help watching the trustworthy visitor from the kitchen door.

When the visitor was about to leave, the widow selected a pair of gourd dippers and strung them together. The visitor, already feeling indebted to her, asked how he could possibly accept them, but the widow pressed him hard to take them and use them, as they were especially sturdy gourds from the previous year.

The traveler began to leave, but the widow came out to the gate and called to him. "Just a moment." She wanted to know where he lived—this visitor who had come in and rent her heart. But when he stopped and turned around, the widow drew near and merely straightened the collar of his coat and stroked his back as if to brush off dust.

"Oh!" cried the visitor, hastily clasping her hand. "Father said that my mother, too, had no ring finger on her left hand!"

With difficulty, the widow spread out the fingers of her other trembling hand.

"Ah, you have even sacrificed your right ring finger . . . Your hands have suffered much."

For a moment, the visitor thought his mother would be just like this woman, if she were still alive.

The visitor looked back several times as he walked away from the village. But when he stopped before turning down the winding road on the ridge, the widow had to cling to the gatepost for support.

". . . You see, there are also widows like that in the world."

Mrs. Pak's hands, neither of which had a ring finger, stopped winding thread for a moment as she turned her head. Her mouth half open, Mrs. Han had been asleep for some time.

tr. NEIL HOYT

SHADOWS OF A SOUND

소리 그림자

Two boys were ringing a bell. Actually, the bellringer, the father of one of the boys, stood pulling the bellrope, while the children, who were moving their arms and bodies as the man did, merely grasped the end. Still, the children were just as elated as if they were ringing it themselves.

The peculiar rhythm of it—the interval between the clanging sound when the rope was pulled and the gonglike sound when it was released and the rather long pause before the next clang. This repeating pattern produced a lingering undertone that complemented the music of the bell itself.

The rickety bell tower was nothing but two tall, straight larchwood pillars facing each other. The bell was suspended from a crossbar on top of the pillars, and the rusty, peaked tin roof rested above like an overturned funnel. The whole tower shook when the bell was rung.

The bellrope was always tied up high on the pillar where only an adult on tiptoe could reach it. This was to keep the village children from playing with it. Still there were mischievous boys who shinnied up, untied the rope, and brought it down to ring the bell. The church members, however, were not deceived; they knew from the rhythm of the bell that someone was playing a prank. One day, however, while the regular bellringer was away, the pastor had to ring the bell himself. But ring though he would, the members did not assemble for their meeting on time, thinking it was those rascal children again. So the pastor was obliged to have the two boys take the bellringer's place whenever he was gone.

I received word that my childhood friend Sŏng-il had died. As I revived my memories of him, groping through the flow of more than forty years, what came back, resounding unexpectedly in my chest, was the dying echo of that bell. Then something else interrupted the bell's sound.

Once, one Wednesday or Sunday evening, for some reason or another, we two boys were supposed to ring the bell in place of Sŏng-il's father. We pulled the bellrope, but there was no sound; the clapper had been tied up against the crossbar. Someone was obviously playing a practical joke. We managed with difficulty to carry a ladder to the tower and lean it against the pillar. Then Sŏng-il climbed up to untie the clapper. When he got all the way to the top, he was gesturing vigorously for me to come up, too. I wondered what was going on.

Some distance from the belfry, across some vacant land, stood the church elder's house where Sŏng-il was pointing beyond the wall. I climbed the ladder and looked. There, under the blossoming apricot tree in the rear garden at dusk, we could see two dogs locked together back to back. One was the elder's Pekingese, and the female was a dog that I had never seen before, several times larger than the Pekingese. The strange dog was walking forward, so the Pekingese was being dragged along, unable to keep its rear legs on the ground. We both started to giggle. This Pekingese was a terribly mean dog. Though we saw it all the time, and the dog knew us, every time we two boys passed in front of the house, it would come out to yap and chase us. If we gestured as if to pick up a rock to throw at it, the dog would run away, only to bark and chase us again when we turned around. Now, this dog, unable to keep its rear feet on the ground, was being dragged helplessly along. The spectacle was so ridiculous, we snickered, unable to contain ourselves.

All of a sudden we heard a shout from below. The elder himself was glaring up at us furiously from the base of the belfry. Before I realized what I was doing, I wrapped my arms around the pillar and slid down. The elder then moved the ladder, so Sŏng-il ended up falling the distance. I merely got splinters from the larch pillar in my hands and arms, but Sŏng-il was cursed by his fall: he became a hunchback.

Not long after that my family moved to Kwangju. I was nine years old at the time.

I do not have what you would call a hometown. The place I lived until I was six does not remain in my memory. Then I lived in the Sŏng-il's village until I was nine. After that, we passed through such places as Kwangju, Yŏng'in, and Paju before finally settling in Seoul. We were forced to move around here and there following my father, who was an elementary school teacher.

If the word "bellringer" had not been written below Sŏng-il's name on the death notice, I would not have realized who the man was. In those forty-odd years we had never even corresponded, much less seen each other. How did Sŏng-il know of me?

The village where Sŏng-il had lived was just off the national highway about halfway between Suwŏn and Inch'ŏn. I couldn't quite connect this place with my memories from when I was a nine-year-old child here. Over forty years of changes gave me the impression that this was a completely different village. There were even electric lights where there had been none before. A grocer, a potter, a pharmacy, and a barbershop all stood on the main street, so it seemed more appropriate to call it a small town now. Maybe it was because of the soldiers stationed on the outskirts of the village that it had changed this much.

The elementary school on the right side of the street, a clapboard building before, was now made of concrete. I turned down the road beside the playground. The earth, muddy from the snow the day before and trampled by all kinds of feet, had changed from the red color I remembered.

As I looked toward a small rise behind the school at the square-shaped stone church in front of me, I had already lost any special feelings I had toward it. I could not have expected the church alone to avoid change and remain as it had been. Long ago it had been an old, traditional L-shaped house with a tile roof. It was arranged so the women sat in one branch of the L and the men in the other. While giving the sermon the pastor could not look at either side squarely since the pulpit was in the angle of the L facing the inside corner.

Of course the bell tower was different now. It stood to one side of the church. A cross with a lightning rod attached extended from the peak of the pointed roof, inscribing a distinct line in the clear winter sky. This scene, however, brought me no special memories. I had not traveled this road groping for reminiscences or nostalgia. I merely left my memories to surface as they would.

Within the outer wall of the church was the pastor's residence. Originally the roof had been thatch, but now it was tile. The old pastor certainly had been a good fisherman. Whenever he had a spare moment, he took his net in hand, and, instead of going out to visit the members' homes, he went down to the stream in front of the village, so the adults called him Reverend Fisherman.

The current pastor was much younger. He looked about thirty or so. As soon as he learned who I was, he said the funeral had been held several days earlier. He also told me that Sŏng-il had asked him before he died to be sure to inform me of his death and had emphasized that he should be referred to as the bellringer.

My coming here had nothing to do with the funeral. The notice had been addressed to the school where I taught, but school was out of session at the time, so it had taken ten days before the message made its roundabout way to me.

I asked the young pastor where Sŏng-il's family lived. That was my main purpose for coming that day. My childhood friend, lost in the tide of over forty years—this friend I had played with as a boy for no more than two or three years—had even known my current place of employment. An indescribable impression grew on me that Sŏng-il had been watching me all my life, and the feeling would not let me leave without looking up his family. The young pastor's answer, however, destroyed my hope. He had no family whatsoever. I could not quite picture Sŏng-il's hunchbacked shape after he became an adult, but he must have become so extremely deformed that he could not have a family.

The young pastor pointed to the place where Sŏng-il had lived alone until he died. It was a small room attached to the main gate. The loneliness and then the pain that this one man had borne for over forty years surged into my breast. Although one might say that I am not totally responsible, that I cannot shoulder the burden for one man's misfortune and loneliness, I felt a flash of remorse that accused me of being nothing more than an indifferent bystander. But what was the use of regretting my error? There was nothing I could do now but visit the dead man's grave before I returned home.

The young pastor seemed to recall something. He went into Sŏng-il's room and came out carrying a rather bulky roll of papers. The pastor told me that these were pictures Sŏng-il had taken pleasure in drawing during his lifetime. I did not recall that he had liked to draw when he was a child. Anyway, Sŏng-il had lived without a family, so he made these drawings his companions.

The pictures were done on charcoal paper with pencil. As I turned over the drawings one at a time, I thought I detected a common element in the simple lines. Something burned within the drawings. Sparks bounded from the entangled tree roots and from every bent and curving line. The countless mouths of the church members in the drawings spouted fire as they sang hymns, and flames rose even from the rugged stones jutting from the side of the bald mountains.

Leafing through the pictures, I saw one in particular that I passed over more quickly than the others. After I had looked through them all, I asked the young pastor if I might take one picture with me as a memento. Having found the drawing I had rushed past just a moment earlier, I rolled it up and put it in my overcoat pocket. Then I left.

Even the house where the elder had lived long ago was now a modern, Western-style house with a brick wall surrounding it. I walked around the wall and looked at the nameplate on the gate. A man named Kim was living there. It appeared the previous owner had been supplanted. The elder long ago was not a Kim. Memory is a curious thing; it cannot be trusted. Though I could not recall what the elder's name was, I was quite certain it was not Kim.

But now, what did it matter what the elder's name was, or whether his descendants were still living here?

The cemetery on a ridge was almost directly across the street from the church. Snow-covered gravestones were spread all over it, some reaching higher than others, but I could not tell which was the new mound. I thought I had made a mistake not asking the pastor a moment earlier where the grave was located; nevertheless, I entered the graveyard, treading across the unspoiled snow. Looking around, I finally caught sight of a new wooden cross at the far end of the cemetery.

It was Sŏng-il's grave marker. But, standing in front of it, I could grasp nothing of the essence of the man. The only thing I could revive was the gaunt figure of a boy, his face veiled with suffering. A kind of rage filled my chest. It was like the rage that entered my heart when I first saw the drawing that I now had rolled up in my pocket. The grave of the elder whose name I could not remember probably lay somewhere among these stones, but I could grasp nothing of his essence either, groping back through these forty years of changes in the world. Now the only thing left in my memory was the shout and the furious expression of that middle-aged man as he glared up toward the top of the belfry.

I walked down the hill and checked the station schedule. A bus came every thirty minutes. I had some time before the next one, so I went into a teahouse. A few people sat around the stove in the middle of the room. Business seemed slack. I took a seat at a bright window.

Having taken but one sip of the water that was brought, I pushed the cup away. Then I pulled the drawing out of my overcoat pocket and unrolled it. In the picture were two dogs. The smaller Pekingese, its hind feet in midair, was being dragged along by a larger dog. There were sparks here, too, just as in the other drawings. From the rendering of these animals, it seemed this crippled man had spewed forth these flames, unable to endure the torment of his deformity. In my chest I felt rage surge anew toward the purposeless punishment one middle-aged man had inflicted on this innocent boy, marring his life.

But my rage was nothing at all compared with the lonely, dark life of the dead man. After all this, why had Sŏng-il gone on to succeed his father as the bellringer?

When the waitress brought some green tea, I spoke to her. "Excuse me. Can you hear the church bell clearly from here?" I wanted to tell the waitress that the sound of the bell must have changed since the old days.

"Isn't today Saturday?" The waitress looked at me as though I were confused and thought today was Sunday. I had asked a futile question.

The people would surely have become accustomed to the sound of the new bellringer, so it made no difference. It was enough that I alone would always cherish the sound of the old bell.

As I pondered these things, suddenly, unexpectedly, a bell began to sound in my chest.

Two boys were ringing the bell. This time Sŏng-il's father was not there, just the two boys pulling the rope together. In the interval between the clang when they pulled the rope and the gong when they released it, then in the rather long pause before the next clang, as this clang and gong repeated, a peculiar trailing sound welled up—beneath, yet essential to the melody. The reverberations, like ripples on the water, filled my heart.

At that moment I saw something. The drawing lying before me was suddenly transformed in an extraordinary way. No, I should not say it was transformed. Rather, I was finally able to discern Sŏng-il's original intent in drawing these pictures. Could working with a brush indeed have been so pleasant? Each of the lines that had looked like sparks to me were, in reality, the rhythms that sprang from unbearable delight. Our pure, innocent giggling came back to life, permeating every mark of the pencil, and we were able to share our laughter of forty years ago.

tr. J. MARTIN HOLMAN

CHRONOLOGY OF STORIES

Reeds	late 1930s
Mantis	late 1930s
Old Man Hwang	autumn 1942
The Old Woman from Maengsan	autumn 1943
The Old Potter	autumn 1944
Snow	winter 1944
Even Wolves	May 1948
Melons	October 1950
Merry Christmas	December 1950
Clowns	May 1951
Cloudburst	October 1952
The Whip	October 1952
Widows	November 1952
Cranes	January 1953
A Man	September 1953
A Peddler of Ink and Brushes	April 1955
The Diving Girl	September 1956
Ringwanderung	February 1958
Time for You and Me Alone	July 1958
Writing on a Fingernail	December 1960

Drizzle March 1961
Shadows of a Sound January 1965
In a Small Island Village August 1965
Blood November 1966
Masks September 1971
A Shadow Solution November 1983